W9-BDH-505

⭑ONE SMALL STEP

P. B. KERR

Margaret K. McElderry Books

NEW YORK LONDON TORONTO SYDNEY

Margaret K. McElderry Books

An imprint of Simon & Schuster Children's Publishing Division

1230 Avenue of the Americas, New York, New York 10020

Book design by Mike Rosamilia

The text for this book is set in Adobe Garamond.

Manufactured in the United States of America

10 9 8 7 6 5 4 3 2 1

Library of Congress Cataloging-in-Publication Data

Kerr, Philip.

One small step / P. B. Kerr.—1st ed.

p. cm.

Summary: In 1969 Houston, Texas, thirteen-year-old Scott learns to fly
from his father, an air-force flight instructor, but when NASA needs him
for a secret space mission, Scott's elation is tempered by concern that
his mother, who has moved to Florida, will find out.

ISBN-13: 978-1-4169-4213-9 (hardcover)

ISBN-10: 1-4169-4213-0 (hardcover)

[1. Air pilots—Fiction. 2. Fathers and sons—Fiction. 3. Space
flight—Fiction. 4. United States. National Aeronautics and Space
Administration—Fiction. 5. Family problems—Fiction. 6. Houston
(Tex.)—History—20th century—Fiction.] I. Title.

PZ7.K46843One 2008

[Fic]—dc22

2007035660

FIRST
EDITION

For William F. F. Kerr

There was a ceiling *of thick cumulus cloud at about five thousand feet. I never liked flying through thick cloud. It was like in* Star Trek *when Captain Kirk finds himself somewhere dreamlike and weird and between worlds. Dad said that when he was in Korea, sometimes he used to hide in a cloud and wait for a MiG to come on by; then he'd wax its tail before it knew what was happening. I can believe that. To me, clouds always seem like they're hiding something. But above eight thousand we found ourselves in clear blue sky with fifty-mile visibility in every direction. Below us the ground had disappeared altogether, and the cloud covering looked less like an ambush waiting to happen and more like thick and fluffy layers of whipped cream. Sometimes that's the best kind of flying there is. The kind where it's just you and the sky, without a hole in the cloud to indicate the way back home. We were in an excellent mood. And in these particular*

circumstances it seemed kind of fitting that there should be no reminder of an Earth that wanted us both tied down or grounded.

"Isn't this something?" said Dad.

"It's great," I said.

"How many thirteen-year-old kids do you figure ever get to do anything like this?"

"I dunno. Not many, I guess."

"I'd say less than not many. I'd say you're the only one, Scotty. Wanna take over for a while?"

"Sure."

"You have control of the aircraft," he said, and let go of his stick.

"I have control of the aircraft," I said, taking hold of mine.

It was probably the best that I had ever flown, a real dollar ride. I did an aileron roll and a loop and a perfect figure of eight. Then I took the Tweet up to thirty-four thousand, which was the highest I'd been in any aircraft. The sky up at that height was the bluest blue—the most perfect sky I'd ever seen outside of that picture of the air above the Island of Skye that was hanging on my bedroom wall. I felt like an angel. I could hardly bear the idea that I was about to give all this up.

"Like I always say," said Dad, "you're a natural stick-and-rudder man. Something born, not made. A true MacLeod."

I whipped the Tweet the length and breadth of Harris County for about an hour before I felt him on the brakes and he said it was time to head for home. I wondered when I would ever again feel such monumental power through my hands.

"You have control of the aircraft," I said.

"I have control of the aircraft," he said, taking the stick and pushing it forward.

Dad dropped down to about seven thousand feet, just above the cloud layer, and then radioed the tower controller at Ellington, who advised him that he was clear to land. So he throttled back and began banking gently to the right, flying in a big wide circle that would bring us in to land from the southeast. Completing his turn, we dropped through the cloud and prepared to make our final approach.

Suddenly, without warning, we found ourselves faced with a flock of about a dozen snow geese flying in a V formation and coming right toward us. There was no time to get out of the way. We were going too fast for that. For me there was no time to do anything except yell and then duck as one of the geese hit the right side of the Tweet's canopy. The Tweet rocked like it had been hit by a surface-to-air missile, and the Plexiglas shattered into a dozen fragments as the goose came hurtling right through the canopy and collided heavily with my dad. The cockpit was filled with a smell like singed hair as another bird, perhaps, or even part of the same bird, was ingested by the air-breathing intakes of one of the two engines.

There was blood and feathers and pieces of Plexiglas everywhere. It was impossible to know how much of the blood and guts spread all over the right-hand cockpit seat was the bird's, and how much was Dad's. The shark pictured on his helmet looked like it had made a fresh kill. Its pointy teeth were dripping with red. It was hard to believe that an ordinary bird could cause such destruction to a jet fighter aircraft. It was equally hard to believe that we were still airborne. But we were. For the moment, at least.

"Dad?" I shouted desperately. "Are you okay?"

His chin stayed on his chest, and his hands remained motionless on his lap. He wasn't holding the stick. He didn't look like he was even awake.

"Dad?" I took him by the shoulder and shook him hard. Restrained by its harness, his body stayed put, but his head lolled alarmingly. I couldn't see his eyes behind his visor, and when I tried to push it up, I found that it was stuck, as if the impact had damaged the hinge. So I reached across and unbuckled his oxygen mask. His mouth was open and full of blood. His tongue was hanging out. A terrible feeling took hold of my stomach. For a moment I felt like throwing up. I was terribly afraid that he was dead. "Dad!"

For a moment I saw his lips move and in the earphones inside my helmet I heard him utter one word: "Eject." Then he was silent.

Instinctively, I reached down beside my thigh, took hold of one of the ejection-seat handgrips, and raised it to the full up position, exposing the trigger the way he had shown me. I felt the shoulder harness tighten. I needed only to squeeze the trigger to launch myself out of the aircraft. Except that I couldn't do it. Despite what he'd said earlier, there was no way I could eject.

For one thing, I could only eject myself, and that would have been like killing my dad. For another, the canopy was a mess. It was supposed to blow off a split second before the seat ejected. But looking at it now I had my doubts about that happening. It seemed just as likely that my seat would be fired straight through the damaged canopy, killing me outright. There could be no question of ejecting. Our only chance was for me to take control of the aircraft and land *it myself—something I had never done. I grabbed the stick as the Tweet gave a little shudder and began to dip to the right.*

"I have control of the aircraft!" I yelled at him.

The trouble was, I didn't. Not by a long shot.

They say your whole life passes in front of your eyes in the moments that precede your own death. But this isn't what happened. Not for me, anyway. Being only thirteen years old, I guess there wasn't that much to remember. Instead, I remembered the last time I'd been really scared. That is, scared enough to think that I might be about to die. It was six months ago, in Miami, before I ever started flying with my dad. Before my life really got started.

Ten . . .

"Just one small step, son," said the teacher. "You can do it. Try not to look down."

The two of us were standing on the second-floor window ledge. I did my best to avoid looking down, but with everyone watching me from the yard, thirty feet below, it was hard not to. Some of the other kids were pointing up at me. Others shouted out, telling me to stop being an idiot and come down, as if maybe they thought I wanted to kill myself. Then one of the teachers on the ground told them to be quiet, and everyone fell silent and waited to see what would happen next. I was curious about that myself.

It was my first day at a new junior high school, in Miami.

The teacher on the ledge was holding out a hairy-looking hand, inviting me to take hold of it. "Come on, boy," he said, reaching toward me. "One small step and then you can grab my hand."

Oh God, oh God, if you help me to get down from here, I promise to be good.

But I stayed frozen to the window ledge. All six inches of it. The school had been built in the late 1950s, and apart from the concrete ledge the building was mostly made of glass. Like a giant greenhouse. There were no handholds to speak of. The teacher, a tall man with lots of blond hair and plenty of teeth, was holding on to the frame of the window I had been heading for, with his fingertips.

How the heck did I get up here?

During the lunch break I'd had a fight with a boy called Lawrence Malley. He wasn't any bigger than I was, but he thought he was tougher. Anyway, we had fought and it was a draw, and then we called it quits. He said he liked me and that I could be in his gang if I had the nerve to accompany him on a walk from one end of the school to the other. It sounded simple enough. There was just one problem. Neither one of us was allowed to touch the ground. This is how I came to find myself out on a window ledge thirty feet above the school yard.

At first the dare had gone well, and I flattered myself that I had probably made a new friend. But then Malley smiled a weird sort of smile and moved along the ledge at speed. He climbed through an open window and closed it behind him, abandoning me to my fate. And that was where I stayed, quite immobilized with fear, until someone spotted that I was stranded there and told the teacher, who opened the same window and came out after me.

The teacher had let go of the window frame and was now

edging his way toward me. His feet were so big only his heels seemed to be on the ledge. "I'm coming to get you, kid," he said. "Hold on."

I closed my eyes for a moment. So I didn't see what happened next. One minute he was beside me, and the next there were several loud screams from the yard below, followed by a muffled thump. The teacher had fallen off the ledge. I didn't look down. My legs felt like Jell-O. The Florida sun was shining brightly on my face, but my skin felt cold and clammy. The only reason I didn't throw up was the idea that I might throw up onto the teacher's dead body.

Bad enough to lose your life trying to help some stupid twelve-year-old kid from falling off a window ledge, but to get covered with his vomit as well is adding insult to injury.

Curiously, the teacher's death seemed to galvanize me, if that's the right word. I gritted my teeth, pressed my hands and back against the window, and started to move again. A few inches at a time. When I got as far as the open window, I felt someone grab me from behind and haul me back inside the classroom. It turned out to be two people, not one: the school principal, Mr. Anderson, and my own homeroom teacher, Miss Kendrick. For a moment I stood swaying in front of them, like I was on the rolling deck of a ship, and then I threw up on their shoes.

They took me to the sick room, telephoned my mother, and told her to come and take me home. By the time I saw her lime-green Oldsmobile pull into the school parking lot, I had learned two things. One was that a privet hedge had broken the teacher's fall, and he wasn't dead at all, but had a broken hip and a concussion. The other was the teacher's name. He was Mr. Diver.

It was April 1968 and I had just moved to Florida with my mom because she wasn't living with my dad. He was still living in our old house back in Texas. They weren't divorced, exactly, but she said that was only because legal things took time. My mom was originally from Miami, and when she left my dad, she decided we should go back there.

I didn't like Miami, I didn't like the house, I didn't like my room, I didn't like Mom's new boyfriend, Gene, who was a widower who lived around the corner, and I didn't like his wire-haired son, Marvin, who Mom said she hoped I would be friends with. I didn't like going to her old church. I didn't like church any more than I liked Miami. I didn't believe in God (maybe I would believe in him if I saw an angel or something). And now that I'd been to my new school, I didn't like that either. All in all, things in my new life in Florida were not looking good.

"What were you doing out on that window ledge, Scott?" Mom asked as we drove back to the house in the Bay.

"Praying," I said. This wasn't so far from the truth, but I couldn't help smiling while I said it.

I saw her glance across at me, and I knew the grin on my face would hardly help her to believe what I had just said. Most of the time when I tried praying on my own, it just sounded like me talking to myself.

"When you really put your mind to it," she said, "I think you can be quite an accomplished liar."

"It's true," I protested indignantly.

"The school principal said they all thought you were trying to kill yourself."

"I might as well be dead," I said. "I hate this place."

"What's to hate? In many ways Miami is just like Houston."

"I wish I was back with Dad," I said.

"Yes? Well I'd like to see how your father would react to what happened back there. That poor Mr. Diver has a broken hip. And a concussion. It's a miracle he wasn't killed. What the heck were you doing, Scott?"

"It was a dare," I said. "One of the guys kind of challenged me to do it with him."

"To do what? Get yourself killed?"

"To walk from one end of the school to the other without touching the ground," I said. "I was trying to make friends."

"With who? The angels?"

"You wouldn't understand."

"So what happened to him?" she asked. "This other lame-brained idiot?"

"Nothing," I said. "He did it. He finished the walk. And I froze up. Simple as that. About halfway across I made the mistake of looking down, and I panicked. I think maybe I suffer from vertigo."

"No, you don't," she said. "A fear or phobia of heights is called 'acrophobia,'" she said, and then proceeded to spell it out loud.

"Vertigo is merely a feeling. A passing sensation. Something very different. Take my word for it."

Take my word for it. It was what she always said when she knew she was absolutely right. Mom said it a lot. She was a fact-checker for the *Miami Herald*.

We got home. It was a Thursday, and Mom always took Thursdays off because she had to work Saturdays. Usually I looked forward to Thursdays because Mom made her ham loaf, which was my favorite meal of the week. Unless of course she had invited Gene and Marvin, which sometimes she did, and that spoiled everything.

Fortunately, on this particular Thursday it was just me and Mom. Despite what had happened that afternoon, she still made the ham loaf, and we ate it in silence. Mom was tired, so she put on her glasses, which didn't suit her at all. They reminded me of the fins on an old Cadillac Eldorado and made her look like a species of beetle. But Mom is a good-looking woman, I think. She's tall, a little overweight, perhaps, with lots of dark hair and nice brown eyes. My Dad says she reminds him of Elizabeth Taylor, which was one of the reasons he married her. He used to joke that she had a temper to match. I'm not exactly sure who Elizabeth Taylor is, but Dad was right about Mom's temper. She and my dad were arguing a lot then, of course. Mostly they argued about the same thing: the war in Vietnam.

My mom was dead against the war. Her elder brother Vern's son, Jimmy, had joined the Marines in 1966 and been killed in Vietnam the same year. He was just nineteen years old. This made it very difficult for my dad, who was an air-force pilot and who was training pilots who were not much older than Jimmy to fly fighter jets.

Things had sort of come to a head when my Mom joined an antiwar movement and started campaigning to get a different president from the one we had. Then she left home. And because my dad was often away on air-force business, I went with her.

After that she joined a whole lot of other antiwar organizations that went under the general heading of the peace movement. She even tried to get me involved in her work. But I wasn't interested. She stopped taking me along to her meetings when I started telling people who asked that when I grew up I wanted to be a spy and work for the Central Intelligence Agency. Like Felix Leiter in the James Bond movies. I love James Bond. I've seen all the movies at least three times. And I don't see anything wrong with wanting to be in the CIA.

After dinner, just before eight o'clock, we settled down to watch *Rowan and Martin's Laugh-In* on TV, which is one of my favorite shows. Mom says it's always the same, but I've told her that the whole point of the show is that it's always the same. Besides, I like things that are always the same. I hate things being changed. Anyway, it turned out that someone called Martin Luther King had been shot at a motel in Memphis. This upset Mom a lot. In fact, she was almost as upset as she was when we left Houston.

"That poor, poor man," she said, and, taking off her glasses, started to cry. I put my arm around her and tried to make her feel better.

"What's the matter with this country, Scott?" she asked me, after about five minutes of really solid crying.

"I don't know," I said. Beyond the fact that King was a black man and a doctor I didn't really know much about him.

"What happened to Dr. King is a reflection of the violence we are inflicting on the rest of the world. In places like Vietnam. What goes around comes around."

Here we go.

"Why does everything with you always come back to Vietnam?" I sighed.

After a moment or two she switched off the TV.

"What are you doing?" I asked, appalled.

"Switching off the TV," she said. "As a mark of respect to Dr. King."

"Respect? For what? He's not dead. He's been shot, that's all. He's in the hospital. That's what they said. He'll probably be okay. You'll see."

"You're just a kid," she said, "but one day you'll understand."

"I doubt it," I said. "When I have kids of my own, I'll let them watch exactly what they want."

So then she went on for a while about how black people in America were being treated like second-class citizens, and when she was finished, I said "Ver-r-ry interesting," in a German accent, the way Arte Johnson did on *Laugh-In*, which by rights I ought to have been watching. She didn't get it, and it was probably as well I didn't add the rest of his catchphrase, which was, "but shtupid."

Then I went to bed, still eaten up with irritation and anger that I hadn't been able to watch *Laugh-In* on TV.

If you ask me, people need to laugh more. Everyone does. Especially my mother. There are times when it seems to me that everyone is angry about this or angry about that. Every time you switch on the TV news, there are people waving signs and protesting about something. And I'm sick of it. The same way I'm sick of Miami and church and Gene and Marvin. I have to get away from it. And soon. Or I'll go nuts too. Just like the guy who shot Dr. King.

In the morning Mom was crying in her Wheaties. She told me that she'd just heard on the radio that Dr. King was dead. I said I was sorry for Dr. King and his family. Then I told her that I didn't want to live with her anymore. I wanted to go back to Houston and live with Dad.

After winning the victory over the Mexicans at San Jacinto that established Texan independence in 1836, Sam Houston decided to found a new town on the west bank of the Buffalo Bayou. That town is now the city of Houston. Once it was famous for oil. Now it's famous because the headquarters of the National Aeronautics and Space Administration, NASA, is about twenty miles south of Houston, in a place called Clear Lake. Before the end of the decade the Manned Spacecraft Center at Clear Lake will guide a man to the Moon. People say that Houston is just two blocks of Manhattan in the middle of a prairie. But I like to think that in the future, whenever anyone anywhere in the world looks up at the Moon, the chances are they are also going to think of our city.

* * *

This was the first time I'd ever flown by myself. Nine hundred sixty-four miles as the crow flies. At the airport in Miami, Mom had cried, and I felt pretty bad about that. She said she thought it had probably been wrong of her to make me try and live a new life with her without asking me first. That it was too much to expect any boy just to pull up stakes and leave all his friends, and his school, and his home. I said that I didn't care about any of those things, and that all I really wanted was for her and Dad to get back together. I didn't tell her what I was really thinking, which was that I figured there was a better chance of her going back to live with Dad if I was living with him. That was my plan, anyway. Maybe if she missed me enough, she'd go back to him.

There were a lot of people at William P. Hobby Airport when I arrived aboard an American Airlines jet from Miami, and I could see that Dad disapproved of them all.

"There are too many goddamned people flying these days, Scott."

That was the first thing he said as we walked out of the airport and got into the car. This was an Acapulco blue Shelby GT 350 with the full "King of the Road" package and ladder bars. Underneath the fancy paint job it was just a Ford Mustang, of course. But it was still a pretty good car.

He threw my bag into the trunk and then slid into the driver's seat.

"Too many," he said. "We got traffic jams on the ground, and if we're not careful, we're gonna have traffic jams in the sky. We've got to watch out for that. We're free spirits, you and I. And the sky's the last place where people like us can really exercise that freedom."

People like us. This sounded good. Like we were two of a kind. As opposed to me being one species and him another, which is how it usually was.

We drove northeast. Hobby is no distance at all from Pasadena. Six miles at most. As usual he drove really slowly. Like it wasn't a Shelby he was driving, but some crummy Datsun. "Any fool can drive fast," he used to say, "but not everyone can drive in control." Whatever that meant. Me, I couldn't see the point of owning a car like the Shelby GT and not gunning it a bit now and then.

"I spoke to Jerry Sherriff," he said. "And explained the situation."

Jerry Sherriff was the principal at my old school, Ima Hogg High.

"Oh?"

"He says you can have your old desk back, no problem. You start tomorrow. Seven forty-five a.m. on the dot. As usual."

"That's great, Dad," I said, trying to conceal my disappointment. I'd been hoping to take a few days off before going back to school. Clearly, my dad had other ideas.

"How is your mother?" he asked after a longish silence.

"She's good," I said.

"I hear you and she were going to church again," he said, half smiling.

"Yes, we did."

"I'm a Methodist, myself," he said. "There's a church on Main Street at Clay. Your mother and I got married there. Before she became a Baptist, that is. Do you want to go to church this Sunday, Scott?"

For a moment I tried to look as though I were actually taking this idea seriously. But the idea of going to church with my dad filled me with horror. I decided it would be best if I offered some kind of household chore by way of an alternative.

"No, sir," I said. "I thought I might try to mow the lawn this Sunday. That is, if I could use the sit-down."

The sit-down was what we called the Briggs and Stratton riding lawn mower. With its four-speed transmission and five horsepower it was as near to driving a car as I was likely to get for now.

"Sure," he said. "Never was much on churchgoing, myself. Not on a Sunday, anyway." There was a longish pause while he turned the car onto the Spencer Highway. "Is she happy, do you think?" he asked, after another long silence.

"No, I wouldn't say that." That seemed to please him. I added, "Especially not now that I'm here with you."

He nodded. "What do you think my chances are?" he asked. "Of getting her to come back to me?"

"Good," I said.

Really, I had no idea. But I wanted him to feel good about having me around again. It seemed to work. He leaned across and tousled my hair like he was actually pleased to see me. Maybe he had the same strategy for getting my mother back as I did. I doubt he'd have thought of a better one. My dad lacks guile. He's a pretty straightforward kind of guy.

"What the hell am I going to do with you, kid?"

"I'll be okay," I said. "You'll see. It'll be fine."

"I'm away a couple of times a month," he said. "Laredo. Fort Worth. Tucson. New Orleans. Sometimes for a few days. It's quite a thing when you're only twelve to find yourself having to handle things on your own. Getting up in the morning. Getting yourself to school. Getting your own dinner. Doing your homework. If this is going to work, I'm going to have to trust you, Scott."

I was looking forward to it, the way he described how my life would be. "You can trust me, Dad, honest."

"I hope so, Scott. Because if I find I can't, that's it, pal. You let me down just once, and it will be once too many. You'll go straight back to Miami to live with your mother. Is that clear?"

"I won't let you down, I promise."

"Then there's no more to be said about it."

For the two of us this had been quite a conversation. Normally Dad never says very much. And he scowls more often than he smiles. Before I left Houston to go to Miami with my mom, there was a competition in my class at school, and I won the vote for having the scariest father. His bark is worse than his bite, of course, but with a bark like that he really doesn't need to bite at all.

Dad isn't a tall man, but I've never seen a man who stands as straight as he does. He never slouches, or leans, or lounges. When he walks, he walks smartly, and never shuffles or saunters.

The way they look at you, his blue eyes are no less straight than his backbone. They go through you like laser beams.

When he's on duty, he wears his uniform. When he's off duty, he wears a short-sleeved shirt and a tie, even when he's at home. My dad is thirty-eight years old, and he comes from Oklahoma City. He sort of fascinates me, like a rare species of animal.

Dad's full name is Kenneth Frazer MacLeod. He hates the name Kenneth, but he is very proud of being a MacLeod and of his Scottish roots. We both are. My grandpaw Hamish MacLeod was a farmer, and Grandpaw's brother Alasdair was a crop duster. He was the one who taught my dad to fly. At the time Dad wasn't much older than me. Dad himself always says that he became a pilot because MacLeod sounds like "cloud" and the sky is in his blood because the MacLeods all came from the Isle of Skye. It's a nice explanation. Talking about flying is about the only time my dad sounds like a really interesting guy. Dad says Skye is a place where the sky never ends. I haven't been there yet, but the photograph of Skye that hangs on my bedroom wall seems to bear him out. My dad took it himself when he went there between wars. In the photograph you can see Kilt Rock, which is called that because it looks like the pleats on a kilt; other than Kilt Rock there's the sea and the sky, and somewhere in the middle there's a join, but it isn't exactly clear where. It looks like the kind of place you could fly around all day and you wouldn't have to share the sky with so much as a lost goony bird.

He joined the air force in 1951 and served in the Korean War. During that time he shot down five MiGs. When he came home, he married my mother. I was born in 1956. From here on in it's a little hazy. He did two tours in Vietnam between 1964 and 1967 and was shot down. He survived in the ocean for three hours before being picked up. The only time he ever spoke about it, he said:

"You want to know why I got shot down? Because I went back to look for someone in my squadron. Nobody gets left behind. That's what I've always believed. A good commander always brings his crew home. If he can. Only the air force didn't agree with me."

Three months after that he was posted back to Texas as a jet flight instructor. And that's pretty much all I know.

My dad's call sign as a pilot was Shark, and that was what everyone called him. The Shark. Only my mom ever called him Ken. Dad liked it just fine being called Shark. Someone said it was because when he was shot down and spent three hours in the sea off the coast of Vietnam waiting for rescue, a shark almost ate him—at least until it found out what he tasted like.

But the Shark himself told it differently. To me, anyway.

"If a shark ever stopped swimming, it would die. It's the same way with me and flying, Scott. If I couldn't fly, I'd die. And don't you ever forget it. You'll understand it better yourself if and when you get a pilot's license."

It felt good to be back home in Houston. Our house is in Pasadena, in the southeastern part of Houston, just a few miles north of Ellington Air Force Base. The house is two stories high on a corner lot, with a carport, a little wrought-iron balcony outside the master bedroom, a double garage, about half an acre of yard, and a fishpond out front surrounded by six weeping willow trees. The fish are long gone, eaten by some raccoon, or possibly a heron. There are plenty of herons in this part of the world. Most of them come in from the beaches whenever there's a storm.

My room was more or less just the way I had left it. There was my empty fish tank, the bookshelf with lots of books, and the desk where I did my homework. Many of the books on the shelves were about animals and birds. When I was a kid, I was quite interested in bird-watching. Next to my bedroom window was a telescope through which I sometimes observed birds, or sometimes the Moon, but just as often I used it to look at the girl who lived next door, Pamela Townshend, who sometimes liked to sunbathe in her backyard.

Above my head were all my dusty Revell model planes, hanging on bits of thread from my ceiling: an F-84F Thunderstreak, a B-29 Superfortress, a Sopwith Camel, a Bell X-5, a B-58 Hustler, and a Lockheed F-94C Starfire. My dad had flown both the Starfire and the Thunderstreak and, while telling me a little about what it was like to handle these fighter jets, he had helped me to assemble the models. Planes are the only models I'm interested in. Nothing else. One time he bought me a model of the Corvette Stingray Sport Coupe, and it's still in the box, unassembled.

By rights they should have made him a colonel when he got back from Vietnam. He was a senior major, with a lot of experience. They should have given him a base to command. It didn't happen.

Ima Hogg High School is one of the oldest public high schools in Texas. It was founded in 1878, which was when most of the teachers were born or last had sex. Especially the principal, Mr. Sherriff, who looks like he's a hundred and two if he's a day. Miss Ima—as people from Houston always call her—is a local philanthropist. This means that she is incredibly rich, having found a gusher of oil in her backyard in about 1920. She's still alive but pretty old, I hear. About eighty-six. Miss Ima seems to have spent the last forty years just giving money away, and it's my opinion that either she has got so much that she'll never actually be able to give it *all* away or she's just plain crazy. I tend to favor the latter explanation.

There's a lot to be said for the school. We have the oldest high-school newspaper in Texas, the *Guardian*, which was started in 1888. Probably this was the last time anyone actually read it, but that's just my opinion. In addition, we have a junior marching band that won some important state contest. When they play, they sometimes march up and down real quick, and look as though they are going to crash into each other, but they don't. They're pretty good, if you like that sort of thing. Me, I always kind of hope that they will actually crash into each other.

There's a lot to be said against the school, too. For one thing there's a uniform, which stinks. Then there's my homeroom teacher, Mr. Porteous, who also teaches math. He calls me Old Mac and seems to think that I'm a character and that I'm not going to amount to very much. But the main thing to be said against the school can best be illustrated by the following imaginary snatch of dialogue. When I say imaginary, I don't mean that it never happens. Actually, it happens all the time. I just mean that I'm not quoting any one particular occasion.

"Hi, what's your name?"

"Scott MacLeod."

"Well, hiya, Scott. What school do you go to?"

"Ima Hogg."

"Well, now that you come to mention it, you do look like one. / All right then, go 'oink, oink.' / I thought there was a nasty smell around here. / Did you make that mess on the sidewalk? / Does the farmer know you're loose? / Gee, a talking pig." Et cetera, et cetera.

See what I mean?

My best friend at Ima Hogg is an amiable giant by the name of Kit Calder. His father is a cattle rancher who got his name in the *Chronicle* in 1965 when he shot and killed a man who'd just held up the Wells Fargo Bank on Travis Street.

Naturally, I had to endure a certain amount of teasing upon my return from the Orange State.

"What's the matter, MacLeod? Florida too cold for ya?"

"Don't they speak Texican in Miami?"

"New school threw you out, huh? Can't say I blame them."

Porteous seemed especially displeased to see me back and decided to give the class a real good laugh at my expense. (I had no trouble remembering what he said; for days my classmates didn't tire of repeating it until they had it word for word.)

"Today we are obliged to welcome Mr. MacLeod back into your simple-minded midst. Some of us had breathed a sigh of relief and thought we were well rid of him. However, it turns out he was merely away on vacation, in Florida, of all places. There may be some of us who suppose that Old Mac's life has been one long vacation. Others might be tempted to imagine that the school he attended in Miami presented him with challenges that were beyond his modest intellectual gifts, and that he has only returned to our bosom so that he might coast through another semester without doing any work. But that would be a mistake. Don't you think so, Mr. MacLeod?"

It was good to be back at Ima Hogg, among the brain-damaged armadillos I called my friends.

On Sunday I mowed the lawn, and then we drove over to Elson's Garden Center on Yale, where Dad got some fertilizer and some roses. On the way back home we stopped at the Sheraton-Lincoln Hotel, where to my surprise he treated us to a proper roast beef lunch in the Cheshire Cheese, which is the name of the restaurant they have there.

"Want anything else to eat?" he asked, after my second plate of trifle.

"No," I said. "I'm really stuffed."

"Good. By the way, what do you think of the view here?"

I looked out of the window and down several stories onto Polk Avenue below and shrugged. "It's okay. But we're really not that high, Dad."

"Exactly. And do you feel like you want to throw up your lunch?"

"No." I wondered what he was driving at.

Then Dad asked me about the incident on the school roof in Biscayne Bay. Apparently he and my mother had already discussed it on the telephone.

"So what went wrong with the dare?"

"The guy I went up with closed the window and left me stranded there," I said. "I lost my nerve. I think I might be suffering from acrophobia."

"Acrophobia?" My dad uttered the word with distaste and shook his head. "You don't suffer from acrophobia. Not if you're up here and looking down. If you did suffer from acrophobia, your lunch would be on the carpet by now. The other guy closed the window and you panicked, that's all. Could happen to anyone."

I nodded silently, surprised at the vehemence with which he had spoken.

"And I'm going to prove it to you. This afternoon. We're going to take all the stuff we bought home. And then we're going to go to Ellington."

"You mean—?"

"That's exactly what I mean." He grinned. "This afternoon we're going down to Ellington. To go flying."

Nine . . .

Ellington is a reserve air-force base. It was here that my dad helped train young pilots from the Reserve Officer Training Corps, many of whom were destined to go to Vietnam. Also he flew all over the country, testing regular air-force pilots in places like Laredo, Tucson, and New Orleans. But his main job at Ellington was the command of two squadrons of Talon twin-jet trainers—the T-38—that the air force had lent to NASA for astronaut training.

Officially, the idea behind the NASA T-38s was that they'd help keep the piloting abilities and judgment of the astronauts from the nearby Manned Spacecraft Center at Clear Lake as sharp as possible. According to my dad, however, astronaut training was deadly dull, with little or no real flying involved, and the Talons had been lent to NASA simply to stop the astronauts from getting bored. They would frequently turn up at Ellington and borrow these supersonic aircraft, often with hardly a word of explanation to my dad. Mostly they were goofing off and joyriding, and sometimes more than that. But astronauts weren't like anyone else, of course. They were special. Everyone knew that.

Dad soon learned to turn a blind eye to what the Apollo boys got up to in the Talons. However, it was hardly surprising that over a period of time Dad developed a low opinion of astronauts. During the early years of the Mercury space program, a lot of spacecraft had been "flown" by chimpanzees. And Dad said that the only reason a man was going to the Moon was because a chimp had more sense. Another time he said that an astronaut was just a chimp with a college degree. Some of the things my dad said about astronauts were even worse than that.

Like most kids of my age, however, I thought being an astronaut looked like the most exciting job in the world.

Dad owns a Cessna 150D that he keeps at Ellington. He bought it in 1965 when he was on leave from the Nam, with some of the money my grandpaw left him in his will. The aircraft is white with a blue racing stripe down each side of the fuselage and has two seats side by side, two control sticks, and two sets of rudders. The air force uses this kind of plane for training new pilots, only it doesn't call the plane the Cessna 150D, but the T-41. That's just the way the air force does things. They have different names for everything. Dad's Cessna has a maximum speed of one hundred twenty-four miles per hour and an operating ceiling of fifteen thousand feet. I knew a lot about Dad's aircraft. Especially when you bear in mind that I had never once been in it.

The reason for this was simple. My mother was scared of flying in small aircraft. Mom wasn't scared of flying in big commercial planes. Just small, private ones like my dad's. Now, Houston is home to the largest flying club in Texas. Consequently, there are always reports in the *Chronicle* of small aircraft crashes. One of these crashes involved Don Pedley, the man who built our house. Don had owned a C-150 just like my dad's. After that, my mom clipped all reports of air crashes from the *Chronicle* and kept them in her purse. And whenever Dad suggested he might take me up for a "spin," she would present her clippings like evidence in *Perry Mason*, and the conversation that followed would go something like this:

"Why do you keep these things?" Dad would ask. "It's morbid."
"Morbid" means having a weird obsession with death and dying.

"To remind me why I don't want Scott to go flying with you," she'd say.

"Honey, there's nothing to worry about," he would reply. "I'm a good pilot."

"Glenwood is full of good pilots," she would say, referring to Houston's oldest cemetery.

"No, they're just the stupid ones," my dad would say. "Look, I don't know about the pilots in these stupid clippings you keep, but Don was a jerk. He was a daytime flier. He simply wasn't qualified to fly an aircraft in the dark on instruments only. He knew that."

My mom, who didn't appreciate the difference, would still not be convinced. And at this point she would usually marshal a reserve argument that my dad found impossible to trump. She used to say, "All right, Ken. Answer me this. If flying is so safe, then how come EFD"—which is what air-force families call Ellington Air Force Base—"is named after someone who was killed in a plane crash?"

This was true. It had happened in San Diego, in 1913.

At this point in the conversation all my dad could say was something like, "Honey, you should have married an insurance salesman, not an aviator." And that was it. Finito. End of story. I was grounded. I guess that my not going flying was just one more thing that came between them. Like the war in Vietnam.

At least I *had* been grounded, until now!

We drove right onto the apron, where he had left the Cessna tied down against the wind, and he left me sitting in the cockpit behind one of the two control sticks while he attended to all the preflight checks: tires, oil and hydraulic fluid on the tarmac, propeller, wheel struts, the leading edge of the wing, flaps and ailerons, tail section.

When he had finished examining the exterior of the aircraft, he got into the right-hand seat, put on a pair of aviator shades, and closed the door. He moved slowly, like he had all the time in the world.

"Most people see an aircraft as a way of saving time," he said. "That's all right if you're some traveling salesman hauling ass on American Airlines. But not if you're a pilot. Folks say that being older means you take more time to do the simplest things. But taking more time to do simple things is the only way a pilot ever gets to be any older. Think about it."

He turned the key, switching the electrics on, and sat there staring at all the gauges and instruments as if he were looking at a delicious buffet.

"You see," he said, "an aircraft isn't anything like a car. It has wheels and seats, but that's the only similarity. A car goes wrong, your journey might come to an end. But if an aircraft goes wrong, it could be your life that ends. So I always assume that the last person to fly this aircraft was an idiot. Even though I happen to know that the last person was me. And you know what? Sometimes I surprise myself. Either way it's a good habit that might save your neck."

Leaning forward he placed his lucky mascot on top of the instrument panel. It was a little rubber troll that I had given him the second time he went to Vietnam. It had a stupid face, big hair, and a little Stars and Stripes in one hand. He took it with him every time he flew. Then he tapped the glass of some of the dozen or more instruments with a brownish fingernail. There was nothing wrong with the clocks, but I sensed he was just making sure that none of the indicators got stuck. It all looked very complicated. But there was a photograph of this same cockpit on the wall of Dad's den, and I had studied it carefully, so I was quite familiar with what most of the clocks were for. He handed me a headset and put one on himself.

"The first important thing is that you're going to tell no one about this. No one at school. No one in the neighborhood. And especially not your mother. This is going to be our secret. Just you and me and the aircraft will know. Is *that* clear?"

"Yes, Dad. Very clear. I won't say a thing."

He started taxiing across the airfield and speaking to the control tower, joking with them, his tone cool and confident. The airforce guys at EFD adored my dad. I think he got away with a lot because of that. Even the astronauts, who largely kept themselves to themselves, liked him. He was what my mom called a real man's man. This means that men liked him more than women.

"You remember how I taught you to swim?" he asked as we approached our designated runway.

"Yes," I said carefully. How could I forget? A year ago Dad had thrown me in a friend's pool and watched as I almost drowned before paddling my way to the side. I knew this was the incident that had given me a fear of the water that endured in the face of all attempts by my schools to teach me to swim properly. He had no idea that I still couldn't swim, of course. Mom had suggested I keep quiet about it in case he threw me in again. He'd meant well, of course. He always did. But I still wondered what was coming next.

"Well, guess what?" he said. "Consider yourself thrown in again. At the deep end. You're going to handle the takeoff of this aircraft. Today is the day you start to learn how to fly."

"Me? Dad? Are you kidding? I mean, is that legal? I'm only twelve years old, remember?"

"Legal?" Dad laughed and started the engine. "While we're in this aircraft, I make the rules. And I say you are ready to fly. Is that clear?"

"Yes, Dad."

"Hell, my uncle Al taught me to fly a Stearman Kaydet when I was younger than you, Scott. And that's a hell of an aircraft."

I swallowed nervously, only partly reassured. And why should I have been? I *was* only twelve years old. I had a slot car racing set and a set of Lego building bricks. I was just a kid, for Pete's sake. Not the "new meat," which was what Dad called the young pilots he would sometimes fly in to Laredo to test and then pass or "wash out."

"Relax," he said, staring down the runway. "There's nothing to it. Landing the aircraft's the difficult part. Taking off is a piece of cake. Anyone who can handle a sit-down lawn mower as well as you do can easily execute a takeoff procedure in a light aircraft. Now put your feet on the pedals. They're what we call the rudders."

I placed my feet on the rudders.

"All right, now take hold of the stick."

I nodded and grabbed the stick like I was planning to wrestle a steer onto the dirt. Through my sweating hands I could feel the aircraft vibrating like some giant crazed insect. The noise inside the cockpit was tremendous.

"See that red button on the stick?" said Dad. "Press that and you can start steering the nose wheel. You push one foot down on the lower part of the rudder pedal and the aircraft will go one way. Push the other rudder to take it in the opposite direction. That lever by your right hand there's your throttle. You push it forward to give you more power. Got it?"

I pressed the button on the stick and pushed the rudder down, and the plane began to turn. For a minute or two I turned the aircraft one way and then the other, and the plane waltzed elegantly around the apron. I was enjoying myself.

Eventually, when my dad figured I had the hang of the steering and brakes, he pointed to our right.

"Okay, you have control. Steer the aircraft that way, in a straight line, until I tell you to stop."

We began to move toward the runway. He flicked a switch on the radio, spoke to the radio tower for a moment, and then turned to me.

"All right, Mr. MacLeod, listen up. I want you to point the aircraft down that runway and then come to a halt."

My heart was in my mouth as I coasted the Cessna to a halt.

"Okay. It's at this point we say to ourselves, 'The Fat Man Pissed Into Someone's Hot Coffee.' That's what we call a mnemonic. A way of remembering important stuff. T for Trim and the Throttle. F so that we know we have enough Fuel and that the Flaps are set for takeoff. M means we have to check the fuel Mixture. P means we check the fuel Primer is in and locked. I for Instruments one last time. Everything looks okay. S means the Switches. Hot means Hatches, Harness, and Hydraulics. The C in coffee stands for Controls, Carburetor, if it's cold, and Cowl flaps, if fitted. Everything looks a-okay. On the top left of your instrument panel you have an airspeed indicator. When I tell you that you have control, you are going to move the throttle forward so that we start to pick up speed in a straight line. You'll be steering us with your rudders. At sixty miles an hour you are going to pull steadily back on the stick so that the nose wheel lifts from the runway. The aircraft will then start to lift in the air. Simple as that. You have control of the aircraft. Take us up."

"Yes, sir."

I pushed the throttle, and the plane began to move down the runway, quickly gathering speed. It was easy to keep the nose wheel in the center, and soon the airspeed indicator was reading forty miles per hour. When it got to sixty, I started to pull the stick back. For a moment nothing at all happened, but gradually the aircraft began to lift off the ground. It seemed miraculous.

The Cessna continued climbing until, at two hundred feet, Dad told me to ease off. The nearly cloudless sky was as blue as a jaybird and the cockpit seemed flooded with warmth and light, as if during takeoff we had punctured some invisible bubble of sunshine. There were several rays as thick as logs shining through the windows.

"What'd I tell ya?" said Dad. "That was a perfect takeoff, Mr. MacLeod. Hell, you're a natural stick-and-rudder man. How does it feel?"

I tried to swallow the carburetor-size lump in my throat but couldn't do it, and I shook my head dumbly.

"I know, I know," said my dad. He was grinning at me. "The first time can be a little emotional. It was the same way for me. Just wait until you go solo. I envy you, boy, I really do."

Eventually I managed to get a word out of my mouth. "Fantastic," I said. And then, "Thanks, Dad."

"Hell, kid, no problem." He pointed out of the windshield. "You want to go higher, don't pull back on the stick like maybe you think you should. Give it more throttle and the aircraft will do the rest. You want to go faster, push the stick forward a little to drop the nose. The air will do the rest."

Glancing out of the window I saw that we were already over the golf course at Clear Lake. A minute later Dad was pointing to a collection of unremarkable modern buildings on the edge of some parkland. "That's the Manned Spacecraft Center," he said. "Better known as Mission Control. Sometimes when you fly over, you can see those astroschmucks getting a tan on the roof."

We were headed out over Galveston Bay, toward the Gulf of Mexico.

"All right," said Dad. "Where do you want to go?"

"How about the Astrodome?" I said. "The baseball game. Astros are playing the Atlanta Braves."

"You sure about that?" Dad was grinning.

"Sure I'm sure. Friday they beat them five-three. But yesterday they lost five-two."

"I have control," said Dad. He kept on grinning, like he knew something I didn't, and then he got on the radio again to clear our flight path.

We approached the Astrodome from the southeast, coming up over Pearland, where he gave me the controls again and told me to fly up the line of Main Street. And then we saw it, glinting in the sun, like a large diamond in a setting of gray and green. We flew right over the famous *roof.* In my excitement I'd forgotten all about the roof. A roof that meant we couldn't see any of the action taking place on the field below.

Dad was laughing now. "Can you see the scoreboard?" he asked. "Who's pitching?"

I grinned back at him. "I forgot about the roof," I said.

"Just a bit," he said.

I continued flying north for a mile or two before Dad took control once again and turned left over northwest Houston.

"Dad?"

"Yeah?"

"I think I've realized something important, Dad. Something that has never happened to me before."

"What's that, Scott?"

"I think I realized that the rest of my life just changed, forever."

President John F. Kennedy got shot in 1963. He was in Dallas, Texas, at the time. Five years later his little brother Bobby was looking to become president, too. But some guy didn't like Bobby, and so he shot him. Five other people got shot as well, but they didn't say who they were. This latest shooting happened on June 5, 1968, in the Ambassador Hotel in Los Angeles. We were asleep at the time. And we heard about it the next morning when we switched on the TV news. They took Bobby to the hospital, but later on he died. This was a bad start to the summer. Bobby had been assassinated. The war in Vietnam was going badly. And every time you turned on the TV news or opened a copy of *Life* magazine, there were students demonstrating against the war in one city or another. I often asked Dad what he thought, but mostly he didn't want to talk about it.

Dad was away a lot for the rest of the month testing pilots in Laredo, but we kept the flying going on weekends when he was back home. I read a lot of books about the principles of flying. *The Air Pilot's Manual*—stuff like that. I read about incipient spins, crosswind operations, descending turns, pilot navigation, and a whole lot of other stuff. When he saw how seriously I was taking it, he fixed it for me to get into Ellington when he wasn't around and use one of the flight simulators they have there. It was against the rules, but Dad said that if it was okay for a bunch of goddamned astronauts to borrow a jet to go shopping, then it was okay for him to let his kid use a sim now and then.

At Ellington all the flight simulators are housed in one room, so all the other pilots can see you when you come in. Each simulator is encased in a large box with a TV screen, a stick, instruments, and some rudders, and once you are in there it's almost as good as the real thing. Almost but not quite. It's not nearly as thrilling, which is the downside. Then again, if you make a mistake, you don't crash and kill yourself. Dad says it saves the air force a lot of money that way. In the beginning I crashed quite a bit, but pretty soon I had it licked and was flying with real confidence. Dad noticed the difference when we were flying for real.

Using the sim meant I got to meet some of the other pilots. They called me Eddie Rickenbacker, after the World War I flying ace who, the story goes, tried to teach himself to fly when he was a kid by leaping off the barn roof with an umbrella, and a lot of dumb stuff like that.

The nicest one of these pilots was a guy called Lee Stervinou. Lee gave me sticks of gum and bought me Cokes, and he gave me some useful flying tips, but he always drew the line at letting me try a cigarette.

"If the Shark found out that I'd let you smoke, he'd have my ass," he said.

From talking to Lee I gathered that there weren't many dog-fights in Nam. A dogfight is when two jet fighters engage in aerial combat.

"That's not the way Charlie fights," said Lee. Charlie was what they called the communist North Vietnamese army. "In the Nam most fighter aircraft missions are to destroy targets that are on the ground, using Sidewinder missiles and napalm bombs."

"But people do get shot down," I said.

"Sure," said Lee. "But mostly it's by antiaircraft fire or surface-to-air missiles."

"My dad was shot down in Nam," I said. "But he won't talk about it."

"I can understand that," said Lee. "A lot of guys come back from Vietnam and don't talk about it. I think maybe they like to forget about it when they come home. But it's hard, you know? With everything that you see on TV."

Before summer vacation I went on the school trip to the Museum of Fine Arts in Houston. But I wasn't really interested in a lot of old pictures. What I was really interested in was Pamela Townshend, the girl next door, who is a year ahead of me at Ima Hogg. She said she thought it was weird that I was more interested in her than in some pictures by Cézanne, but I could see she was a little flattered all the same. And I spent a lot of the trip trying to make her like me. This proved to be quite difficult. Because she's taller than me. And beautiful. Absolutely the loveliest thing I've ever seen.

"You're too small to be thinking about girls," she said.

"I'm not much smaller than you," I said. "Maybe you're a little older, if that's what you mean."

"I'm a whole year older than you," she insisted.

"That's not so much. My dad is five years older than my mom." I shrugged. "Anyway, I'm not thinking about girls. I think about you, Pamela. Other girls mean nothing to me." I told myself that the girls of *Playboy* did not count. Besides, they weren't really girls. They were the stuff that certain dreams were made of. "You're the only girl I ever think about."

"Do you really mean that, Scott?" she asked.

"Of course I mean it, Pamela."

"If only there wasn't this gap in our ages," she said. "It would be easier."

"Look, what if I did something that would really impress you?"

"Like what?"

"I dunno." Of course, I was thinking that maybe one day, when I was a little bit older, there might be a way of persuading Dad to let us take her up in the plane. With me flying. "But I'm determined to impress you in some way."

"I don't think that's very likely," she said. "Do you? You're just a kid. But when you're ready to impress me, don't hesitate to call, Scott. And I'll be there."

"You promise?"

"Sure," she said. "I promise. Just don't forget to ask, okay?"

When I wasn't thinking about Pamela Townshend, I spent most of the time thinking about the sim at Ellington. Or wishing I could go flying with Dad. That same week he presented me with my very own USAF-issue K2-B flying coveralls. Made of light gray-green cotton, the K2-B is flame-retardant, but Dad said I shouldn't let that fool me. Dad said he'd had to phone around every USAF store in the country before he'd found a size small enough to fit me. He also gave me my own pair of Ray-Ban aviators. These sunglasses were developed specifically for pilots.

By now I was able to land as well as take off. Landing an aircraft is much more difficult. My first few landings were far from perfect. They were what Dad called balloons and bouncers.

Toward the end of summer we were practicing stalls. A stall happens when there is insufficient airflow under the wings and the aircraft starts to fall. The weight of the aircraft overcomes lift. The first time we did it, Dad pulled the throttle out until the engine was just ticking over, dropping our airspeed to less than fifty miles per hour. The aircraft started shuddering like an old stagecoach, which is something you don't get in the sim. Then the stall-warning signals started, which I hadn't heard before. It was all quite alarming. Next thing the nose of the aircraft dropped like a stone toward the ground. A big stone. And my heart started to beat at probably two or three times its normal rate. Seeing me swallow nervously, Dad smiled and relaxed his grip on the stick for a moment.

He pushed the throttle back in and, pulling the stick back toward him, recovered control. We were level again.

Then it was my turn. I practiced the maneuver several times until he decided I had it right.

After we landed, I let out a breath and shook my head. My shoulders were aching from all the pulling on the stick. And when I took off my new flying suit, my shirt was soaked with sweat. Dad smiled and said, "Flying is one sure way to find out if you have a heart condition or not."

Eight . . .

It was my thirteenth birthday. Mom came back to Houston from Miami. *On the train.* We all met for lunch at Brennan's, on Smith Street.

For my birthday Mom gave me a Polaroid Land camera. It has a built-in timer to let you know when your picture is ready. After lunch we walked over to Tranquility Park, where, reluctantly, they agreed to pose for my new camera. They stood apart and looked kind of stiff, like they were standing on the medals podium at the Olympics in Mexico City. Of the two, Dad seemed more cheerful; Mom looked like maybe he'd won the silver and she'd had to settle for the bronze. When she'd gone, I asked Dad if he thought there was any chance she might come back. He shrugged and didn't answer for a while, as if he was really thinking about his answer.

Dad gave me a Skyscope, which is a Newtonian reflector telescope with an aperture of three and a half inches and focal length of f10. With it you can see the polar caps on Mars, the belts and large moons of Jupiter, and Saturn and its rings and three of its moons. It cost forty-five dollars, but Dad said it'd be worth every cent if I get to see some dumb astronaut fall on his ass when he's walking on our Moon.

That night I looked at the Moon for almost an hour. Once upon a time people had just looked at it, written poems and music about it. Some of them had even worshiped it. But no one had thought of actually going there until Jules Verne had written a novel about it, almost exactly one hundred years ago, in 1865. Even then the thought remained little more than a dream: science fiction. Who could have imagined that a president of the United States would turn Verne's dream into a reality? "We choose to go to the Moon in this decade and do the other things, not because they are easy, but because they are hard . . ." John F. Kennedy said that. There was hardly a person in Houston who didn't know these words by heart, because they had been spoken right here in Houston, at Rice University, on September 12, 1962. *By the end of the decade.*

Now, if Kennedy had said we'd get to the Moon before the end of the century, then a lot more people might have believed it could be done. As it was, there were quite a few who thought Kennedy's "Moon choice" was foolhardy. Even now, more than five years after Rice, there were folks in Houston—my Dad included—who thought Kennedy had taken leave of his senses when he'd said that.

"If you ask me, Jack Kennedy's idea would probably have been quietly dropped if he hadn't got himself assassinated in Texas," he said.

As I continued my observation of the Moon's plaster-of-Paris surface, another thing that occurred to me was this. Even the most powerful telescope we have, the two-hundred-inch Hale Telescope at the Mount Palomar Observatory, couldn't actually see a spacecraft landing on the surface of the Moon. *So how are we going to know for sure that it has actually happened? I mean, the TV pictures of the Gemini missions were pretty crummy-looking. I don't know what kind of cine-camera they're using on the spaceflights, but they want to get a better one. Because if NASA is not careful, we might get some people who say that it didn't happen at all.*

But whatever happens, the more you look at the Moon, the more incredible going there actually seems.

"Which one was Moonwatcher?" asked Kit Calder as we came out of the movie theater.

"He was one of the apes," I said. "The one that used the jawbone of the animal to kill the other ape."

"Oh. You mean the ugly one."

"That's right. The nutcase."

Kit and I had just been to see *2001: A Space Odyssey* for the second time, in the hope that we might understand it a bit better. We didn't. At the same time, however, I felt I'd experienced something special.

"I thought that one of the best things about the movie," I said, "was those scenes with the apes at the beginning."

"Yeah," he said. "What was that all about? And how did they train them to do that?"

"Do what?"

"You know. Touch the monolith. And use tools and stuff."

"You make it sound like they were real apes," I said.

"Awww, go blow your jets," he said. "They *were* real monkeys."

I shook my head and smiled. "With the exception of two baby chimpanzees," I said, "all of the apes in the movie were played by human beings dressed up in animal skins." This was perfectly true. I'd read about it in a magazine. "They filmed all of that stuff in London, apparently." But Kit wasn't having any of it.

"Crap," he said. "That was never filmed in London. And those were real monkeys. Had to be."

"Yeah? Well, first off they weren't monkeys; they were apes. Monkeys have tails. Apes don't. And how come all those apes have names in the list of cast credits at the end of the movie?"

"I didn't see any names."

"What about Moonwatcher?" I asked. "He had a name. He was played by someone called Daniel Richter. If he's an ape, then how come he has a human name?"

"All right, maybe that ape was a human," said Kit. "But the rest had to be all apes. Anyway, what makes you such an expert on apes and monkeys?"

I might have said that it had long been my dearest wish to own a pet chimpanzee, but that of course my dad had said no.

"As a matter of fact," I said, "we've had a family membership at the Houston Zoo ever since I can remember."

"That figures, looking at you, pal."

"The primate section is one of the oldest and my most favorite parts of the zoo," I said, also neglecting to mention the toy chimp that still sat on my bed. His name was Jacko. Anyway, what was there not to like about our nearest relative? "But I don't think you have to be an expert to know the difference between a real ape and some guy in a suit," I told him. "Look, I don't know why you should have a problem believing any of this, Kit. Didn't you see *Planet of the Apes*? This is the same thing. Men in monkey suits."

"As I recall, it's largely thanks to you, MacLeod, that I once believed the apes in *Planet of the Apes* were real."

I grinned, remembering that this was true. "Despite the fact that they could talk," I said.

"The funny guy," he said, and putting his large hands around my neck he pretended to throttle me. "You're full of crap, MacLeod, do you know that? This is just another one of your stupid stories to make me look like an idiot."

"You don't need one of my stories to do that," I said, and Kit began throttling me again.

Well, it's true, of course. I do like to tell a tall tale. The taller the better. After all, I was born in Texas. We've got tales taller than the ALICO Building. But Kit was easy prey. He was one of the most gullible people I'd ever met. And really it wasn't very difficult convincing him of anything.

✪ ✪ ✪

There is something about skimming over a bank of cumulus clouds that seems exactly like a wonderful dream. Midway between heaven and earth is a very peaceful and dreamlike place to be. And somehow being above the world helps you appreciate it a little more. To realize how it might be without you. When you're detached from the ground, watching people and cars coming and going far below, the closer proximity to the Sun and the Moon is inclined to make you more contemplative and thoughtful. Perhaps it's no wonder that as soon as man was airborne and defying gravity, he wanted to take the dream as far as he could, across the Atlantic from Long Island to Paris, even as far as the Moon.

By now I had at least thirty flying hours in the Cessna. In less than six months I had learned to take off, land, handle a power-on stall and a power-off, fly a figure of eight, fly on instruments—you name it, I could do it. But there was one thing I hadn't yet done. And that was go solo. Going solo is when you fly without anyone in the cockpit alongside you. It's a big moment for every novice pilot. I knew I was ready, and so did Dad, but, as usual in life, there was a problem. My age.

"If you were older, I'd let you do it," said Dad. "Hell, I've got new meat coming to learn how to fly Tweets that aren't up to your standard, boy. *But.*"

A Tweet is a twin-engine jet used for training pilots. The air force calls it the T-37, and it's supposed to give student pilots the feel for handling the larger, faster Talon.

"*But* the thing is this," said Dad. "Because you're only thirteen, we can't apply for you to have a private pilot's license. Not yet. You have to be fifteen to take the written test, and seventeen to get a private pilot's license. I know, I know, you're ready now, but that's just the way it is, son. Until you're fifteen, you're going to have to sit tight and be patient."

"That's two years," I said.

"I never figured on you becoming such a competent aviator as quick as you have," he admitted. "Frankly, I'm astonished at the progress you've made."

He could see that I was disappointed.

"Tell you what I'm going to do," he said. "I have to go over to Laredo on Sunday." He made it sound like it was just across the street. But it was more than three hundred miles to Laredo. "Why don't I take a Tweet instead of a Talon, and you can come along for the ride. How's that?"

"You mean it?"

"Sure I mean it."

"Won't the air force mind?"

Dad looked awkward for a moment, like he was trying to remember where he had parked the car. "The hell with them," he said, shaking his head. "What do they know what goes on at Ellington? Those goddamned astronauts treat the place like a goddamned taxi stand, anyway. But we'll leave early in the morning, so no one will be any the wiser."

He nodded. I could see how he was thinking out all the possible pitfalls. "Then, when we get to Laredo . . . well, hell, kid, I'm a major. No one but a bull colonel's going to challenge me."

It was a Monday when he said this. And the days before Sunday dragged like they had a chute flaring out the back. On Thursday night Dad was away in Dallas, and I had the house to myself. Kit came over for the evening and I made us both TV dinners, which we ate while we watched TV. Then we searched Pamela Townshend's bathroom window with my new telescope to see if behind the frosted glass we could detect some sign of her naked body, or perhaps her mother's.

"Hey," said Kit, after we had scanned the window fruitlessly for almost half an hour. "How about we help ourselves to some of your dad's cigarettes?"

"Okay," I said.

We went into the den, and I let Kit have a good snoop around for a while because I was quite proud of the way it made my dad look. There were lots of pictures of him in uniform and standing beside jets and stuff like that. But Kit picked up a little framed piece of poetry my dad had on his desk.

"'Oh! I have slipped the surly bonds of earth,'" he said, reading it aloud. "'And danced the skies on laughter-silvered wings.' What's that?"

"Poetry," I said. "It's by some fighter pilot called John Magee who got killed in a Spitfire during the Battle of Britain in the Second World War. He was nineteen years old."

"It's nice."

"My dad says it describes what his life is all about."

I flipped open the lid of the silver cigarette box. "Help yourself."

Kit took one and let me light him up. And then I lit up myself.

And then Kit did his perfect lisping impersonation of Arte Johnson doing the German in the jungle on *Laugh-In*, which was the best of all his stupid voices. Somehow it worked better with a real cigarette as a prop.

While we smoked our cigarettes, I fetched the key to Dad's secret closet and showed Kit the top shelf, where all the *Playboys* were hidden. And his eyes lit up like he was Larry on *Bewitched* and I was Darrin working some cute miracle, with Samantha's secret help, of course.

While Kit amused himself with a year's worth of Playmates of the Month, I took a more leisurely look through some of Dad's other stuff. There were several flight manuals, a rack of wine, some cameras, a Bullworker home-exercise system, and more piles of magazines: *Sports Illustrated* and *Life*. But it was the boxes of papers I was interested in. Of special interest to me was a manila envelope with the word "NASA" scrawled on the front. Inside was a letter from the Pentagon ordering my dad to report to Washington on February 2, 1959; another letter ordering him to report for "medical evaluation" at some place called the Lovelace Clinic, in Albuquerque, and then astronaut training at Wright-Paterson Air Force Base in Ohio; and last, a letter from NASA, dated June 1960, telling Captain Ken MacLeod "with regret" that he had not been one of the seven men chosen for Project Mercury, but that NASA was very grateful to him for volunteering for what promised to be a very difficult assignment. "The impression you made on the selection committee was favorable. Overall, however, we did not feel your qualifications met the special requirements of the astronaut program as well as those of some of the other outstanding candidates." Project Mercury had been the USA's first manned space mission; it had seen its climax on February 20, 1962, when John Glenn became the first American to orbit the Earth. Even now, six years after his orbit, John Glenn was just about the most famous man in America.

I read the letter several times just to make sure that I was reading it correctly. But the letter was only one paragraph long, and there could be little room for doubt.

My dad was a reject from the astronaut program.

I felt a pang of regret for him. But it helped explain a lot. Such as why Dad was always making jokes about "astroschmucks" and their seemingly endless privileges, like low-priced Corvettes, and the free tickets for the Oilers—for some reason that had always really irritated him. He was jealous of them. Had to be. Every time he saw an astronaut, he was probably thinking that it could have been him. And maybe wishing that it had been.

"What's up?" asked Kit. "Has your old man got a dirty secret? Do tell."

Hurriedly I returned the letter to the box, and then I shook my head. "It's nothing," I said. "Nothing at all."

My face must have told a different story. Either way, Kit wasn't convinced. Sometimes my friend was much more perceptive than I gave him credit for. Friends often are. He looked squarely at me, trying to read what was in my mind and heart.

"You want my advice? Whatever it is you found in that box,

don't ever mention it. Not ever. Sometimes, what's in the box needs to stay in the box. You just found that out the hard way."

Kit was right. And I decided to say nothing about what I'd discovered. Least of all to my dad. For one thing I figured that if I asked him about the NASA application, then he'd guess I'd been raking through his private stuff, go nuts, and bawl me out. But most important of all, of course, I didn't mention it to him in case he decided not to take me to Laredo in the Tweet. Stupid I was not.

Going to Laredo in the Tweet was going to be great. I had no doubt about that. For my dad it was a clever card to play. Compensation for not being allowed to go solo didn't come much better than a ride in a military jet. But I have to confess that the fact that I was four years off getting my license still really bugged me. It was so unfair. In order to impress him with my knowledge of another airplane, I decided to familiarize myself with the Tweet's instruments and flight controls before my trip.

Tweet was short for Tweety Bird, after the little yellow cartoon canary who's always being chased by Sylvester the cat. You know, the one who says, "I tawt I taw a puddy tat." Built by Cessna as a side-by-side jet trainer, the Tweet wasn't the fastest or largest aircraft ever built, but according to the books it *was* one of the most maneuverable and best-loved jets in the air force. Hence the name. I kind of liked the name myself. It sounded cute and friendly. Probably they ought to have painted it yellow. Instead it was the same colors as Sylvester the cat: black and white. Which seemed a shame.

There was nothing cute about the Tweet's flight manual, however. For one thing the first page made clear that it was illegal for an unauthorized person like me to read or even have possession of the manual. (I'd borrowed it from the closet in my father's den.) All the time I was reading the manual, I half expected some air-force policemen to appear behind me and clap me in irons. No less intimidating to me was the size of the manual, which was a massive three hundred eighty pages long. Also it was full of graphs about things like descent times that looked more complicated than anything in your worst math homework. I might have been put off reading such a huge and complicated book but for an early paragraph entitled "Sound Judgment." This explained that the instructions in the manual were for "a pilot inexperienced in the operation of these airplanes." Well, that was me, all right. The flight manual also made it clear that it provided anyone flying the Tweet with "the best possible operating instructions under most circumstances." In other words, short of actually flying the Tweet I had only to read the manual to know everything there was about this airplane.

Of course, as well as reading the manual I also managed to persuade Lee Stervinou to show me the controls in the T-37 simulator at EFD. He'd already seen me use the T-41 simulator, the one just like my dad's Cessna 150—all the other pilots had—and he knew that I could handle a propeller-aircraft sim okay. But that didn't stop him from teasing me a little. Especially when he saw the flight manual under my arm.

"You after my scarf, kid?" As a pilot who'd soloed a Talon T-38,

Lee was entitled to wear a scarf that was white with red polka dots. Around Ellington that kind of thing marked you out as special.

"Maybe," I said. "But I'd rather have that gold Corvette that's parked outside."

"Oh, that," said Lee. He pointed to a guy in a flying suit with blue eyes and not much hair. He was coming out of the Talon simulator. "The 'vette's his."

"Wow," I said, because I knew that with a car like that the guy just had to be an astronaut. All the astronauts had to practice regularly on the Talon sim before flying the real thing. Dad insisted on it.

Grinning broadly, the guy came over. He had a gap between his front teeth that was just like mine. And he was only an inch or two taller than me. "I know there's a war on," said the guy, looking me up and down. "But the air force is taking them kind of young, these days, isn't it?"

"This is the Shark's kid," said Lee. "Scott MacLeod."

"Chip off the old block, huh?" The guy held out his hand. "Pete Conrad," he said. "Nice to meet you, Scott."

"You're an astronaut," I said dumbly. "You were on *Gemini Five*. And you were the commander on *Gemini Eleven*. You set a world record for flight altitude."

"So they tell me," said Pete.

"Are you're going to the Moon, sir?"

"They tell me that, too," said Pete. He grinned and added, "But I'm not so sure. None of us is. Sometimes it seems like a pretty tall order."

"I'd like to be an astronaut, sir," I said. "When I grow up."

"I don't know that growing up is all that important for what we do," said Pete. "If it was, then maybe we'd be doing something else. But you're in the right place, Scott." He nodded at the flight manual under my arm. "And from the look of things, you're going to get there before me." He glanced at a watch that was as big as a paperweight. "Well, I'd better be running along. I have a lesson to go to back at MSC. Computer programming. By the time you grow up, Scott, they won't need pilots at all. The spacecraft will be flying themselves."

We watched him go. The gold Corvette took off with a tire-burning launch that Lee reckoned was mostly done for our benefit. Which only made me appreciate it all the more.

"I liked him," I said. "He was okay."

"Pete is a real friendly guy," said Lee. "That is, for a navy man."

"He's in the navy?"

"U.S. Navy pilot. Lot of those astronauts are navy men."

"You ever thought of becoming an astronaut, Lee? Going to the Moon?"

"Naw. I like it down here. 'Sides, I'm going to Florida this weekend." He grinned at me and tousled my hair. "I ain't got time to go to the Moon."

Lee and I went back into the sim center. I took my place inside the Tweet simulator, with Lee kneeling alongside. It was dark in there. It had to be dark for the simulation to work. It was easier to make a sim that way. After all, it was just a lot of little lights on a black background. The idea was that you were flying at night. Lee switched on the sim, and our faces turned green from the lights, of the instruments on the control panel. We looked vaguely sick, which reminded me that it was possible to make yourself sick if you stayed in a sim for long enough.

"Moving from a prop to a jet is quite a step," said Lee. "Think you can handle it?"

"What can happen?" I shrugged. "It's a sim, right?"

Even with Lee sitting beside me, the simulator was a lot harder to "fly" than I had figured. In a propeller airplane like the T-41 there's a lot more time to do stuff. You can look out the window of the aircraft—bank the wings for a while and enjoy the view from two thousand feet. Once the airplane is trimmed—that just means adjusted for speed and height—it almost flies itself. But in a jet everything happens so quickly. Takeoff was simple enough, just like before: I pointed the aircraft down the runway, pushed the throttle up, and then kept the nose straight until I had enough speed to lift off. So far so good. But from then on everything was much harder to control. Everything. It was a little like finding yourself in the saddle on an extremely fast stallion that quickly ran away with you.

For example, after takeoff the Tweet was up to fifteen thousand feet in just a couple of minutes. And, despite my efforts with the stick, it kept wanting to go up even higher than that. In a straight line things were easy enough. But as soon as I turned, I found myself turning too far and then having to correct the course the other way. Landing seemed almost impossible.

Even at the lowest revs my final approach to the runway felt like an express train. In the real T-41 I had been able to pick a spot on the runway from about two or three miles out and land on it every time. Sometimes it was like landing a kite. But in the Tweet simulator my final approach was always too high and too fast.

I crashed. And I crashed again. I turned too low, stalled, and took the wing off. I overshot the runway and went through an aircraft hangar. One time I demolished the passenger terminal at William P. Hobby.

"Congratulations, kid," said Lee. "You just killed yourself and everyone in the airport. The Federal Aviation people will be here to arrest you any second for culpable manslaughter."

He thought that was pretty funny.

Of course, it was just a simulation. Luckily for me. Not to mention all the people at William P. Hobby Airport. Still, I couldn't help feeling a tinge of guilt about what had happened. That was the thing about the simulators at Ellington. They were very realistic. Everyone said so.

"I'm never going to get the hang of this," I complained.

"Sure you will," said Lee. "You're a kid. Kids have got all the time in the world. Which is why kids get the hang of everything eventually. Especially the things they're not supposed to be able to do until they're older."

That night I dreamed I went flying. I was going solo in the Tweet. As I took off and climbed up into the sky, the golden mosaic that was the Earth seemed hardly there at all, and my connection with it almost irrelevant. There was just me, the instruments, the stick in my hands, the sound of the engine, and, dead ahead of the Tweet's pointed nose, the Moon. Not a yellow moon, but a brilliantly white one: the type of white that is so unearthly. This, I told myself, was the sight that would surely greet the Apollo astronauts, the Pete Conrads of this world, when they finally set out for the Moon.

I pushed the throttle in all the way, pulled the stick back as far as it would go, and aimed squarely at the Moon.

Surely, it was just a matter of going there. It seemed simple enough. Why hadn't anyone thought of doing this before? And the higher I climbed, the more it seemed that I was already half-way there.

For a long time I kept the Moon in sight in front of me, like the lucky mascot Dad always placed on his instrument panel whenever he was flying. At about twenty-five thousand feet my ascent slowed significantly, but still I kept the airplane pointed at the Moon. After a while the airplane leveled out, and each time I tried to pull back on the stick to keep on course for the Moon, it started to bounce around in front of me like the telescopic-sight gunshot that always starts off a James Bond movie. Something was pulling me back to Earth.

Gravity. Of course. The engines aren't powerful enough.

Then I stalled. All sorts of warning lights and loud noises came on in the Tweet's cockpit. But it was too late. I was losing control. The airplane fell away in the sky like a dying bird.

A Tweety Bird. And there was nothing I could do. I spiraled toward the ground like one of those whirlybird seeds from a maple tree. Everything rushed toward me. The sky below me and the Earth above. And then the other way around. Until I couldn't tell one from the other.

I cried out, hauled the blankets off my sweating head and body, sat up in bed, and let out a loud breath of relief that I was back on Earth, and still very much alive.

"You'll need an HGU," said my dad. "You can use this one."

An HGU was a pilot's helmet. Don't ask me what HGU stands for; I haven't a clue. Dad's helmet was white, with a picture of a shark on it. The one he gave me was plain white. It had a visor, an oxygen mask, and a built-in radio receiver. I held it in my hands like it was something holy. It hadn't occurred to me that I would need a helmet to fly in the Tweet. But now that it had, my first thought was that it should become mine.

"Can I keep it?"

"Sure," he said. "Why not? It's been kicking around the base for a while. Too small for the astroschmucks with their big heads, I guess. It should fit you fine."

"Gee, thanks, Dad." I hadn't yet told him I'd met the astronaut Pete Conrad, just in case he said something bad about him.

"Go ahead," he said. "Try it on. Let's see what you look like."

I put the helmet on and let Dad adjust the chin harness. The inside of my HGU smelled strongly of leather and cigarettes. It was a smell I liked a lot. Now that I was wearing the helmet, I felt like a real fighter pilot. I was already wearing my flying suit, of course. I checked myself out in Dad's bedroom mirror and then gave him a thumbs-up sign.

"You'll do," he said, and then grinned. "As a matter of fact, with that visor down you could probably pass for an astronaut." He laughed wryly. "There's none of them that you could call tall, exactly." He nodded thoughtfully. "You know something? That's what we're gonna do. When we get to the airfield, you just keep that visor down until I tell you, and no one will be any the wiser. It'll save the need for any awkward explanations about why you're going up in a military jet trainer. Got that?" He punched me gently on the side of my helmet.

"Yes, sir," I said, and saluted him.

"If your mother could see you now, she'd kill me," he said. "You know that, don't you?"

I nodded.

"Hell, she'd probably think I was trying to turn you into some kind of boy soldier or something."

Behind the visor, I grinned. Being a boy soldier sounded just fine to me.

We drove down to Ellington. It was a fine, sunny Sunday morning. We passed some people going to church, which sort of reminded me how lucky I was to be going flying with my dad instead of stuck inside listening to someone going on and on about hell. At the airfield we parked the car and collected our survival vests and parachute harnesses from the pilots' office. The harness weighed a ton. We both put our helmets on and walked to the line office, where Dad signed a yellow sheet for the aircraft. Outside the office our Tweet was waiting for us. Next to the Tweet was a start cart and a guy from the ground crew whose job was to help us get airborne. The start cart provides the power needed to activate all the Tweet's electrical components and spin the two engines. The bubble-glass canopy was already open, and I climbed up into the Tweet without a word to the crew chief. No one seemed to pay me much attention.

Unlike most military jets, this one had a cockpit wide enough to seat two pilots side by side. I took the left seat as I'd been instructed, strapped myself in, and had a good look around while Dad spoke to the crew chief for a while. It was a bit higher off the ground than the Cessna 150, but not much. The instrument panel was lower down, so I could see much better.

Dad walked around the aircraft checking the fuselage, the tires, the wings, and the tail before releasing the grounding wire attaching the Tweet to a hook in the tarmac. As usual he was taking his time about things. Then he climbed aboard and flicked a switch that brought every instrument in the cockpit instantly to life. Having completed the first stage of the pre-start checklist he waved his left forefinger at the crew chief, moved the throttle into idle, and pressed the left-engine starter button. Then he started the right engine. With the canopy still open we taxied slowly away from the flight line. We were almost ready to go.

While we taxied, he showed me how to connect my hose to an oxygen block on the parachute harness and how to plug in to the radio. There were earphones inside my helmet, and there was a microphone in my oxygen mask. That way we could hear each other over the engine noise, which was pretty loud.

"Okay, listen up," he said. "First I have to introduce you to someone called Martin Baker. Martin Baker is an Englishman who makes rocket ejection seats. If you were a trainee pilot, you would have been exhaustively schooled in the use of the Martin Baker. But to be honest there's really not much to know. When the handgrips on the seat beside your thighs are raised to the full up position, they lock there, exposing the seat-ejection triggers and locking the shoulder harness. Squeezing either trigger will initiate canopy jettisoning and seat ejection. Martin Baker will handle everything from then on in. The seat will eject approximately one third of a second after the trigger is squeezed. If I tell you to pull those triggers, you do it, boy, and do it real quick, because your life will depend on it. Understand?"

"Yes, sir." I knew where the triggers were already, of course. There were a couple of diagrams explaining their use in the manual. But I didn't tell him that. I didn't want to sound like a smartass. Or to put him on alert that I had taken the Tweet's flight manual out of his closet.

All the time he spoke, his feet were moving the rudders that steered us toward the takeoff runway.

"The only other thing I have to point out is the canopy breaker. That's it there, on the canopy bow. It's a knife you use to break through the bubble during an emergency, such as if the canopy fails to jettison. To remove it, first pull the pin at the end of the handle. Got that?"

"Yes, sir."

"That's the theory, anyway," he said. "People say the knife doesn't actually work. Let's hope we never have to find out for ourselves."

Mention of the ejector seat made me realize how much more dangerous flying in a jet was than flying in a propeller aircraft like the Cessna 150. In the Cessna you didn't even get a parachute, because if the engine died on you, there was every chance you could still fly it to the ground. None of that was at all likely in a jet. If the engine died, *you* died. At least you would without the ejector seat.

I'd never sat in an ejector seat before, and it gave me a funny feeling. Like I was that Chinese henchman in *Goldfinger*—the one who gets ejected out of the roof of the Aston Martin DB5, which has to be the best scene in any James Bond movie. Of course, my ejector seat had a parachute attached to it, and the one in *Goldfinger* didn't. All the same, it still gave me a funny feeling. I thought of a whole load of dumb questions about accidental ejection and then kept them to myself. Dad wasn't ever very tolerant of dumb questions.

He braked at the edge of the runway, lowered the canopy, and radioed the control tower for clearance to take off. It being a Sunday morning, the airport was quiet, and our clearance came through immediately. Dad taxied out and stopped the Tweet facing down the runway. With the brakes still on he pushed the throttles all the way up and waited for a moment while all the gauges went up to the maximum.

"Check the instruments for anything in the red," he told me.

"They're all green," I said.

"Then let's go."

He lifted his toes off the brake pedals, and we started rolling, Dad's feet keeping the nose wheel on the centerline of the runway. Pretty soon the airspeed indicator showed us doing seventy-five miles per hour, and Dad was pulling back on the stick, and we were heading straight up into the sky like a bat out of hell.

We leveled out at fifteen thousand feet, in less time than I'd have thought possible. As a pilot I'd never been higher than five thousand feet. *Fifteen thousand.*

"What do you think?" he asked, after radioing the tower.

"Fantastic," I said. "Absolutely fantastic."

He grinned as if I'd said something funny.

"The whole purpose of the Tweet is to train you to fly the Talon," he said. "That goes twice as fast as this plane. Believe me, kid, next to the Talon this aircraft feels like a bicycle ride. Which is one of the reasons I like it so much. This is a real nice aircraft." He paused for a moment. "Want to take the stick?"

"You're kidding."

"That's what you said the last time," he said.

He showed me how to trim the Tweet for level flight, how to climb, and how to perform a descending turn, and gradually I started to let him know that I knew what all the various gauges were for, and that I already understood the basic principles of how a jet aircraft worked. By then we were approaching Laredo. I flew along the Rio Grande, which wasn't much to look at, quite frankly.

Maybe there are other places where it looks grand, but Laredo isn't one of them. It's just a river there, and not a very wide one.

Dad took back control of the aircraft and explained the principle of flare, which is when you pull the nose up slightly while the airspeed is coming down so that you land just before the aircraft stalls. Which is different in a jet from a prop.

Then we landed.

Laredo was even quieter than Ellington. Dad went to the pilots' office and was there for about half an hour. I stayed put in the seat while the ground crew refueled the Tweet. I kept the visor on my helmet down and ignored the crew the way my dad had told me. "If you don't talk to them, they won't talk to you," he said. "They'll just assume we're in a hurry. The way pilots are, sometimes." I could hear the guys talking while they worked. They were talking about the president and what an idiot he was for letting the war escalate and how it was time someone else got into office who could fix things before they got any worse. Stuff like that. The cockpit smelled of burned wiring, hydraulic fluid, and sweat. It was a little uncomfortable waiting there in the sun, but I didn't mind. When Dad returned, we took off again. And that was when part two of my unofficial lesson got underway.

"You're a fast learner, son," he said. "A born stick-and-rudder man."

"I've got a good teacher," I said.

He made flying a jet seem easy, of course. Easy and safe. Which of course it wasn't. As I was soon to learn.

✪   ✪   ✪

According to the accident board of inquiry later on, Lee Stervinou had logged a couple of problems with the T-38 he had been flying, although the aircraft was almost brand-new. Arriving at Patrick Air Force Base in Florida he had noted an inoperative transponder, which was a minor technical problem. And just before returning to Houston he had discovered that the T-38 had a flat battery. The battery had been replaced. The transponder remained unfixed, however. This wasn't a problem so long as you stayed below a certain height—about 22,500 feet. In other words, low enough to use a visual flight plan rather than fly by the instruments.

Somewhere over the Gulf of Mexico the aileron control must have jammed solid. An aileron is part of the flight-control system—a sort of flap that helps to balance the aircraft. Lee's aircraft began to spin almost vertically. But for some reason he chose not to eject right away. Dad said that what probably happened was that the high speed stopped the spin and persuaded Lee, wrongly, that he was bringing the Talon under control. Anyway, somewhere over the Mississippi Delta Lee decided that he could not bring the Talon under control after all, and he decided to eject. By this time the Talon was only fifteen hundred feet off the ground, which was much too low to the ground to eject safely. Not only that, but the aircraft was almost vertical when he ejected, which meant that Lee ejected horizontally. His parachute started to deploy, but Lee was going too fast and headed straight for the ground. At high speed his body slammed headfirst into a ploughed field on the edge of a forest, two hundred yards from the downed aircraft. He was killed instantly.

The board said that if the transponder had been working, he'd have been higher up when the aileron had jammed and higher up when eventually he'd ejected, and that being higher up would have saved his life. The jet made a crater forty feet wide and fifteen feet deep. Lee was just twenty-five years old.

The news stunned everyone at Ellington. I'd never had a friend who had been killed. My dad was aware of my friendship with Lee and let me come to the requiem mass that was held two days after his death at the Assumption Church in North Houston. As the service neared its end, a squadron of T-38s flew over as a mark of respect. I wasn't sure if this was such a good idea. The Talons were going pretty fast, and as they passed overhead the whole church shook, as if one of the jets had hit the ground. That's what it sounded like to me, anyway. To my eyes Lee's parents looked a little upset to be reminded of how their only son had met his death. Probably the last thing they wanted to see as they came out of the church was a T-38. The air force meant well, of course, but . . .

When Dad and I got back home, he poured himself a drink and didn't say much for a while. Neither of us did. And for the first time I began to understand why he never talked about the war. I realized that he must have lost friends before. Lots of them, probably. And it must have been painful talking about the war. Just thinking about Lee made me want to cry. After a while I stopped trying not to cry and just let it go. Dad nodded somberly and handed me Lee's pilot's scarf. The white one with the red polka dots.

"Better not tell your mother what happened to Lee," was all he said. And we never mentioned him again.

Seven . . .

That fall I went flying with my dad in the Tweet on several more occasions. Each time he taught me something new about flying a jet. Meanwhile, I continued to use the simulator and to study the flight manual as if it were holy writ. As if I were a student pilot looking to get a certificate of competence to fly the T-37. One time we took a NASA Talon up, and he let me hold the stick. The Talon felt very new and very powerful. And, in view of what had happened to Lee Stervinou, a little bit scary, too.

But the scariest thing of all was when Dad tried to show me how to handle a spin in the Tweet. Spin in a propeller airplane like the Cessna 150 is frightening enough. But in a jet moving at three hundred fifty miles per hour it's damn near terrifying. He would take us out over the Gulf Coast, climb up to about twenty-five thousand feet so that we had plenty of room to "fool around" (as he put it), throttle way back, and pull on the stick so that the nose stayed up. Then he would stamp on the right rudder, and we'd start to go down. Slowly at first. But quickly speeding up.

"You can't fly out of this kind of spin just on your stick," he would say on the radio, quite coolly, as we began to spin toward the Earth like that little maple seed. Only a lot, lot faster. "You gotta use your brain, boy. You gotta figure the direction of the spin, keep the stick into your belly, and then use the rudder in the opposite direction." He pushed his foot down hard on the left rudder and kept it there.

The spin slowed down, a little.

"At the same time you gotta find a point of reference on the ground. Like that sand spit down there. It can be anything at all, just so long as you keep your eyes on it and don't lose your cool. Not so easy if there's a lot of cloud around. Okay, there's the sand spit again. That's our cue to jam the stick forward, real hard, all the way, and recover the aircraft."

The Tweet now entered a steep dive, and we began pulling negative g's, which felt like the sensation you get in an elevator when it goes down fast and your stomach gets left up in the air. It was the same in the Tweet, except that it wasn't just my stomach that lifted up, it was anything lying loose on the cockpit floor: chewing gum wrappers, bits of dried mud, coins. Dad brought the wings level, pulled us slowly out of the dive—rather too slowly for my comfort—added some throttle, and he was back in control. Not even a little out of breath.

"If you haven't recovered the aircraft by ten thousand feet," he said, "then proper procedure calls for you to eject. But that's just for rookies like you, boy. In the Nam I pulled out of spins at just five thousand feet."

I tried it a couple of times, but I found it hard to work out which way we were spinning, and I never did get the hang of breaking a spin. And every time we did this maneuver, I thought of poor Lee, wondering if this was how his last moments in the Talon must have seemed.

"You'll figure it out eventually," said Dad. "After a while, breaking a spin is as easy as falling off a log."

The negative g's were the worst part of breaking a spin. Sometimes they made me feel like I wanted to throw up. And Dad said I was just getting a little taste of what the astronauts went through on the "vomit comet"—the passenger jet NASA used to simulate the weightless conditions of space.

By now I had a better understanding of Dad's nickname, the Shark, and the underlying idea that you had to keep flying or die. Despite my dislike of negative g's this was exactly the way I felt about it too. Flying meant everything to me. It occupied my every waking thought. You might have thought it would have affected my schoolwork, badly. Instead it seemed to have the opposite effect. For one thing, understanding some of the principles involved in flying required me to pay more attention in science and math. And for another, I had come to a decision about my future: When I was seventeen years old, I would go to the United States Air Force Academy near Colorado Springs.

"That's great, Scott," said Dad when I told him. "But for Pete's sake, don't tell your mom. She'll have my guts."

Toward the end of 1968 I started to believe that they were going to get back together. Mom came back to Houston for Thanksgiving, and that went pretty well. She stayed with us at home instead of in a hotel. She even cooked our Thanksgiving dinner. That particular weekend it felt like we were a real family again. Neither of them so much as mentioned the war. This was good because it meant that they didn't argue. Not once. Before she went back to Miami, Mom asked me what I'd like for Christmas, and I said that what I wanted most was that she and Dad would be together again. At this she smiled thinly and said that anything was possible, but in a way that suggested that it might not be.

Then in November there was an election. The president we had was retiring or something, and we were going to have a new president sometime in January.

At the end of December, Mom came back to spend the holidays with us after all, and like every other normal family in America we spent Christmas Eve watching the *Apollo 8* astronauts on TV. Frank Borman, Jim Lovell, and William Anders became the first humans to leave Earth's orbit and to orbit around the Moon. Things got pretty tense when they went around the far side of the Moon and out of radio contact with Mission Control. On the third time around they all read a bit from the Bible, and Mom cried and said it was the most special Christmas she could remember.

I got a Hot Wheels car racing set from Dad, and from my mom a guitar. I started learning to play "Home on the Range."

This time when she went back to Miami we all had the impression that it wouldn't be for long. Dad told me that he thought it likely she would come back and live with us again permanently, and that he appreciated my efforts to get her back, especially as it would very likely entail a major sacrifice on my part.

"How do you mean?" I asked. "What kind of major sacrifice?"

"You do understand that she'd never let me take you up in a jet if she was living back here," he said. "No way on earth."

I could see he was right, of course. There was no way Mom would ever tolerate my going in the Tweet with him. Let alone the idea of me actually flying it. That was unthinkable.

Dad nodded slowly. "Exactly," he said. "That's what I'm talking about, Scotty. It'll mean the end of you flying. At least until you're old enough to go for a license."

I considered the matter for only a second or two. "Even if I have to give up flying," I said, "I still want Mom back here, living with us. For her sake as much as ours." I paused for a moment and then added, "Don't you want that too, Dad?"

"All the time, Scott. All the time." He swallowed a lump in his throat. "Besides, it wouldn't be possible anyway. I mean for me to take you flying. Not if I do what she's asking *me* to do."

"What's that?"

"To leave the air force and get a job with TWA," he said. "As a commercial pilot." He grinned. "You know. Flying fat salesmen out of Urbana, Illinois."

"Is that what you want?"

"Hell, I dunno." He shrugged. "But I'm not going anywhere in the air force. With an honorable discharge, my war record, and my medals, I should be able to get a decent job. She's right about that. I might even get on one of those transatlantic routes."

"But the air force is your life, Dad."

"It sure used to be," he said ruefully. "These days I'm not so sure. Wet-nursing kids in the air reserve, testing new pilots, trying to keep an eye on the astroschmucks. It's not what I signed on for. I'm a fighter pilot, Scott. Not a teacher."

"You're a good teacher, Dad," I said.

"Thanks, Scotty."

"So what *are* you going to do?"

"Tell you what," he said. "Tomorrow, why don't we take a trip over to Anahuac? Like we've been meaning to do since you got back from Miami. To clear our heads and think about it. How does that sound?"

"Just fine, Dad."

For the past ten thousand years or so, snow geese have wintered on the Texas coast. Some of them fly up to two thousand miles to get there from their arctic and subarctic summer nesting grounds. Every January, Kit Calder's dad organizes a shooting party to go after them, and every year he invites me and my dad. But Dad has never been much of a hunter. Nor am I. I like birds and I like animals. I certainly wouldn't want to shoot anything as beautiful as a snow goose. Instead we drove down to Anahuac National

Wildlife Refuge, on the northeastern edge of Galveston Bay, and spent a whole day watching the snow geese drift over the winter-browned coastal marshes. They lock their wings and parachute down from hundreds of feet up, and as soon as they land, they start swallowing small pieces of gravel to help their gizzards grind the seeds and roots they like to eat. "Maintaining the aircraft" is what Dad calls it. "Just like controlling the fuel mixture in your engines," he says.

Anahuac is a beautiful place. Sometimes there can be as many as one hundred thousand snow geese at Anahuac. And not just snow geese, but ducks, ibis, herons, bobcats, otters, raccoon, opossum, and alligators. It's exactly the kind of place to go when you need to do some serious thinking.

"Would you like a pet, Scotty?" he asked me as we drove back to Houston.

In truth I had always wanted a chimp or a monkey, but I knew that wasn't the kind of pet he would approve of. So I said I'd like a dog, and he said that we would get whatever kind of dog I wanted. And I said I'd always liked Irish setters. And he agreed and said he'd always liked them too. Of course, as soon as he asked me if I wanted a pet, I knew he had decided to do what Mom had asked and resign from the air force. I figured the pet was meant to make me feel better about having to give up flying, at least until I was a little older.

Before all that could happen, however, we decided to go flying in the Tweet one last time.

✪   ✪   ✪

There was a ceiling of thick cumulus cloud at about five thousand feet. I never liked flying through thick cloud. It was like in *Star Trek* when Captain Kirk finds himself somewhere dreamlike and weird and between worlds. Dad said that when he was in Korea, sometimes he used to hide in a cloud and wait for a MiG to come on by; then he'd wax its tail before it knew what was happening. I can believe that. To me, clouds always seem like they're hiding something. But above eight thousand we found ourselves in clear blue sky with fifty-mile visibility in every direction. Below us the ground had disappeared altogether, and the cloud covering looked less like an ambush waiting to happen and more like thick and fluffy layers of whipped cream. Sometimes that's the best kind of flying there is. The kind where it's just you and the sky, without a hole in the cloud to indicate the way back home. We were in an excellent mood. And in these particular circumstances it seemed kind of fitting that there should be no reminder of an Earth that wanted us both tied down or grounded.

"Isn't this something?" said Dad.

"It's great," I said.

"How many thirteen-year-old kids do you figure ever get to do anything like this?"

"I dunno. Not many, I guess."

"I'd say less than not many. I'd say you're the only one, Scotty. Wanna take over for a while?"

"Sure."

"You have control of the aircraft," he said, and let go of his stick.

"I have control of the aircraft," I said, taking hold of mine.

It was probably the best that I had ever flown, a real dollar ride. I did an aileron roll and a loop and a perfect figure of eight. Then I took the Tweet up to thirty-four thousand, which was the highest I'd been in any aircraft. The sky up at that height was the bluest blue—the most perfect sky I'd ever seen outside of that picture of the air above the Island of Skye that was hanging on my bedroom wall. I felt like an angel. I could hardly bear the idea that I was about to give all this up.

"Like I always say," said Dad, "you're a natural stick-and-rudder man. Something born, not made. A true MacLeod."

I whipped the Tweet the length and breadth of Harris County for about an hour before I felt him on the brakes and he said it was time to head for home. I wondered when I would ever again feel such monumental power through my hands.

"You have control of the aircraft," I said.

"I have control of the aircraft," he said, taking the stick and pushing it forward.

Dad dropped down to about seven thousand feet, just above the cloud layer, and then radioed the tower controller at Ellington, who advised him that he was clear to land. So he throttled back and began banking gently to the right, flying in a big wide circle that would bring us in to land from the southeast. Completing his turn, we dropped through the cloud and prepared to make our final approach.

Suddenly, without warning, we found ourselves faced with a flock of about a dozen snow geese flying in a V formation and coming right toward us. There was no time to get out of the way.

We were going too fast for that. For me there was no time to do anything except yell and then duck as one of the geese hit the right side of the Tweet's canopy. The Tweet rocked like it had been hit by a surface-to-air missile, and the Plexiglas shattered into a dozen fragments as the goose came hurtling right through the canopy and collided heavily with my dad. The cockpit was filled with a smell like singed hair as another bird, perhaps, or even part of the same bird, was ingested by the air-breathing intakes of one of the two engines.

There was blood and feathers and pieces of Plexiglas everywhere. It was impossible to know how much of the blood and guts spread all over the right-hand cockpit seat was the bird's, and how much was Dad's. The shark pictured on his helmet looked like it had made a fresh kill. Its pointy teeth were dripping with red. It was hard to believe that an ordinary bird could cause such destruction to a jet fighter aircraft. It was equally hard to believe that we were still airborne. But we were. For the moment, at least.

"Dad?" I shouted desperately. "Are you okay?"

His chin stayed on his chest, and his hands remained motionless on his lap. He wasn't holding the stick. He didn't look like he was even awake.

"Dad?" I took him by the shoulder and shook him hard. Restrained by its harness, his body stayed put, but his head lolled alarmingly. I couldn't see his eyes behind his visor, and when I tried to push it up, I found that it was stuck, as if the impact had damaged the hinge. So I reached across and unbuckled his oxygen mask.

His mouth was open and full of blood. His tongue was hanging out. A terrible feeling took hold of my stomach. For a moment I felt like throwing up. I was terribly afraid that he was dead. "Dad!"

For a moment I saw his lips move, and in the earphones inside my helmet I heard him utter one word: "Eject." Then he was silent.

Instinctively, I reached down beside my thigh, took hold of one of the ejection-seat handgrips, and raised it to the full up position, exposing the trigger the way he had shown me. I felt the shoulder harness tighten. I needed only to squeeze the trigger to launch myself out of the aircraft. Except that I couldn't do it. Despite what he'd said earlier, there was no way I could eject. For one thing, I could only eject myself, and that would have been like killing my dad. If he wasn't dead already. For another, the canopy was a mess. It was supposed to blow off a split second before the seat ejected. But looking at it now I had my doubts about that happening. It seemed just as likely that my seat would be fired straight through the damaged canopy, killing me outright. There could be no question of ejecting. Our only chance was for me to take control of the aircraft and land it myself—something I had never done. I grabbed the stick as the Tweet gave a little shudder and began to dip to the right.

"I have control of the aircraft!" I yelled at him.

The trouble was, I didn't. Not by a long shot.

What happens in a spin is that the aircraft gets very slow in the air. There's not enough wind coming over the wing to act against the raised aileron at the rear edge. The aircraft stalls. The wing dips, but not enough to let the nose drop the aircraft into the kind of accelerating dive you can fly out of. Instead the aircraft starts spinning like a sheet of paper falling through the air. You can't fly out of a spin. That's what Dad had taught me. So I had to break the spin, which was also something I hadn't done before.

The ground beneath us was moving from right to left. This time I was sure of that. Which meant we were spinning to the right. Which meant . . .

I stamped the left rudder as hard as I could, held it there, looked for a fixed spot on the ground, and prayed to a God I wasn't even sure existed that I'd made the right call.

The spin slowed a little, and then I saw it. The Clear Lake Golf Course, just a mile or two northwest of Houston's famous space center. If I got this wrong, I was going to put America's manned space program back by years, probably. I waited a moment as the whole of Clear Lake City moved from right to left. And then I saw the golf course again. Very likely there were astronauts down there teeing up even now.

I lifted the rudder, rammed the flying stick forward, right to the bottom of the hinge, and the nose dipped, slamming me forward against the harness. Dad's chin dropped hard on his chest. Blood dripped from his nose into the oxygen mask, which hung underneath his mouth like a broken jaw. With one eye on the swiftly approaching golf course and one eye on the little *W* that was the attitude indicator, I tried to bring the jet's horizontal wings level. Gaining speed and pulling negative g's, the Tweet screamed toward the ground like a meteor.

The wings were level!

I was pulling back on the stick now. Pulling back with all my strength and more. If I could just bring us out of the dive, we might have half a chance. For a long moment the *W* stayed firmly in the DI-VE zone. I pulled even harder than before, until I thought my arm might come out of its socket.

The nose started to come up. Slowly. Slowly. The *W* was in the CL-IMB zone. But had I left it too late? I had the Manned Spacecraft Center in my sights. If I'd been on a bombing or strafing run, it would have been perfect. And then the nose was lifting higher. At almost three hundred miles an hour we were going to miss the Manned Spacecraft Center by no more than a hundred feet. I pushed the throttle all the way up and steered the airplane into a steep climb, away from the ground.

As I let out a long breath, I felt the sweat pour off my forehead and into my eyes. I couldn't wipe it off because of my visor. I'd broken the spin. Now all I had to do was land.

"Mayday, Mayday, Mayday," I said.

Really, I wanted to cry, but I was trying to keep it together, trying to sound as cool as possible, the way my dad always did. Like a real pilot worthy of a license. I figured that if I didn't panic, then at least we had a chance of getting down in one piece. As Dad always said, "Any fool can land an airplane. Gravity will see to that. But not everyone can do it and walk away." I had to stay focused on that one thing. Landing the airplane safely.

"Ellington Tower, this is Volkswagen Three," I said. "Nine

miles northeast with X-ray, on a go-around, after a bird strike. The pilot is unconscious, possibly dead. We have negative ejection capability. Repeat: negative ejection capability. Requesting emergency checklist. Ellington, this is the first time I've tried to land one of these birds outside a sim."

There was a longish pause before Ellington Tower came back on the squawk: "Victor Whiskey Three, this is Ellington Tower. Say again."

I didn't blame them for asking me to repeat what I'd just told them. Probably they had been enjoying a nice quiet Sunday until I popped up on the squawk and spoiled it. I almost hated to say it all again. But I did.

"Roger that, Victor Whiskey Three," said the Ellington controller. "Is this some kind of goddamn joke? There's no record on Victor Whiskey Three's flight plan of any student pilot or passenger. Please identify yourself."

"Ellington Tower, this is Victor Whiskey Three," I said. "This is not a joke. My name is Scott MacLeod. I'm the Shark's son. I know I shouldn't be here, but I am."

"Roger that, Victor Whiskey Three," said the controller. "Stand by for further instructions."

Another longish pause.

"Ellington Tower," I said, a little impatiently. "This is Victor Whiskey Three on a go-around with a broken canopy and an unconscious instructor pilot. My dad is hurt. Maybe he's dead; I don't know. But you've got to give me some help here, sir, or I'm going to crash this bird. I'd like to remain in the pattern while I set up and then make a landing on runway 35R, soonest. I think I know how to fly this thing, but I'm not one hundred percent sure how to land, which is why I'm requesting emergency checklist."

"Roger that, Victor Whiskey Three. How old are you, kid?"

"Ellington Tower, this is Victor Whiskey Three," I said. "Sir, I'm thirteen years old."

"Roger that, Victor Whiskey Three. Son? Please confirm your negative ejection capability status."

"Ellington Tower, this is Victor Whiskey Three. The canopy is badly damaged above the right-hand seat. I don't think it will blow if I squeeze the trigger."

"Roger that, Victor Whiskey Three. Scott. What does your fuel gauge and altimeter show?"

"Eleven hundred ninety-five pounds, sir," I said. "And four thousand feet." I reeled off the other gauges for good measure.

"Scott? Now listen carefully. Do you know how to turn the aircraft?"

"Yes, sir."

"And how to throttle back?"

"Yes, sir."

"I want you to decrease your speed by fifty percent and make a descending turn to two thousand feet. When you get there, drop your landing gear. Copy that?"

"Yes, sir."

"You're lucky, kid," said the controller. "You're in the easiest jet to fly that there is. Nothing to it. Okay?

"Yes, sir."

"My name is Fred, kid. And you're doing fine."

Throttling back, I began a slow left turn. At the same time I pulled the gear handle that would lower the Tweet's wheels. I wished I was back in the Cessna 150. I could have landed that airplane on a dime. I looked at Dad's lucky mascot—the troll I had bought him before he went to Vietnam the second time—and touched it for luck. I was going to need it.

Fred began to reel off a series of questions as he and I went down the checklist of everything I had to get right. At his prompt I throttled back a little more and watched the airspeed drop again. Eventually I was ready. I was now flying at right angles to the runway, the opposite way from the direction I was going to land. I caught sight of some fire trucks that were creeping toward the far edge of the runway. Their warning lights were flashing. It wasn't an encouraging sign.

I knew that the secret of landing well was to pick a spot for touchdown, well before you got there. I picked one and then flew straight ahead for a short distance. Then, as instructed, I made another 180-degree turn that would put me on a final approach. Fred, the Ellington flight controller, was telling me what to do. But I already knew what I was supposed to do. I'd seen Dad do it often enough. The difficult thing was *doing* what I was supposed to do. I had to get the heading and airspeed right before I got over the runway so that everything would be set for touchdown. The right airspeed was slow; the trouble was that to my inexperienced eyes the "slow" in a Tweet still seemed way too fast to even think of landing. And that was what I had to forget.

I started my final approach, pulling the stick back and keeping the nose up just short of a stall to stop the aircraft from fully descending, holding the wheels just a few feet above the runway. But I flared too soon, and the Tweet leveled off several feet too high. The Tweet was gliding just above the runway like a paper airplane. Then the airspeed declined abruptly, and the Tweet dropped like a stone onto the runway. Everything shuddered, not just in the airplane but in my bones and dental work. It was a hard landing, but we were down. I let the landing gear run for about fifty yards and then stamped on the brakes. The Tweet came to a halt. Just like that.

Fire trucks and an ambulance surrounded us as I secured all the switches. Outside the aircraft a helmeted fireman was giving us the thumbs-up, probably to indicate that there was no sign of fire. Then I looked across at my dad. He was sitting up now, holding his jaw like someone had socked him and looking at the ruins of the canopy. I guessed that the heavy landing must have jolted him back into consciousness.

"What the hell happened?" he asked, unstrapping himself instinctively.

"Bird strike," I said.

"And you landed it?"

I nodded and opened the canopy.

"The hell you did." He grinned. "Outstanding," he said.

"How do you feel, Dad?"

"Punchy," he said, taking off his helmet. "But I guess I'll live."

Two ambulance men helped Dad out of the aircraft and then

laid him carefully onto a stretcher. I stood up and then climbed out. But not before picking up Dad's lucky mascot.

"Well, what do you know?" I muttered to myself. "It works."

The ground crew and firemen were now joined by several people in uniform running from the control tower. They were all looking at me. I took off my helmet. There seemed little point in keeping it on. By now they all knew who and what I was. And me, I knew I was in trouble. Big trouble. When two of the men grabbed me, I half expected them to put me in handcuffs or throw me in the brig or something. Instead they hoisted me up onto their shoulders. And everyone crowded around and started to smile at me. Some were nodding, too. And then they all began to applaud. Like I'd done something impressive. Like I was some kind of a hero. One of them said, "You know what you did, son? You just saved your daddy's life." And another said: "Not just his daddy's life. That goddamned Tweet might have come down on the Manned Spacecraft Center, or someone's house." At which point the applause grew louder. They carried me to the control tower, where a tall, red-haired man wearing a sergeant's uniform came out and shook me by the hand.

"I'm Fred," he said. "You must be Scott MacLeod."

"Yes, sir," I said. I was smiling. But by now there were tears in my eyes too. I guess I was just sort of waking up to the reality of what had just almost happened. Of how my dad and I had almost been killed.

Fred shook my hand gravely. "That was a hell of a bit of flying, kid," he said. "Your mother will be very proud of you when she finds out what happened here today."

"I'm not too sure about that," I said, grinning through my tears. I could almost hear my dad saying, "For Pete's sake, don't tell your mom. She'll have my guts."

Someone tousled my hair. Someone else clapped me on the back. Everyone was cheering. I looked around for my dad and saw him get out of the ambulance and start walking a little unsteadily toward me. I made the ground crew put me down and ran to my dad and hugged him tight. I think he was crying too.

"A born stick-and-rudder man," he whispered, sounding kind of choked. "I'm proud of you, Scotty. Real proud."

I didn't know it then, but our troubles were just starting.

Six . . .

The Judge Advocate General's Corps investigated the incident. Air force JAGs had the power to order a court of inquiry or a court-martial. There were three types of court-martial: a summary court-martial, a special court-martial, and a general court-martial.

Dad was advised that he would probably face a summary or special court-martial for teaching an unauthorized person—namely me—to fly a military aircraft. The summary court-martial carried a maximum penalty of one month's confinement, forfeiture of two-thirds pay for a month, and reduction in rank. The special court-martial carried a maximum sentence of twelve months' confinement, forfeiture of two-thirds pay for twelve months, reduction in rank, and a bad-conduct discharge.

A bad-conduct discharge was, he was advised, an unlikely

outcome. But if he was found guilty, almost any of the other punishments Dad might receive would prevent him from applying for the job at TWA. You needed a clean military record to work for any airline. Dad said there could be no question of him resigning from the air force without that job. Piloting a TWA jet was bad enough, but at least he would still be in the air. Flying was his whole life. So both he and I knew what it would mean if he was found guilty of misconduct. It would mean that Mom was going to have to reconcile herself to being married to an air-force man if she came back to live with us. And that seemed hardly likely.

Dad was also advised, however, that as far as his defense was concerned, there was one significant factor in his favor: me. The officer defending him said he was planning to argue that if I hadn't been in the cockpit, the Tweet—a plane worth $164,854—would undoubtedly have crashed, and a USAF major would have been killed, which also would have incurred some considerable cost to the air force. He said there was also the possibility that the Tweet might have crashed on a house or the MSC, possibly killing someone else besides my dad. It might even be argued, said Dad's legal advisor, that the excellence of his abilities as a teacher, and hence his indispensability to the air force, were ably demonstrated in me: After all, if Dad could teach a thirteen-year-old boy to fly a military jet, then it might be said that he was too valuable to let go.

While all this was going on, the air force was trying to hush up the facts of what had happened. Dad and I had been sworn to secrecy. When I asked him why, he said it was because they were embarrassed. They were mainly worried that the American public, alarmed at the idea of thirteen-year-old boys flying military jet fighters, might demand the resignations of officers much more senior than my dad.

"The Tweet's only a trainer," said Dad. "But it only takes some dumb newspaperman to suggest you might have had access to an airplane with an atom bomb on board for the whole thing to get blown out of all proportion."

In the early days of January 1969 these were all factors that seemed likely to give the air force JAGC some pause for thought.

Pending the outcome of the inquiry the air force suspended Dad from full-time duty, which meant he stayed at home all day, watching TV, reading, mowing the lawn, and generally getting grouchy.

Mom called and asked if Dad had come to a decision about the TWA job. Naturally, we hadn't told her about the accident. Dad said he was still thinking about it, which left her pretty annoyed with him, I think. But what else could he do?

Trying to pretend that nothing had happened I went to school, as usual, and kept my mouth shut. For my dad's sake. But it's not easy being a kind of hero and unable to say a damn thing about it. Not even to your best friend. Kit sensed there was something I wasn't telling him. And it certainly wasn't easy seeing Pamela Townshend and not being able to impress her, like I'd promised to do, with an account of what had happened. But this was nothing compared with what was to follow, of course.

One evening a few days after the "incident" we were at home watching *Rowan and Martin's Laugh-In* when the doorbell rang. I scrambled off the couch the way I always did and answered it. Outside the door were two men in neat gray business suits. One wore a white shirt and a white tie, and the other wore a white shirt and a red tie. Behind them, in the driveway, was a large station wagon, and, beyond, on the road in front of our house, there was a big black Lincoln Continental limousine. The man in the white tie was tan, with silver hair. He smiled a lot and did most of the talking. When he smiled, you noticed his mouth was full of metal teeth. The other man wore glasses and carried a box about four feet long under one arm.

"You must be Scott MacLeod," said the man with the metal teeth, in a vaguely foreign accent.

"Yes, sir."

"Is your father at home, Scott?"

"Yes, he is."

"Who is it, Scotty?" asked my dad, appearing in the hallway behind me.

"My name is Dr. Brown," said the man, handing him a business card. "And this is my colleague, Dr. Stewlinger. We're from NASA."

"NASA?" Dad looked at the man's card with a mixture of suspicion and incredulity.

"That is correct."

"I guess you'd better come in," he said.

Half of me was thinking that they might have reconsidered his earlier application to become an astronaut, and half of me was thinking that perhaps while pulling the Tweet out of the spin I had come closer to hitting the Manned Spacecraft Center than I had earlier believed.

We went into the living room. Dad turned the TV off and faced our visitors with folded arms.

"What's all this about, gentlemen?" he asked.

"We heard about . . . the incident," said Dr. Brown, those metal teeth smiling at me. I wondered what it would be like to be bitten by him. "That was a brilliant bit of flying you did, young man. Very, shall we say, intrepid?"

Dad shook his head. "I'm afraid we're not permitted to talk about that," he said. "With anyone outside the United States Air Force."

"Of course, of course," said Dr. Brown. "We understand *everything*."

"We brought the boy a present," said the other man. He was foreign-sounding too. "As a small token of our admiration."

"A present? What kind of a present?"

"Is it permitted?" asked Dr. Brown. "After all, he did steer the aircraft away from the Spacecraft Center."

Dad rubbed his jaw uncertainly. And then he shrugged. "I guess it would be okay," he said.

The other man handed the long box to Dr. Brown, who handed it to me with a stiff bow. He kept on smiling broadly as I lifted the lid and heard myself gasp.

Inside the box was a model of a NASA rocket. A *Saturn I*—the kind of two-stage rocket that had launched all the Gemini space missions. But this wasn't just any cheap Revell-kit model. This was a scale model, perfect in every detail. The kind of model a real rocket scientist might have on his desktop.

"Wow," I said. "The *Saturn One*. Thanks a lot, Dr. Brown."

Dr. Brown seemed pleased that I recognized it. "You know this rocket?"

"Do I! The first stage has eight engines, generating one-point-three million pounds of thrust. That's the rocket that the *Saturn Five* is based on."

"Excellent," said Dr. Brown. "It would appear that Scott's expertise is not limited to jet aircraft. He knows rockets, too, yes?"

Dad nodded, apparently happier to talk about my more conventional boyish interests than my love of flying military jets. "Scotty's a real space buff, Dr. Brown," he said. "Aren't you, Scotty?"

"Yes, Dad."

"He's got all sorts of books about space exploration, and a pretty good reflector telescope."

"I should like to see your telescope, Scott," said Dr. Brown. "Very much."

"Sure," said Dad. "Go ahead, Scotty. Show them." He paused. "Maybe you and your colleague would like some coffee, Dr. Brown?"

"Coffee would be wonderful, Major MacLeod," said Dr. Brown. "And please, call me Wernher."

Dad went into the kitchen, and, still carrying my model rocket, I led the way to my bedroom. The two men admired my telescope for a minute and glanced admiringly up at the model airplanes; they even took one or two books off my shelves and examined those. But most of all they seemed to look at me, as if sizing me up in some strange way. I placed the rocket carefully on my desk and stood watching them watching me.

"Tell me, Scotty," said Dr. Brown. "I may call you Scotty, may I?"

I shrugged. "Sure."

"Are you in good health, my boy?"

"I guess so. I sure can't remember the last time I was sick."

"And school?" asked Dr. Stewlinger. "How is everything at school?"

"I'll be honest, sir," I said. "If you'd asked me that question six months ago, I'd have said it was lousy. But lately, since I got interested in flying—well, I seem to have discovered a new appetite for math and science."

"Excellent," said Dr. Brown. "Excellent. You are an interesting little fellow, Scott. Very interesting."

At first I had thought that Dr. Brown and Dr. Stewlinger might be English. It was only when I heard him say "very interesting" that I realized he sounded just like Arte Johnson doing his impersonation of the Nazi soldier on *Laugh-In*. The two men were German.

We went back into the living room, where Dad was serving coffee. The two Germans sat down.

"It is my impression that perhaps Scott wishes to become an air-force pilot when he grows up," asked Dr. Brown. "Like his father, yes?"

"Yes, sir," I said. "And after that maybe an astronaut. That is, if you'll have me, sir."

The two Germans exchanged a look.

"Oh, I think there is no question about that," said Dr. Stewlinger.

"As a matter of fact, that is why we're here," said Dr. Brown. "Major MacLeod. We would like young Scott here to come and fly for us."

"Say again, doc?" said Dad.

"Please," said Dr. Brown, smiling. "*Wernher.*" He looked at me. "We should like to offer your son, Scott, a position in NASA's astronaut program, with immediate effect."

I felt my jaw drop like a trapdoor. And my ears were ringing like someone had socked me one. For a moment I thought I had misheard him. And I was about to say as much when Dad said, "You're kidding."

"No, no. This is not a joke, Major," said Dr. Stewlinger. "We are serious. Very much so. We think your son has what it takes to serve his country. Courage. A cool head under pressure. The ability to work precisely to a checklist. All of the very special qualities that are needed to make a good astronaut."

"Me? An astronaut?" I was grinning like I was fit to bust. "When do I start?"

"Excellent," said Dr. Brown. "That's the spirit."

"Hold on a minute," said Dad. "Look, Dr. Brown. *Wernher.* Don't think we're not mindful of the great honor of what you're suggesting. Most pilots would give their right arm to join the space program. But Scott is only thirteen years old." He smiled uncertainly. "Just when were you thinking of sending him up into space?"

"Four months from now," said Dr. Brown. "Depending on how his training goes. By all accounts Scott is an exceptionally fast learner."

"Four months?"

Dad sounded shocked. So was I. Four months was hardly any time at all.

"We think in May or early June," said Dr. Brown. "That would be best. Naturally, he would have to leave school for a while. He would be going to a different kind of school. Astronaut school."

"What, are you crazy?" Dad was shaking his head. "He's just a boy."

"He's a boy whom you thought sufficiently competent to fly a jet aircraft," said Dr. Brown. "Is it not so?"

"Under my instruction," said Dad. "With me sitting beside him. There's a hell of a difference."

"I believe that when Scott landed the aircraft for the first time, you yourself were unconscious, yes?" asked Dr. Stewlinger.

"But what about the risks?" Dad was still shaking his head. "With all due respect, gentlemen, being an astronaut is dangerous. Maybe you've forgotten that back in 1962 fewer than nine out of ten Atlas launches were successful."

"Would you say it was any more dangerous than being a jet pilot?" asked Dr. Brown. He paused. "In Vietnam, for example? No, of course not. Even here in Texas, flying a jet is not without its hazards. There was an accident at Ellington just the other month, was there not? I believe you both knew the pilot who was killed-- Herr Stervinou. And you yourself were almost killed the other day. But for Scott's presence of mind you would not be here now."

"Piloting a Tweet is one thing," said Dad. "But flying a space-craft is something else."

"It might seem that way," said Dr. Stewlinger. "But piloting a jet fighter might actually be more difficult."

"The flying part of NASA's space missions has perhaps been exaggerated by the newspapers," said Dr. Brown. "Ever since the Mercury program we have been obliged, for political reasons, to foster the impression that the spacecraft are flown by the astronauts rather than guided by controllers here on Earth." He shrugged. "In order to spare the pride and the feelings of the pilots who are involved. In truth there never has been very much flying involved. Computers do almost everything."

Dad stood up as if he had heard enough.

"I'm sorry, gentlemen," he said. "But I'm afraid the answer has to be no. I think I'd be failing in my duty as a parent if I said yes. That's my final word."

The two Germans quickly finished their coffee and stood. "Very well," said Dr. Brown, and bowed stiffly to me and then to my father. "We shall not trouble you anymore. If you change your mind, then you have my card."

When they were gone, I went to my room, closed the door, and lay down on my bed, seething with anger and disappointment that Dad had turned down the biggest opportunity of my life. Of *any* boy's life. That he of all people should have treated me like a child seemed too much to bear. After a while there was a knock at the door.

"Scotty?" he said. "Can I come in for a moment?"

"Go away!" I yelled.

He opened the door anyway and came in.

"I don't want to speak to you!" I yelled at him. "Not ever."

"Look, Scotty, some of these guys at NASA have been training for years to become astronauts. *Years.*"

"Don't you mean astroschmucks?" I said. "That's what you usually call them, isn't it?"

"But *four months* of training before you go into space." He shook his head. "It just didn't sound right. Still doesn't."

"*Dad,* you didn't even ask me," I said. "You didn't ask me what I thought. It's my life, Dad. And if I want to risk my life, that ought to be my decision. Not yours."

"Scotty, listen to me," he said. "Don't be in such a hurry to grow up, son. You're just a boy."

"Where does it say that you have to be an adult to do something important? What about all those kings who were just boys? David was just a shepherd boy when he beat Goliath with a slingshot. And there were boys who fought in the Civil War who weren't much older than me. Where does it say that you have to grow up to serve your country?"

"This is different," he said.

"How?" I asked. "You know what I think, Dad? I think you're jealous they asked me and not you. Because you didn't get to be an astronaut yourself, you hate them. You hate all those astro-schmucks. They rejected you, Dad. And you can't bear the idea that it's me they want."

After I said that, he was pretty quiet for a moment. He turned away and walked out of my room. And, feeling a little guilty at what I'd said, I followed him back into the living room.

"But why do they want *you*, Scott?" he asked. "Just stop and think about that for a moment. Why do they want a thirteen-year-old kid to join the space program? It doesn't make any sense."

"I guess we'll never know, will we?" I said. "Not now that you turned them down flat."

And then the doorbell rang again.

The man standing at the door was a big man. Bigger than either of the two Germans, bigger than my Dad, and certainly bigger than I had ever imagined. He wore metallic-framed glasses, a pale brown suit, a white shirt, and a reddish tie with yellow bucking broncos painted on it. He wore a lot of gold, too. A big gold watch, gold cuff links, and a big gold belt buckle. In one hand was a gray, broad-brimmed Texas Stetson hat, and in the other a cigarette. I had never met him before. But I recognized him immediately: He was the president of the United States of America. At least for five more days he was. After that he would be handing over the office to the man elected to be the next president. The sweaty one. Whose name I had already forgotten.

"Can I come in?" he asked.

"Yes, sir," I said, and stepped smartly aside.

The president dropped his cigarette, ground the end out on our doorstep with a handsomely stitched cowboy boot, and then came inside. He stood patiently by my side, filling the hallway, while I closed the door.

"You from Texas, son?" he asked quietly.

"Yes, sir," I said.

"Well, that's a start. Where's your daddy?"

I pointed down the corridor.

"Let's go talk to him."

We walked into the living room, where Dad was standing looking out of the window at the back lawn, probably wondering if he should risk cutting it twice in one week. He turned, saw the president, and almost dropped the glass of scotch he was holding. "Mr. President," he said. "What are you doing here?"

"If that's whiskey you're drinking, Major," said the president, "I won't say no."

He sat down. Dad poured him a drink. The president liked it with ice and soda. Watching them both I wondered what Mom would have thought of my dad sitting down in our living room and having a drink with the president. This was the man she held personally responsible for the war. Probably she'd have stood out on the lawn with a bullhorn and shouted about peace and stuff like that. I sure don't think she'd have fetched them a bowl of pretzels.

"I expect you can guess why I'm here, Major," said the president. He had a real Texas drawl. Just like Kit Calder's dad, as a matter of fact.

Dad was still looking blank. I knew he guessed the president's being in our home must have something to do with the two NASA officials who'd left a few minutes earlier, but it was hard to imagine that the president would take a personal interest in the future of one small boy. I was having a little trouble with that myself.

"The air force's top space expert has predicted that the Moon will be a military rocket base for either Russia or the U.S. within ten years," he said, "and I do not believe that this generation of Americans is willing to resign itself to going to bed each night by the dirty yellow light of a communist Moon."

He lit a cigarette and let it hang off his lip, cowboy-style. As he spoke, he laid his fingers down to make a point—one, two, three. Like one of the teachers at Ima Hogg.

"No, sir," said Dad. "Absolutely right."

"The Moon will provide a base of unequaled advantage for raining sure and massive destruction on Earth," said the president. "We simply have to get there first. The plain fact of the matter is that whoever controls the Moon controls the Earth. Our experts predict that if the goddamned Russians do get there first—and intelligence sources indicate that it's possible that they might—they could actually claim ownership of the Moon. That is what we are facing unless the Apollo Moon mission is successful this summer. So we're going to leave nothing at all to chance, and before I leave the White House, I'm doing everything I can to make certain that the mission will succeed. As the man who founded NASA and who's been in charge of the space program since 1961, I don't want anything or anyone to screw it up."

Dad nodded. "Makes sense, sir," he said.

"Throughout the Apollo program we've been shadowing all the space missions with a secret space program called Caliban. After the ugly guy in some play by William Shakespeare. Everything we've done with Apollo we've done first in the Caliban program, using monkeys. Just in case anything went wrong. If it did, we'd be handing those godless red Ruskies a propaganda victory on a hog-sized plate. Then there's the sheer cost of the program. At this stage any kind of accident will leave Apollo's enemies an opportunity to close the program down on the grounds of its enormous expense.

"In May, *Apollo Ten* is going to test the procedures for a rendezvous between two spacecraft in lunar orbit, ahead of an actual landing by *Apollo Eleven* in July. But it won't answer any of the sixty-four-thousand-dollar questions about a Moon landing. For example, can two men land on the Moon and take off again? Will the lunar module sink in the Moon dust? Will rock samples from the Moon burst into flames as soon as they are exposed to oxygen inside the module? Will the lunar module's engine work in low gravity? What we still don't know could fill a ten-gallon hat.

"Before *Apollo Eleven* ever takes off, *Caliban Eleven* is going to try to provide answers to these questions, and a whole lot more besides. We're going to land two monkeys on the Moon, in secret. A third monkey was going to pilot the command module in orbit around the Moon. Unfortunately, the goddamned thing has become aggressive and unmanageable. Started biting people. And we cannot tolerate an astronaut that bites. Which is where Scott comes in. And why I'm here now, Major. To ask you to reconsider your decision. We'd like your son to take command of *Caliban Eleven*. To pilot the command module around the Moon while the two monkeys descend to the lunar surface.

"That's about the size of it, in a nutshell. And naturally, it goes without saying that all of this is extremely hush-hush and confidential. I'm sure you'll agree we don't want anything to take away from the national prestige that's riding on a manned lunar landing in July."

"Let me get this straight, sir," said Dad. The vein on his forehead was throbbing ominously. He looked like he was trying hard to control himself. Out of courtesy to the president. And perhaps to me, too. "You want my son to take a monkey's place on a spaceflight to the Moon?"

The president crossed his legs and began to scratch his chest and under his arm, like one of the very monkeys he had been talking about.

"I never had a son myself," said the president. "But if I had, I'd sure have wanted him to be someone who could have a real influence on events. Someone like your boy, Major. I will not minimize the risks involved. You're an air-force pilot, and you know all about the fallibility of complex machines. But, after the success of *Apollo Eight* a couple of weeks ago, the people at NASA now believe that the risks involved in orbiting the Moon in the command module and returning to Earth are more acceptable. He'll have to train hard. Like a real astronaut. But the dangerous part will be down to the monkeys."

"Then why not send a regular astronaut to command the mission?" Dad asked. "Why do you need Scott?"

"The Caliban lunar module and command module are only half the size of Apollo," explained the president. "This means that a regular-size astronaut simply won't fit in the spacecraft. We've tried to recruit a midget or a dwarf to command the mission. But the plain fact of the matter is that there isn't a midget or dwarf in America who's qualified like your son is qualified, Major. That is, a midget with the know-how to fly a jet. Believe me, we've looked everywhere."

"I dunno, sir," said Dad, shaking his head. "I mean, it all sounds kind of risky."

"America needs this Moon landing to happen, Major," said the president. "She needs to feel good about herself again. Especially right now, with the war we're fighting against the communists."

"I'd like to do this, sir," I said, and shot Dad a look before he had a chance to contradict me. "I want to do this. For my country."

Dad bit his lip.

"I see you've brought your boy up well," said the president. "He's courageous and independent. A true American."

"Well, sir, he's apt to be a mite impetuous and overconfident at times," said Dad. "To be honest with you, sir, if Scott does go around the Moon, like you ask, I'm a little worried what I can tell his mother."

"You can leave all that to the Secret Service, Major," said the president, and turned to me. "We'll let them figure out a good cover story for you, son." He allowed himself a grin. "Hell, they've been pulling my nuts out of the fire for the last eight years."

It was my turn to grin. My life had just changed out of all recognition. Not only did it look like I was going to be an astronaut and orbit the Moon, it also looked as if I was going to have my own Secret Service cover story. At the same time I realized something important. The fact that the president had turned up in person to ask me to do this must mean that they needed me very badly. Very badly indeed.

"I'll do it, sir," I said. "Only I have two small conditions."

"Let's hear 'em," said the president.

"One is that there's to be no court-martial for my father."

Dad tutted loudly. "Scott," he said. "You can't bargain with the president like that. Besides, there's air-force rules and regulations to consider. I broke them. So there has to be an inquiry."

"Hell, no," said the president. "The boy's absolutely right. But for you teaching him to fly a jet, Major MacLeod, we wouldn't be where we are now. With me asking you for a favor. It's absurd to think that you might be disciplined for bringing about a situation that helps us out. As the commander in chief of U.S. military forces for another five days, it's within my power to do this for you both. Consider it done."

For a moment I thought Dad was going to argue with him. Instead he swallowed and said, "Thank you, sir."

The president grinned. "Spoken like a true Texan, Scott. Family comes first, whatever we do, right?"

"Yes, sir," I said.

"And your second small condition?" he asked. "What's that?"

Five . . .

Kit Calder stared at me, openmouthed with surprise and disbelief. I could see that he wanted to call me a liar but that he was having a hard job doing it in front of my dad. We were at the local McDonald's where he and I had just eaten two burgers. Each. Finally, the urge to challenge what I had just told him proved too much to bear.

"This is one of your stupid stories, MacLeod," he said, shaking his head. "And I'm not buying it. Both of you must think I'm a total idiot." He paused and looked fiercely at me and then uncertainly at my dad. "Come on, guys. It's a joke, right?"

"It's no joke," I said. "Tell him, Dad."

"It's no joke," said Dad.

"It has to be a joke," he said. "You don't really expect me to believe that the president came to your house and asked Scotty to go to the Moon with two chimps? Do you?"

"That's exactly what happened," said Dad.

"It's no joke, Kit," I said.

Kit smiled wryly. "I think it's a bit sneaky of you, MacLeod," he said. "Bringing your dad in on a story like this. I can't call *him* a damned liar."

"Show him your security pass," Dad told me.

I took out the plastic NASA ID card given to me by Dr. Brown and slid it across the table to Kit. You were supposed to wear it on your breast pocket whenever you were at a NASA or USAF facility. It said SCOTT MACLEOD. ACCESS ALL AREAS.

Kit looked at it skeptically. "I don't see what this proves," he said. "You could have faked this."

"You've been watching *Mission: Impossible*," I said. "But as it happens, this *is* actually a secret. And we will deny it if you tell anyone. More importantly, so will NASA and the government. This is all very hush-hush, Kit."

"Yeah, sure."

"Look, I don't blame you for not believing me. If I were you, I probably wouldn't believe me either. The only reason I'm telling you about this is that I want you to come with me. Then, of course, you'll know that what I'm telling you is true."

"You want me to come to the Moon?"

"No," I said. "Not to the Moon. NASA won't allow that. No, I want you to be my buddy through the training. Which is going to be pretty intense. It'll mean us both cutting regular school for three months."

"Count me in," said Kit. "Only don't expect my parents to say yes. They have old-fashioned attitudes about me cutting school to go and work for the government."

"Leave your parents to me," said Dad. "And to Special Agent Bragg."

"Who's he?" asked Kit.

"The guy from the Secret Service," said Dad, "who's been assigned to Scott to help come up with a cover story that will explain his absence from school for three months."

"A Secret Service agent." Kit shook his head with wonder. "Wow." For a moment Kit looked thoughtful. "Hey," he said, "does that mean what I think it means? That I'd get a cover story as well? Like a secret agent? Like . . . James Bond?"

"Of course," said Dad. "It'd be just like James Bond."

"Wow," said Kit. "I always did want to go undercover."

Secret Service Special Agent Hank Bragg was based on Sawyer Street in Houston. He said he was originally from the oldest town in Texas, which is called Nacogdoches. He had thick red hair, a twinkle in his eye, a large nose that was the shape and color of a piece of bubble gum, and a way of speaking out of the side of his mouth that reminded me of Popeye. He came to the house, asked Dad and me and Kit a lot of questions, wrote several pages of notes, drank a lot of coffee, smoked several cigarettes, and seemed especially interested in an old friend of my dad's who was a teacher at some school in Scotland. Then he went away again in a blue Plymouth Fury. This is a nice enough car, but it's not what I'd drive if I were a Secret Service agent.

The next day Agent Bragg came back and pitched us the story with which he proposed to cover our absence from school. I didn't know what Dad had said to Kit's father, but it had worked, and Kit was now a member of the team.

"This Canadian guy you know who lives in Britain," he said. "Jimmy Winthrop. The one you met in Korea, Major? It seems that he's the assistant principal at a famous boarding school in Scotland called Gordonstoun. Knowing this, I enlisted the help of the commander of the Air Force Academy Prep School in Colorado Springs, Colonel Walter Sutherland, to speak to him. Sutherland and your friend Winthrop have agreed to set up an exchange program for students between your school and the one in Scotland. Paid for by the American taxpayer, of course. Winthrop has agreed to officially offer Scott and Kit places at Gordonstoun for one semester, with immediate effect. In order to cover his absence from school here in Texas. It's perfect for us. The school's in the middle of nowhere. It's a tough, typically British sort of place: cold showers, hard beds, lousy food. And the boys are only allowed to write home once a week. It's a bit like the army, but worse."

Dad shook his head. "I don't know if Scott's mother will go for any of that," he said. "She's always kind of disliked the idea of Scott being away from either of us for very long. Even when he was at summer camp last year, she insisted on calling him every week."

Agent Bragg looked at me with—it seemed to me—a question in his eyes.

I nodded back at him. "Embarrassing but true," I said. "Dad's right. She might not be so easy to sell on this."

"Take my word for it, Scott," said Agent Bragg. "I've spent the last three years guarding the president's wife, the first lady. And if there's one thing I know about, it's women. As soon as your mama hears that Gordonstoun is where the queen's son Prince Charles goes to school, she'll just love the idea of your going there too. There are two women that other women the world over seem to get really excited about. One is Jacqueline Kennedy Onassis. And the other is Queen Elizabeth of England. Don't ask me why, but they do. The idea that you might end up rubbing shoulders with royalty will overcome any doubts she might have about you being away from home for a few months."

"Maybe so, but she's bound to ask me questions about it," I said.

"Yeah," agreed Kit. "Won't it look kind of odd if we don't know anything about the place?"

"Don't you worry about that," he said. "That's my job. I'll write you a briefing document so that you two boys can learn up on it. By the time I've finished, you'll think you actually did go to school there."

Agent Bragg was wrong about Prince Charles. Charles had left the school in July 1967. But he couldn't have been more right about my mom. I guess that's why the Secret Service in some countries is called Intelligence. She bought every word of the story he'd dreamed up, including Prince Charles.

"My son going to the same school as a prince," she said on the telephone when Dad called to tell her the news. "It's amazing. Perhaps you'll be friends."

To my surprise she didn't seem to smell a rat. Dad was a terrible liar. By which I mean he wasn't very good at it. Instead of lying he usually preferred to say nothing. Or just mumble. He only just managed to go through with it because Agent Bragg wrote down what to say and he read it out on the phone. He didn't care much for the way we were deceiving her, but neither of us could see any alternative. There was no way she would ever have permitted me to go on a spaceflight. She certainly wouldn't have forgotten the deaths of Ed White, Gus Grissom, and Roger Chaffee. Mom's own dad was originally from Mitchell, Indiana, which was also where both Gus Grissom and his wife, Betty, came from. She hadn't known either one of them there, but Grissom's death and Betty's bereavement touched her in some deep, dark, weird way. When it happened, she kept all the newspaper clippings, and for days afterward every time the *Apollo 1* fire got mentioned on TV or radio, Mom had sighed, "That poor woman," as if there had been only one widow instead of three. About the only thing Mom regarded as more dangerous than flying an airplane was being an astronaut.

"This could be the opportunity of a lifetime, perhaps," she added.

"It's only for one term," I said. "That's what they call a semester over there." I'd been reading the briefing document Agent Bragg had prepared for me.

"English people have such a lovely way of speaking," she said.

"I guess so," I said. My own exposure to English accents was limited to Sherlock Holmes movies.

"Are they going to write about you and Kit in the *Houston Chronicle*?" she asked. It seemed like a reasonable question, especially given that my mom worked for a newspaper, but it was one that none of us, including Agent Bragg, who was listening on the other telephone, had even considered.

I looked at him. He was nodding vigorously.

"I guess so," I said vaguely.

"Make sure you send me the clipping when they do," she said.

Apart from that, everything seemed to go as planned. And the only possible fly in the ointment was that Mom said she would have to speak to me by long-distance telephone call on a weekly basis. I tried to explain that there weren't many phones in Scotland, but she was not to be dissuaded.

"Don't worry about it," said Agent Bragg when the call was over. "We'll fix something up. If we can speak to an astronaut orbiting the Moon, I'm sure we can make your mama think you're calling her from Scotland."

I began my astronaut training at the Manned Spacecraft Center at Clear Lake. It was a collection of modern buildings made of dark glass and white stone and surrounded by small lakes and nice-looking lawns. I guess you could say it looked pretty futuristic.

The astronaut office was on the top floor of Building 4. Building 30 was the famous one, the Mission Control Center. Dad came with me. And so did Kit.

Most of the other astronauts were in another part of the building, but Pete Conrad was waiting for me. Also waiting there for me were the two German scientists, Dr. Brown and Dr. Stewlinger. They were both wearing white coats. It turned out that Dr. Brown wasn't Dr. Brown after all, but Dr. von Braun. Apparently the "von" meant that he was a German baron, like the Red Baron von Richthofen, but Dr. von Braun told me that this kind of thing was no longer of any importance to him. He said it was a very long time since he had lived in Germany and that he couldn't really remember much about it. Besides, he said, that was all in the past: The United States of America was now his home. Dr. Stuhlinger—not Stewlinger—was of the same opinion. And both of them told me how much they preferred living in America to living in Germany. Which was kind of nice, I thought.

"First of all," said Dr. von Braun, "I should tell you that we have assigned an experienced astronaut to help you understand these procedures. I believe you've already met Captain Pete Conrad."

"Yes, sir," I said.

"Hello, Scott," said Pete. "Nice to see you again."

"Captain Conrad is the only astronaut who has been briefed regarding your mission, Scott. For reasons of astronaut morale. If the human astronauts going to the Moon in July were to discover that two chimpanzees had been there first, they might feel a little ticked off, yes?"

"A little ticked off is right." Pete Conrad laughed.

"So we must ask you please to be keeping your mission a secret, yes? For the moment at least. In a year or two, when it's all over and you're officially part of the space program, there will be no need for secrecy, and it may be possible to talk about this then."

"Yes, sir," I said. "But won't that be difficult?"

"Not at all." Dr. von Braun grinned his metallic grin. "We kept *Apollo Seven* a secret from the other astronauts without any problems at all. At least until it was underway. Besides, we shall not train you here in Houston, with the rest of the astronauts, but at Cape Kennedy, in Florida."

Dr. von Braun then described how my training would proceed:

"First you will go to the Lovelace Clinic in Albuquerque," he explained, "for a complete physical examination. To find out just how healthy you are, my boy."

I felt my lip wrinkle with disgust. I'd always hated physicals at school.

"I sure hope I don't have to have a physical," said Kit. "It always seems to come down to one thing: dropping your shorts."

Dr. von Braun smiled thinly. "No," he told Kit, "you will not have to have a physical. What would be the point? You are not going into space." I could see that he slightly disapproved of Kit being along for the ride. But of course there was nothing he could do about it now. Not after the president himself had okayed it.

"There's nothing to it, kid," Pete told me. "The worst part of the whole deal is having to stay in Albuquerque."

"I have an aunt who used to live in Albuquerque," said Kit. "The place sucks."

"Quite so." Dr. von Braun smiled uncertainly. "Then you will go to Johnsville, for psychological and stress testing."

"To find out if you fall apart under pressure," said Pete.

"Not him," Kit said loyally. "Not Scott."

"After this you will go to Florida for procedures training. In the spacecraft simulators."

"That's the fun part," said Pete.

"Any questions, my boy?" asked Dr. von Braun.

"Yes, sir," I said. "When do I get to meet my crew?"

"Your crew?" Dr. von Braun looked blank. Then he looked at Dr. Stuhlinger. It was obvious that neither of them had given the matter any thought.

"The two chimpanzees I'll be flying with, sir," I said.

"Scott's right, Wernher," said Pete. "As commander of this mission he should get acquainted with his fellow astronauts as soon as possible. After all, he's going to be spending a week in space with them. Perhaps he should meet them straight after his medical. At the Cape."

"Yes, of course he should." Dr. von Braun was smiling uncertainly. "A very good idea, Scott. So then. You will also get acquainted with, er, your crew. At the Cape."

"That should be fun too." Pete said this in a way that made me think it might not be fun at all. "Talking of which." He pushed a square box across the table toward me. "All astronauts get one of these. Standard issue."

I opened the box and gasped. It was a watch. And not just any watch, but an Omega Speedmaster Professional. The official astronaut watch. I wrestled it out of the box and put it on.

"Wow," said Kit, admiring it on my wrist. "You know how much these cost? A hundred and seventy-five bucks."

"You're kidding," I said. "For a wristwatch?"

"Your whole life now runs according to that watch," said Pete. "It keeps time, exactly. The exact time to get up. The exact time to eat. The exact time to go to the bathroom. The exact time to go to bed. Everything you do as an astronaut has to be done exactly. Heck, it's just one order after another." Pete glanced at Dr. von Braun and grinned. "Eh, Wernher?"

Dr. von Braun shrugged. "Orders are orders," he said.

"That's right. If you thought being a kid was just a lot of people telling you what to do, then you're about to find out that being an astronaut is ten times worse."

Four . . .

The Lovelace Clinic, in the high, dry air of Albuquerque, was founded by some nuns, for people with tuberculosis, in 1901. As well as treating New Mexicans, the clinic carried out "aerospace medical" work for the government. But an unpleasant discovery awaited me at the pueblo-style building on Gibson Boulevard. All of the physicals I'd had at school only ever lasted about an hour. This one was scheduled to last a whole week.

"A week?" I said, when Pete told me. "Are you kidding?"

"'Fraid not, kid," he said. "This is something that you're going to have to put up with if you want to make it into space. Look, we all did complete physicals at Lovelace. Shepard, Glenn, Carpenter, me. And now you. My advice is to start thinking of yourself as a kind of guinea pig. You get a lot of that as an astronaut. Particularly here at Lovelace. These are the people who look up the ass in NASA."

Sometimes Pete had a real neat way of putting things.

"What about Kit?" I asked.

"He'll see you when you're done here," said Pete. "At the Cape."

I hated the Lovelace Clinic the minute I got there. The doctor running the place was called Schwichtenberg, but everyone at Lovelace called him General Schwichtenberg, so I presumed he was a general as well as a doctor. And my time at Lovelace began with him asking me a lot of questions, which seemed to take all afternoon.

He asked me if I'd recently traveled to an area where parasitic diseases were common. I told him the only place I'd been lately was Miami. I said I didn't know what other diseases they had in Florida but that there were sixty cases of malaria in Florida every year because of all the mosquitoes they have down there in the Everglades.

"And that's a fact," I said, because I knew I was quoting my mom on this, and she was never wrong about something like that. There had been an article in the *Miami Herald* about it.

Then he wanted to know what I dreamed about, so I made up a whole load of stuff about how I dreamed about going into space. Mostly it was the plot of *2001: A Space Odyssey*, which is a bit like a dream anyway in that none of it makes very much sense. But there was also a bit of the plot from the last Bond movie, *You Only Live Twice*, about stealing rockets, and that interested him quite a lot.

"When you dream of space rockets, do you also dream about girls?" he asked. Seeing me looking blank, he rephrased the question. "Do you ever dream of girls before you dream of space rockets? Or do you ever dream of girls after you dream of space rockets?"

I pretended to give this some careful thought. "When I dream of space rockets," I said, "I sometimes also dream of ice cream."

"Ice cream?" He sounded surprised, but he wrote it down anyway.

"Ice cream," I said. "A huge ice-cream sundae. With a cherry on top."

Then he asked a lot of stupid questions about my mother and her attitude to hazardous flying, and I said that she regarded all flying as hazardous and that she got nervous at the sight of a paper airplane. He seemed especially interested in her relationship with my dad and asked me if I thought it wasn't a bit strange that someone who was so nervous about flying should have married an air-force pilot.

"Of course it's strange," I said as politely as I could, because Schwichtenberg was a general, after all. "But you know something? Maybe that's why they're not living together."

Over the next few days I was treated like a secondhand car. As if they hoped to find some hidden fault. I had an eye test and a hearing test, part of which involved filling my ear full of water. That was none too comfortable. I had several X-rays—head and chest. They examined my nose and my throat. One morning breakfast was just a beakerful of glucose so that they could see how much sugar remained in my blood sample. And I hate needles. My reflexes were tested, exhaustively, along with my lung capacity. For several hours they had me sit on an exercise bicycle, pedaling away like mad, while they measured my heart rate and how much oxygen I was pumping out. Stuff like that. They even measured my body density: This involved weighing my naked body in a bath of water while I concentrated on breathing in and out to my maximum capacity. One way or another I spent a lot of time naked as a jaybird. Or having things shoved up my butt. Worst of all was that every time I went to the bathroom, I had to collect both one and two in separate receptacles, which isn't as easy as you might think. These were then taken away for analysis. Which sounds like a really swell job to have. Especially near lunchtime.

The stupidest test was when a guy in a white coat showed me a series of inkblots on squares of cardboard and asked me to describe what I saw. "And don't say inkblot," he said, anticipating my first answer. "Just try to articulate what each shape looks like. What you think it reminds you of." The thing was, they pretty much all reminded me of a bat. Sometimes the bat had a small putz, and sometimes the bat had a large putz, but I swear they all looked like bats: happy bats, evil bats, upside-down bats, flying bats, dead bats, squashed bats, and kissing bats. He asked me if I was afraid of bats. I said I wasn't.

"What do you think it is that makes you think of bats so much?" he said, his eyes narrowed as if there were some great significance in my choice of answer.

I thought for a moment. Then I pointed to the cards. "They do," I said. "Those cards."

People get paid to do this stuff.

Pete Conrad had been right, of course. When I wasn't feeling like a putz, a guinea pig was what I felt like. Except that guinea pigs are cute, and the people at Lovelace didn't make me feel very cute at all. Most of the time I just felt embarrassed. And angry that it didn't seem to matter much to these people that I was just a thirteen-year-old kid who had volunteered for all this. They never even so much as acknowledged the fact.

"I guess you think you know all there is to know about me now," I told the general on the day Pete Conrad came back to the clinic to pick me up and fly me to the Cape.

"Pretty well, I think," he said cheerfully.

"Inside and out," I said.

"Inside and out," repeated General Schwichtenberg. "That's about the size of it, Scott."

I shook my head. "You don't know me, sir," I said. "You just think you do."

"Oh?" The general seemed amused. "And how do you work that out?"

"You don't know what my favorite color is," I said. "My favorite dinner. My favorite TV program. You don't know if I have any pets or not. You don't know if I believe in God. Or what baseball team I follow. You don't know if I prefer Pepsi to Coke. Or what my room looks like at home. You don't know what books I like to read. My favorite subject at school. All that you know about me are samples and results. What can fill a bottle or be examined under a microscope. All you know are some numbers on my final evaluation, sir. You got some blood. And you certainly got a lot of piss. But that's not me. That's not me at all."

"I think I can know that you're in excellent physical shape," said the general. "That's what those numbers are meant to determine, Scott. I know you well enough to say that. Surely."

"It's not much," I said. "Not much at all. Not in a week."

Pete took my bag and walked me outside to the jeep he'd left parked in front of the entrance. "I guess you told him," he said. "That bad, huh?"

"It was the worst week of my entire life."

"I figured as much," he said, opening the passenger door. There was a brown paper bag on the seat. He handed it to me. It was full of candy bars, comic books, paperbacks, pens, and assorted souvenirs of the kind that would make me feel vaguely human again, and not like some kind of lab rat.

"Thanks, Pete." I tried to hold back the tears in my eyes. But it was no good.

"You know, I was here ten years ago, with five other guys," he said. "We had each other to keep our spirits up. And that was tough enough. But you did it on your own. And in my book that already marks you out, kid. A lot of other people in your position would have thrown in the towel and quit."

"You're kidding," I said, and forced a smile. "Was that really an option?"

At Albuquerque Airport we climbed into NASA's Gulfstream II jet and flew east to the Florida coast and Cape Kennedy. I sat in the cockpit with Pete, but he wouldn't let me take the stick. I told him this seemed kind of weird, given that I was supposed to be training to fly to the Moon, but he said he had specific orders from NASA not to let me fly and there was no point trying to change his mind about it.

In the Gulfstream the flight took less than three hours, and it was the first time I saw the Cape, perched right on the edge of the Atlantic Ocean and sandwiched between Port Canaveral and Cocoa Beach. As we flew over, Pete pointed out the Launch Operations Center, the huge Vehicle Assembly Building, and the two rust-colored launchpads—39A to the south and 39B to the north—from where the *Saturn V* rockets took off for the Moon. Otherwise it was a featureless place of long, straight highways under a cyanide-blue sky; from the air it looked like a perfect spot to launch a rocket, but a bad spot if you were a chimpanzee. There were no trees. None. Not for miles. Just sand and sea. And after Lovelace I was a little worried about what I was going to find down there.

We landed at Patrick Air Force Base in Cocoa Beach and drove onto the Cape. At the guardhouse a security man handed me a second NASA pass and advised me to keep it pinned to my chest whenever I was on the base. Then we drove over to the astronaut headquarters in the building known as Hangar S.

"That's where we live during the final preparations for a flight," explained Pete. "But most of the time that we're here we prefer to stay at the Vanguard Motel on Cocoa Beach. That's where I'll be for the next few days if you need me."

Hangar S was like a large sprawling ranch house, with bedrooms, a kitchen, a living room, a TV room, a dining room, a swimming pool, and several bathrooms. Kit was already there, watching TV with a large bowl of popcorn on his lap. We shook hands warmly, and after I had told Kit all about Lovelace, he gave me the tour of the house.

"This place is just fantastic," he said. "For a start there's someone who cooks you whatever you want, whenever you want. And the icebox is always full of stuff. There's even a private theater where you can watch all the latest movies. I watched *Bullitt* five times. It's a great movie. Plus there's no one telling you when to go to bed and when to get up."

"So what have you done for the last week?" I asked him.

He shrugged. "Watched TV. Watched movies. Played the slot machines at the motel. I won twenty bucks! Played pool with Pete."

"Your friend is quite a little hustler," said Pete.

"I don't know why they'd want to stay at that motel," said Kit. "It's so good here."

"You can be around this place too much," said Pete. "After months and months of being here, you need to get away for some rest and recreation."

"You mean R and R?" I said.

"That's right."

"In *Playboy* magazine it says that in Vietnam, R and R is what our troops call having sex," I said.

"You read *Playboy?*"

"Well, I don't exactly read it," I said.

"Neither do I," said Kit.

"My dad gets it," I said. "He doesn't know I look at it."

"I guess that explains why you're such a hot flier, kid." Pete grinned awkwardly. "Our idea of R and R is maybe a little different here from R and R in Vietnam. Mostly it's just the boys drinking beer, staying up late, driving up and down Route A1A a little bit too fast. Rat racing, we call it. That's R and R, Cocoa Beach–style. But I'm glad your friend likes it here. While you're on the Cape, this is where you'll both be staying, so you boys make yourself at home. And then we'll go find your crew."

I threw my bag onto one of the beds. "Okay," I said, "I've made myself at home. Let's go find my crew."

At the back of Hangar S was what looked like a fenced-in trailer park. There were two long trailers, the kind you might see at a carnival or a circus, except that these were painted white and had blue lettering on the side. One said NASA-AC-3 and one said NASA-AC-4, and these two trailers were hooked up end to end like a train. At the end of the farthest trailer was a large cage. Surrounding the two main trailers was a variety of other smaller trailers and vans. Outside one of these other trailers was a clean-cut sort of man dressed like a dentist, wearing a short-sleeved white smock and baggy white pants. He was sitting in a white plastic chair, enjoying the sunshine, reading the newspaper, and smoking a cigarette. Seeing us enter the compound, he stood up, threw away his cigarette, lifted his shades, and stared at us with narrowed eyes. He was tall. He reminded me a bit of Clint Eastwood. He nodded at Pete warily and said, "I guess you're Captain Conrad." Then he looked at me and Kit and said, "And one of you two boys must be Tarzan."

"Tarzan?"

"You know," he said. "The story about the kid raised by apes in the jungle?" He shrugged. "No disrespect, but that's the code name we were given for you by the Secret Service. On account of you being so hush-hush 'n' all."

Pete pointed at me. "This is Tarzan," he said. "But he also answers to the name Scott MacLeod."

"Pleased to meet you, Scott." The man sort of smiled and held out a big strong hand, which I took. "I'm Ed Deayton. I'm the head veterinarian at Hangar S. From the Aeromedical Research Lab at Holloman Air Force Base in New Mexico. Nice to meet you, too, Captain Conrad."

"Didn't I get a code name?" asked Kit.

"Nope," said Ed. "We weren't expecting two kids. Just the one."

"This is Scott's friend Kit," explained Pete. "He's here to make sure Scott doesn't get lonely."

"Is he now?" Ed shook hands with Kit and then looked back at Pete. "Heard a lot about you."

"You mean you guys have never met before?" I said.

"Nobody on the base has much of an idea what we do," said Ed. "People tend to leave us alone. Which suits us just fine, Caliban being a secret project 'n' all. There are twenty of us here. Twenty humans, that is. We work in shifts, four of us at a time, twelve hours on and twelve hours off. Right now it's me and Maurice looking after our simian guests."

"How many chimps are here?" I asked.

"Six."

Ed smiled as he saw the surprise on my face.

"I know what you're thinking. Twenty guys looking after six chimponauts. Seems a lot, doesn't it? Well, for one thing, they're very valuable to the United States government. A pile of money has gone into their training. For another, a chimp is very like a human. They take a lot of looking after. We've learned a great deal about their welfare since we used them in Project Mercury. But there are a couple of important things you gotta remember when you're dealing with them, Scott. One is that they're clever. Very clever. Escape is always an option where a chimp is concerned. The other thing you've got to remember is that they can be dangerous. Which is why we use young chimps. None of the chimps at Hangar S is more than eight years old. But it doesn't take them long to acquire bad habits and turn nasty. Like T. C. did."

"T. C.?" I said.

"T. C. is the chimponaut who was due to command *Caliban Eleven*," said Ed. "The chimponaut you're here to replace, if you don't mind me putting it that way."

"I don't mind," I said. "It's true. What happened to him? To T. C.?"

"C'mon," said Ed. "I'll introduce you."

He led the way around the far side of the trailer.

"Like most of our primates," said Ed, "T. C. came from the

Cameroons, in West Africa. He was one of our oldest and most experienced chimponauts. One of the original six from Project Mercury. Which is why we wanted to use him again. But somewhere between Mercury and Apollo, T. C. developed an alcohol and tobacco problem. Someone back at Holloman thought that they were being kind to him, probably. All these little guys like a treat. Usually we give them banana pellets. Or sometimes candy. But T. C. got himself a taste for beer and cigarettes."

Pete grinned his gap-toothed grin. "Sounds like just one of the guys to me," he said.

"Right," said Kit.

"But worst of all," said Ed, "he got himself a ghost."

"A ghost?" I said. "What do you mean, a ghost?"

"He's always looking over his shoulder to see if there's anyone there. That's disaster for a chimponaut. It means you can't get him to concentrate."

On the far side of the first trailer was a cage about the size of a large closet. The cage appeared to be empty but for a curious-looking pile of newspapers in the corner. And it was only when we neared the pile that Pete and I realized the sheets of newspaper were being very carefully held in place by a small hairy hand.

"He uses the paper to keep the sun off," said Ed. "Or maybe just to hide from us. We're not exactly sure."

Ed dropped down on his haunches. Kit and I did the same.

"How are you today, T. C.?" said Ed. "Do you want to say hello to our guests?"

At the sound of Ed's voice T. C.'s other hand appeared from

between two sheets of newspaper and came through the bars of the cage. The leathery black palm was flat and open to the sky. He appeared to be begging. Like some old hobo or bum you might see outside a railway station. Seeing it made me feel sad. I could see that Kit felt much the same way.

"It's too bad," said Ed, "because T. C. was the best of the bunch. He was the quickest to learn and could operate the spacecraft console like no ape we ever saw before. We simulated an eight-day Moon mission, and he was outstanding. Came through with the lowest blood pressure for a chimponaut ever recorded. In a way T. C.'s the only reason we thought the *Caliban Eleven* mission was ever feasible."

T. C. lifted the sheet of newspaper from his head and looked out for a moment. He pinched his fingers together and tapped them against his lips like he was smoking a cigarette or, more likely, asking to be given one. At the same time he kept glancing over his shoulder just as Ed had described: as if he thought there was someone there.

"And then he cracked," said Ed. "He treated every physical examination as if it were an assault."

"I can understand that," I said.

"He couldn't stand being cooped up," said Ed, "or confined in the capsule. Not even in the simulator, and they get to kind of enjoy that."

Pete nodded. "It's like they suddenly develop acute claustrophobia," he said. "I've seen it happen to astronauts. They just go nuts."

"Not like this you haven't." Ed grinned. "Even a young chimp like this one is as strong as a man. A fully grown adult is maybe five times as strong. Anyway, T. C. started biting. A bite from a chimpanzee, even a young one, can be very dangerous. You can lose a finger. Part of your face. To say nothing of the toxicity of their saliva. Blood poisoning is a real hazard in working with chimps. It took three of us to handle and restrain him, and he still managed to bite us. But, more importantly, he started biting the two chimps in his crew. Beating them up."

Kit inched backward a bit.

"Why'd he do that?" I asked, feeling more than a little sorry for T. C., who was still tapping his lips with his fingertips suggestively.

"Why?" Ed shrugged. "Chimps are naturally aggressive, that's why. T. C. has just grown up a little more quickly than we had bargained for, is all." Ed took out his cigarettes. "I'd better give him one, otherwise he'll start to become really agitated." He lit a cigarette and handed it carefully to T. C., who took it and, turning his back on us, smoked it with obvious pleasure. "In time he'd probably have killed one of the others," said Ed, "so we had no choice but to segregate him from the rest and retire him from the program."

"He really likes his smokes, doesn't he?" said Kit.

"Isn't smoking bad for him?" I asked.

"Sure it is," said Ed. "But so's beating his head against the bars, which is what he'll do if I don't give him one. And I can't bear to see that."

I smiled as out of the corner of my eye I saw Kit quietly beating his head against the bars, as if he hoped his behavior might earn him a cigarette. If Ed saw it too, he didn't let on. And in silence we watched T. C. smoke for a while.

"When you see him smoke," observed Pete, "it kind of makes you think how like us they really are."

"More than anyone ever suspects," said Ed.

"What'll happen to him now?" I asked.

"Well, that's an interesting question," said Ed. "Despite having been bitten and even on one occasion hospitalized by him, I'm very fond of this little fur-ball. Like most of my colleagues I'm of the opinion that after his several spaceflights he's earned his retirement at a nice zoo somewhere. But there are some people in the air force who would like to see all of the apes in the Caliban space program eventually sent back to Holloman for use in further experimentation. Until the issue has been resolved, he stays here, with people who love him."

Ed ushered us into the first of the two big white trailers. It was air-conditioned, which came as a relief after the sticky heat of the Cape. There was an office, two procedures simulators, and a mock-up of the interiors of two spacecraft. Another man dressed in white was sitting in the office, listening to the radio and making some notes on a clipboard. He was black, with a large mustache and heavily lidded eyes that made him look a bit like a snake. His black shoes were polished as if he'd been on parade.

"This is Maurice," said Ed. "Maurice, say hello to Tarzan. Better known to himself as Mr. Scott MacLeod."

As I shook Maurice's hand, I realized that I'd never before actually met a black man.

"Mind if we just call you Tarzan?" said Maurice. "Matter of fact, I think our chimpanzees might prefer it that way. Could help them take to you more quickly." He held up a Tarzan comic book. "'Specially as how I've been reading them this at bedtime since we heard you were coming."

"I don't mind," I said. "I always did like Tarzan."

"Yeah, but which one?" asked Maurice. "Johnny Weissmuller, Jock Mahoney, or Ron Ely?"

"Weissmuller, of course," I said.

"Is the right answer." Maurice grinned back at me. "Who are these other Homo sapiens?" he asked Ed, looking at Pete and Kit.

"This is Tarzan's buddy, Kit," said Ed. "And the slightly taller one is Captain Pete Conrad. The astronaut."

"An astronaut?" said Maurice. "Damn. Never met one of those before. Not in all the time I've been here on the Cape. How about that?"

Maurice shook their hands in turn and then turned back to me. "You met your predecessor yet, Tarzan?" he asked. "T. C?"

"Just now," I said.

"Best damned astronaut I ever saw," said Maurice. He looked at Pete Conrad and shrugged. "No offense to you, Captain."

Pete grinned his grin. "None taken, Maurice."

"Tell me, Captain. Those other Apollo astronauts. They really don't know about our astrochimps? The Caliban program? Any of it?"

"I didn't know about it myself until a few days ago," said Pete. "The other *Saturn Five* launches? They told us those were unmanned probes. Satellites. That kind of thing."

"Now that you *do* know," said Maurice, "what's your opinion of what we're doing here?"

Pete shrugged. "I can see the logic behind doing it," he said. "After all, an ape was the first Mercury astronaut. And that didn't detract from what Shepard and Glenn did at all. So I don't think it will matter much that we're going to put an ape on the Moon before a man." He shook his head. "I'm more concerned with the long-term future of the space program. If there's another accident I don't see space exploration in this country having any future at all."

Maurice nodded and got up from behind his desk. "Come and meet all the gang," he said.

We followed Maurice and Ed into the next trailer and saw six cages, each of them numbered and about eight feet square and all but one home to a small chimpanzee. In front of each cage was a color TV. Ed noted my surprise.

"Chimps watch a lot of TV," he said. "Keeps them from getting bored."

"Me too," said Kit.

From under his eyelids Maurice shot me a look. "And you?"

"Sure," I said. "The way I see it, a man who's tired of TV is tired of life."

"Got that right too," said Maurice. "You like *Top Cat*, Tarzan?"

"*Top Cat?*"

"You know, the cartoon on ABC television."

"Sure."

"The six chimpanzees we got in here we named after T. C. and his gang. We got Choo-Choo, Fancy, Brain, Spook, and Benny the Ball. T. C. you already met."

"I was wondering why he was called T. C.," said Kit. "Now I know."

"That's as far as the similarity goes," said Maurice. "Like the Brain we have here? That isn't ironic. All of these cats are smarter than the average bear. If you get my meaning."

"Then I guess that makes you Dribble," I said. "I mean Dibble."

Maurice grinned at Ed. "I like this boy, Ed. I really do. He's fast. Maybe as fast as a chimp. A chimp's average response to a given physical stimulus is seven tenths of a second. Man's average is five. Don't know what a boy's is. Not yet. But we'll find out, Tarzan."

Ed had opened a cage and was leading one of the chimps out by the hand. Walking like a cowboy who'd just dismounted a horse after a long ride, the little ape came quietly, and after only a few steps it climbed up Ed's body and put an arm around his neck. "Hey, Benny," said Ed, "this is Tarzan. The guy we were telling you about. Remember?"

Benny looked at me.

"Tarzan? Say hello to Benny the Ball. Benny is going to be one of the two chimponauts in *Caliban Eleven*'s lunar module. Isn't that right, Benny?" Ed nodded at me. "You can shake his hand, if you'd like. Benny is very friendly and polite. He likes to shake hands when you meet him."

I held out my hand and took the chimp's hand in mine. Benny's amber-colored eyes looked into mine, and in a strange way I felt us connect. I was imagining it, perhaps. But maybe he felt it too, because he held on to my hand for several seconds and then quite spontaneously let go of Ed and climbed onto me.

Ed was pleased. "How about that?" he said.

"Looks like you've made a friend, Tarzan," said Maurice in a pretty good impersonation of Benny's squeaky little voice on *Top Cat*. As it happened, Maurice could do all of the voices perfectly. Including Officer Dibble. Kit was impressed. We both were.

Maurice handed us some banana pellets to give to Benny and, keen to continue making common ground with the chimp, I tried one myself.

"Not bad," I said.

"Go easy with those," said Maurice. "We steal 'em from the air force chief of staff. The general finds out you've been eating his personal supply of banana pellets, he'll come down here and give you a rocket."

I guessed this was a joke, but with Maurice it was hard to know when he was joking and when he was not. Most of the time he was smiling, whatever he said. He opened another cage and dropped down on his haunches in front of a different chimpanzee. This one was wearing a little gray-white lace-up suit and had a darker-colored, more resigned face than Benny.

"This is Choo-Choo," said Maurice, and collected the ape in

his arms. He did the voice to help me remember him. "Choo-Choo is the other chimponaut going to the Moon with you, Tarzan. He's a year older than Benny."

"They're not actually going to set foot on the lunar surface, are they?" I asked.

"I was kind of wondering that myself," said Pete.

"Hell, no," said Maurice. "If we let them out of the LEM—that's what we call the lunar module—we'd never get them back in again." He grinned. "'Sides, we gotta leave something hugely momentous and important for our human astronauts to do. Otherwise there would be no point in them going, now would there?"

"What's with the romper suit?" asked Kit, stroking Choo-Choo's hairy arm.

"The what did you call it?" asked Ed.

"The romper suit," said Kit. "My kid sister wears one like that."

Ed laughed. "Each g suit was hand-tailored to fit the wearer," he said. "At a cost of several hundred dollars apiece."

"No wonder the space program costs so much," said Kit. "A romper suit would have been a lot cheaper."

"Choo-Choo spent the morning on the procedures trainer," Maurice said patiently. "We always make them wear their g suits when we put them in the simulator. It helps condition them to know when it's time to go to work. Say hello to Tarzan and his little friend, Choo-Choo."

I stood closer to Maurice and Choo-Choo and said hello.

Choo-Choo stared at me for a moment and then looked away.

"He's a little tired, I guess," said Maurice. "Right now you wouldn't know it, but Choo-Choo's more of an extrovert than Benny. He likes to let his hair down and party when he can."

"He sounds like my kind of chimpanzee," said Kit.

"Benny's the steadier of the two," added Ed. "He has less stamina than Choo-Choo, but you can throw any kind of a situation at him in the simulator and he doesn't panic."

"The two of them work well together," said Maurice. "Better than any other pair we've got. Including you two monkeys. Which is why they've been selected to crew the LEM."

"From the sound of things," said Pete, "I could use them on my crew."

"I don't know about that," said Maurice. "Chimps are kind of picky about who they fly with."

"It's a cinch that Tarzan here is okay with Benny the Ball," said Ed.

"True. But it sure looks like the jury's still out on him as far as Choo-Choo is concerned," said Maurice. "I guess he's gonna reserve judgment for a while. See how Tarzan shapes up at Johnsville. Choo-Choo already passed all his tests there. Maybe Tarzan has gotta earn his respect and do likewise. Then he and Choo-Choo can meet each other as equals."

After a couple of days on the Cape the time came for Pete to fly me and Kit to Johnsville, in Pennsylvania. Kit and I sat in the sumptuous passenger cabin of NASA's Gulfstream jet, helped ourselves to pretty much everything that was in the icebox—including the beers—and generally fooled around.

"Will you look at this?" Kit said excitedly. "A color TV in an airplane. And a reel-to-reel tape deck. Jeez, Mac. This cabin is better than our living room at home."

His delight with our private jet and its many luxuries lasted only until we began taxiing for takeoff. It was at this point that I noticed he'd adjusted the buckle on his seat belt extra tight and was gripping the leather armrests as if he were clinging to the edge of a tall building. As the engines reached full power in a whistling crescendo of wind and turbine, and the jet gathered speed, sweat started to roll down my friend's face like rain on a windowpane. "We're not going to make it," he said through clenched teeth.

"Of course we're going to make it," I said, squeezing his forearm. "There's nothing to worry about. Pete Conrad's as good a pilot as ever held a stick. They don't come any better, Kit. Except maybe my dad. Besides, this is a brand-new jet."

He nodded grimly. But his nervousness lasted until after we were airborne, when he seemed to relax and become himself again.

"You should have told me you were afraid of flying," I said when we had leveled out above the clouds.

"I'm not afraid of flying," he said, unbuckling his seat belt. "It's takeoffs and landings that scare me. It's the uncertainty I don't much care for. But I'm perfectly okay with the bit in the middle. The actual flying part. I'm all right now, as you can see."

I kept on looking at him.

"What?"

I shook my head.

"Anyone would think I barfed all over the plane," he said irritably, "the way you're staring at me." And then he put his fingers into his mouth and pretended to barf all over the plane.

"Hey," he said. "What's the speed of this airplane?"

"About five hundred and sixty-five miles per hour," I said. "Why?"

"There's something I always wanted to do," said Kit. "My own little Superman experiment. Only my parents would never let me."

"What is it?"

Kit marched to the back of the jet and assumed the crouched start position of a sprinter. He waited for a moment, got himself set, and then took off running up the aisle of the plane. He ran about fifteen yards and then stopped. "Okay," he said. "What speed was I doing?"

"I dunno. Maybe ten miles an hour."

"Wrong," said Kit. "If I was running at ten miles an hour, I was going ten miles an hour faster than this plane. Therefore I was doing five hundred and seventy-five miles an hour. Well don't ya geddit, MacLeod? I was going faster than the plane. Just like Superman."

I grinned. "You're crazy, do you know that?"

"Me?" He laughed. "Me? You're the crazy one, MacLeod. You're the one who's going to the Moon with a couple of goddamned chimpanzees." He grinned and rubbed his hands. "Now, then, what's on TV?"

☆ ☆ ☆

The Naval Air Development Center in Johnsville is home to the Aviation Medical Acceleration Laboratory and the largest human centrifuge in the world. This centrifuge is known as the Wheel. It has a four-thousand-horsepower motor, a fifty-foot arm, and a forty-g capability—one g being equal to the normal force of gravity on Earth. At the end of the arm is a passenger capsule, inside of which is a mock-up of the Apollo cockpit, and the idea is that you're strapped inside and then spun around like a stone in a slingshot—the difference being they don't actually throw you out at maximum speed. To me it looked like something in a Bond movie. The kind of machine Goldfinger might have used to torture 007. But the point of the Wheel was not to torture me but to simulate the kind of forces encountered by a human body during takeoff on board a *Saturn V* rocket and reentry into the Earth's atmosphere at twenty-five thousand miles an hour. So that I'd know what to expect when it happened. And not just me. I'd managed to persuade them to let Kit have a go too.

Pete Conrad had described the Wheel with a certain amount of awe and said he'd almost blacked out at fifteen g's when he'd done it the first time, in the summer of 1963. But Kit and I were looking forward to it in much the same way we might have looked forward to riding the Flying Coaster at Six Flags AstroWorld.

The Wheel itself was in a building that resembled a giant hollowed-out flying saucer. In the circular ceiling above the arm there was an engineer in a little plastic pod operating the ride, just like the guy at the amusement park. I put on a helmet, and some other naval engineers helped me into my pressure suit. It was the first time I had worn one. Kit said it made me look like a real astronaut. Then they attached some sensors, wires, hoses, and microphones to my body, and I climbed inside the capsule. They closed the hatch and left me alone with the voice inside my helmet.

"Scott, this is Johnsville control," said the voice. "Do you read me, over."

"Johnsville, this is Scott," I replied. "Reading you loud and clear."

"We can fix that, too," said the voice. "During the simulation we play the sound of an actual Saturn rocket firing, so you'll get a pretty good idea of what it might feel like actually to take off. The g counter is just above your eye line. And we'll be watching you on a closed-circuit TV camera. All you have to do is answer when we speak to you, and push a few switches when you see a light come on above them. Simple as that. If at any time you decide you've had enough, just hit that chicken switch beside your right hand."

"Roger that, Johnsville."

"Roger that, and good luck."

Now that I was in the capsule, my greatest fear was not that I would black out but that I would hurl in the capsule. The same capsule where the likes of Alan Shepard, John Glenn, and Pete Conrad had been tested. What I didn't realize until the centrifuge began moving quickly was that it was physically impossible to hurl inside the capsule on the Wheel.

I didn't know how many g's I'd felt pulling out of that spin in the Tweet after the snow goose went through the canopy, but this was many times worse. In only a couple of minutes we were up to five g's, and my arms were almost immovable by my side. It was nearly impossible to press any buttons at all. But I managed a couple. And with my chest pressed back against my spine I couldn't have hurled, even if I'd wanted to. Still the speed and the g-forces mounted. *And the noise.* The noise was incredible. Like an atom bomb inside a garbage can.

"Scott, this is Johnsville, how do you read?"

"A-okay!" I yelled. "This is the original dollar ride!"

At twelve g's my eyeballs started to vibrate inside my skull. "It's like the end of the movie *2001!*" I shouted. "The light sequence. When Bowman goes into the monolith." At least, that's what I wanted to say. It might have come out different on account of the fact that my cheeks were forced back underneath my ears. My face must have looked like a skull. At fifteen g's I felt like an elephant was sitting on my chest. I'd never experienced anything like it. Each breath was an effort. I saw my finger stretch for the chicken switch. I was certain I was close to blacking out.

"That was good, Scott," said the voice. "You were up to seventeen g's without blacking out."

The simulated launch noise had stopped abruptly. And then I was decelerating. Breathing became slightly easier. I managed to close my mouth again and lift my spine off the back of the seat. And when finally the Wheel stopped, I felt like I had been trampled by a whole football team. The inside of the g suit suddenly felt wet as I started sweating again.

"Seventeen g's is something of a record," said the controller. "People mostly black out at around fifteen or sixteen g's. But then they're usually a lot heavier than you too. Body weight may have a lot to do with how we cope with these kinds of stresses."

Then the hatch opened and it was Kit's turn.

The engineer said he wouldn't be taking Kit up to seventeen g's. Nothing like it, in fact. It turned out that the U.S. Navy had forbidden him to go above five g's. Which is fast enough, especially when you keep it up for as long as Kit did. He spent the whole time laughing and screaming by turns, so that by the time his ride was over, the engineers were almost crying with laughter themselves. That was the great thing about Kit. He made everything seem like fun. And when he emerged from the capsule, a little unsteady on his legs, as I might have expected, he was ready with one of his terrible jokes:

"What did the test pilot say when he got into the Johnsville centrifuge? I'll see you around."

Kit and I had managed to enjoy ourselves. Even the recorded noise of the mighty *Saturn V* had seemed more fascinating than intimidating. But it was hard to imagine how the same would have held true for the chimps from Hangar S. I couldn't help thinking that a chimpanzee from West Cameroon—especially a young chimpanzee—would have found the whole Johnsville experience truly terrifying. To say nothing of what they would think of the real thing when it finally happened.

I came away from Johnsville determined to achieve two things. One was that nothing on earth was going to stop me from going into space as commander of the *Caliban 11* flight. The other was that somehow I was going to improve the lives of Benny the Ball and Choo-Choo and all the Hangar S chimps.

"It says here," said Kit, "that the old house in which Gordonstoun School is located was built in the eighteenth century by Sir Robert Gordon, the Wizard of Gordonstoun."

We were heading back to Houston for a trip on a very different airplane from the jet we were on now. I was reading a book about astronomy, which was part of the stuff I had to learn for the astronaut classes I was soon to have. Kit was reading the briefing document specially prepared by Agent Bragg on the boarding school we were supposed to be attending. Kit was fascinated by what he read, and there were times when I thought he would almost have preferred to be going to Scotland instead of the various NASA training facilities that were dotted all over the United States.

"Maybe the place used to be a school for wizards," I said. "If you believe in that kind of thing."

"I believe in UFOs," said Kit.

"Really?" I said. "I'm not sure I do."

"But not in wizards. Besides, the school was only founded in 1933. By a German called Kurt Hahn."

"A German?" I said. "It sounds a bit like NASA. That's run by Germans too."

"There's a picture of him in the file here," said Kit.

He showed me a photograph of a rather sinister-looking old man with a bald head, sunken eyes, and a thin, cruel mouth. It was easy to imagine the man wearing a German helmet. "He looks . . . very interesting," I said. "But not so stupid."

Kit grinned. "You don't suppose he was a Nazi, do you?" he asked. "He looks a bit like a Nazi."

"Remind me to ask Dr. von Braun about it," I said. "I expect he would know. Perhaps they were friends."

"Boys at the school have to have a cold shower every morning," said Kit. "Can you imagine it? Having a hot shower every morning would be bad enough. But a cold shower . . ." He shivered. "Ugh."

"Why does it have to be a cold shower?" I wondered aloud.

"Perhaps Germans just like making the British take cold showers," said Kit. "As revenge for them losing the war. Either that or maybe they're just trying to save money on electricity." His eyes widened with surprise. "On second thought, ignore that. Money's not a problem for these people. Have you seen how much it costs to send a kid there?"

"Expensive, huh?"

"Very. By the way, there are no girls there."

"Maybe that's why the showers are cold. Can you imagine a girl taking a cold shower?"

"All the time." Kit grinned and slapped my hand. I liked the way he was always ready with a joke if I set him up with one. "For breakfast they eat something called muesli."

"What the hell is muesli?"

"Says here it's rolled oats, bran, nuts, and raisins."

"Hamster food."

"And if you do something wrong, you're sent on a long walk. As a punishment."

"How long?"

"Miles, probably. It wouldn't seem like a punishment if it was a walk around the garden. *Jesus.*"

"What? How many miles is it?"

"No, not that. On Sundays boys are expected to wear a kilt when they go to church," he said. "A kilt is a kind of skirt for Scottish men, isn't it?"

"Why do you have to wear a kilt?"

"I dunno." He shrugged. "I'm not exactly sure why women wear skirts, let alone men."

"What about miniskirts?"

"What about them?"

"I mean it's obvious why women wear those."

"Is it?"

"So men can see their underwear. Or not. Depending on whether they're wearing any. I mean, you do see their underwear when they're wearing miniskirts. So that must be what they want. Otherwise they wouldn't do it."

Kit nodded. "Hey, what do you know? The school has its own coast guard and fire department."

"That's Germans for you," I said. "They think of everything."

"I sure hope so, MacLeod," said Kit. "For your sake, I hope so."

The KC-135A Stratotanker is a passenger-size jet built by Boeing and based at Ellington Field. The procedure is that the airplane gets up to about twenty-six thousand feet. Then the pilot makes a parabola. This requires that he fly the aircraft straight up at a forty-five-degree angle, during which time a passenger will pull about 1.8 g's. After about half a minute of going straight up, the pilot levels out briefly and then flies straight down, at an angle of about thirty degrees, for about eight thousand feet. The airplane's acceleration then matches the Earth's acceleration of gravity. In other words, the airplane flies down as fast as you can fall, making everything inside weightless for up to half a minute. The idea is that you get some idea of what it's like to be in space. The people at NASA call the airplane the "weightless wonder." But according to Pete all the astronauts call it "the vomit comet."

"Why's it called the vomit comet?" I asked Pete as we sat down on the floor and strapped ourselves to the wall. Inside, the plane was built like a padded cell in a nuthouse. Everything was cushioned to stop you banging your head. Some of the cushioning carried some ominous-looking red and yellowish stains. "Are we gonna throw up?"

"Not everyone does," said Pete. "But it's a possibility, sure."

A NASA official wearing white overalls and chewing gum handed us each a plastic sick bag and told Kit and me to put them in the pockets of our flight suits. The name on his ID tag said Elliot Sickorez. I could see Kit had noticed it and wanted to make a joke about it, and I had to shoot him a look. Instead he smiled at me and then asked what he thought was a sensible question:

"Mr. Sickorez? How long have you worked on this plane?"

"I've been on the KC since 1959," he said.

"Do people ever miss their sick bag, sir?"

"All the time," sighed Mr. Sickorez.

"So, in almost ten years," continued Kit, "how much puke would you say you've had to clean up in here?"

Mr. Sickorez blinked slowly. "Maybe seventy-five gallons of puke."

"Seventy-five gallons!" I looked at Kit with astonishment. "Seriously?"

"You bet seriously," said Mr. Sickorez. "It's always serious when you've got to clean up someone else's puke, wouldn't you say?"

"You got that right," I said.

The aircraft took off, and we began our slow climb to twenty-six thousand feet.

"Can you tell who the pukers are going to be *before they hurl?*" Kit asked Mr. Sickorez.

"There's no way of telling until they do it." Mr. Sickorez smiled thinly. I could see that he was becoming a little tired of the subject of barfing. "So you'd best keep your sick bag handy, huh?"

Somewhere over the Gulf of Mexico we reached twenty-six thousand feet. For a while longer we remained sitting down as the aircraft climbed steeply. Then, at the signal from Mr. Sickorez that the first parabola was upon us, we all unbuckled.

After thirteen years of feeling the pull of gravity, I found its absence more than a little strange. One second we were sitting on our butts, and the next we were floating up in the air like flying gurus. The weirdest thing of all was that it was impossible to change direction once you'd launched yourself one way. And the only way to check your progress along the interior of the aircraft was to grab hold of one of the straps on the fuselage wall or ceiling.

"Isn't this great?" I yelled at Kit as he launched himself, one fist extended ahead of him, just like Superman in the crummy TV show.

"Faster than a speeding bullet!" he yelled back at me.

It was a one-hour flight, and we were scheduled to make about twenty weightless parabolas. But by the fifteenth parabola both Kit and I were feeling distinctly queasy. My stomach couldn't decide where it was going, up or down. It wasn't the weightlessness that affected us so much as the aircraft leveling out and then climbing back up. It was like riding up and down, again and again, in a really fast elevator—times ten. After a while we had both had enough, and we buckled ourselves to the wall, holding the sick bags to our mouths, certain that we were going to barf. Pete and Mr. Sickorez watched us with amusement.

"I think we'd better call it a day," Pete told him. "I expect these boys will be wanting some lunch. I hear they've got Mexican in the canteen today. Chicken fajitas and beef burritos, both with lots of cheese, and jalapeños and salsa. Followed by ice cream with chocolate sauce and pistachios. And all washed down with lots of fizzy Coca-Cola. Right, boys?"

Kit swallowed uncomfortably and tried to suppress a groan. Then he belched and sort of barfed all at once—a quite spectacular maneuver that instantly filled the bag with vomit, as if the entire contents of his stomach had been moved there in less than a second. The sight and sound of what had happened to Kit was so revolting to me that I did the same.

We sealed the sick bags and handed them to Mr. Sickorez. He handed us some tissues, and we wiped our mouths. "I think we'd better call it a day," agreed Mr. Sickorez, and he radioed the pilot, telling him to take us back to EFD. Much to our relief.

"Does this mean I can't become an astronaut after all?" I asked Pete.

"Hell, no," he said. "Lots of guys throw up. Even on a space-flight. Rusty Schweikart threw up on *Apollo Nine*. Twice. And I don't expect he'll be the last. Just don't barf in your space suit. That's what they say. There's nowhere for it to go but back in, somehow."

"Sounds like good advice," I said, dabbing at my mouth and trying to imagine the horror of being locked inside a helmet with a mouthful of vomit floating around like a cheesy liquid asteroid.

Kit was looking as pale as a bank of cumulus cloud. He smiled weakly. "I guess now I know why Mr. Spock is green," he said.

Three . . .

"Are you getting enough to eat, honey?" asked my mom.

"Yeah," I said. And told her about the muesli.

"Well, that sounds nice and healthy," she said.

"Healthy, yes," I said. Bragg's file was open on the table in front of me. "Nice, no. Fortunately, we're allowed a kind of private food store we keep in a box. It's called a tuck box. You know, like Friar Tuck in Robin Hood. If I get hungry, I just help myself from that."

"I know what a tuck box is," she said. "What's the weather like over there?"

I looked out of the window. The sun was shining and the temperature was in the seventies. It was a typical Floridian day.

"Cold," I said. "Yesterday we had to play field hockey in the snow."

"Did you remember to pack your warm coat?"

"Are you kidding? I wear it all the time. We have to take a walk before breakfast. They're very big on walks and fresh air here."

"It all sounds very healthy. What are the other boys like?"

"They're okay, I suppose. Most of them are from really rich families. Three boys in my class have dads who own Rolls-Royces."

"That's nice. Have you met him? Prince Charles?"

"No," I said. "But I see him around sometimes. Everyone says he's okay. For a prince."

"I never got that clipping," she said. "From the *Houston Chronicle*. About you and Kit going to Gordonstoun."

"No?" I said. "I have one here. I'll mail it. Only it might take a little while. The mail here is kind of slow. Everything is kind of slow here."

"Maybe so," she said. "But this is an amazingly clear telephone line. Normally a transatlantic call sounds like you're speaking to someone in a submarine."

"I wouldn't know," I said. "I never made this kind of call before."

"The school doesn't mind you making a transatlantic call?"

"It's part of the bursary," I said. "That's what they call it here when they give you a scholarship."

"I know what a bursary is, Scott," she said.

"It includes all kinds of stuff. Free food, free clothes, free travel, free phone calls, you name it, Mom."

"Maybe you should call more often."

"We're allowed one phone call a week," I said. "That's the rule."

"So what are you learning about in school?" she asked.

I hadn't actually discussed this with Agent Bragg. Both of us had kind of assumed that children in schools learned the same sort of things the world over. But now that she'd asked, I thought it seemed unlikely that this would be the case. From the little I'd read about them, the Scots seemed like a remarkably clever race having invented the television, the telephone, penicillin, the pneumatic tire, the telegraph, the steam engine, the refrigerator, hypodermic syringes, and anesthetics. And it hardly seemed probable that a Scottish school would bother teaching anything much except science and engineering. Which just happened to be what I'd been studying in my NASA classes at the MSC in Clear Lake. So I decided to tell her that.

"I've been learning about astronomy," I said. "And aerodynamics, rocket propulsion, communications, medicine, meteorology, physics of the upper atmosphere, guidance and navigation, mechanics, survival skills, geology, and digital computers."

"Survival skills?" Mom sounded surprised.

"The school has its own mountain-rescue team," I said. Remarkably, this was true. "On account of all the hill walking that gets done here."

"You won't do anything stupid, will you, Scott?"

"No, Mom, of course not."

Unless you count being blasted into space and going around the Moon as stupid.

"Apart from that it all sounds very scientific," she said.

"It's very scientific here," I said. "Scottish schools are really big on science. Much more than American schools."

"And are you enjoying it there, Scott?"

"Sure, Mom," I said. "Although it does get dark very early in this part of the world."

"What about Kit?" she asked. "Is he enjoying it too?"

"The dark?"

"The school."

"Apart from having to wear a kilt on Sunday," I said, "Kit loves it too, Mom."

"You have to wear a kilt on Sunday?"

"They don't let you into church without one," I said inventively. "It's the law in this part of the world."

Mom was laughing. "What does Kit look like in a kilt?" she said.

"Scottish, I guess," I said. "He looks very Scottish."

Telling Mom the truth about where I was and what I was really doing would have meant the end of my Moon mission, not to mention the end of my dad's chances of getting back together with her. She would have been furious. I felt bad lying to her like that. She deserved better. But what could I do? Every time I looked at the *Saturn V* being assembled on the launchpad and considered the enormous cost and effort involved, I told myself there was no way I could let everyone down. It was something I was just going to have to live with. Assuming I survived, of course.

A *Saturn V* rocket is made up of several different sections.

The command and service modules (CSM) are two parts working together: the conical-shaped command module, better known as the capsule, in which we three astronauts would make the 480,000-mile journey to the Moon and back; and the cylindrical service module containing the fuel and oxygen tanks. The CSM sits right at the top of the *Saturn V* rocket, like the torch in the hand of the Statue of Liberty. (In fact the CSM is sixty feet higher than the torch held by the Statue of Liberty.) The *Saturn V* rocket has three stages. The first stage is the largest and most spectacular—the part that blasts the astronauts off the ground at Cape Kennedy. Along with the second stage it falls away as its fuel runs out, so it's the third stage that pushes the CSM into orbit above the Earth. Once orbit is achieved, the third stage reignites a second time, sending the CSM on its way to the Moon.

About fifteen minutes later—and about six thousand miles from the Earth—the rear section of the CSM separates from the third stage of the *Saturn V* and turns around so that the nose of the capsule is pointed at the top of the third stage. These two sections then connect with each other, like vacuum-cleaner attachments, in a procedure called docking. The CSM then reverses so that it can withdraw the lunar module, which is the spider-shaped spacecraft we were counting on to land two astronauts on the Moon. The third stage then falls away, leaving these two oddly connected spacecraft—the CSM and the LM—"drifting" toward the Moon at twenty-five thousand miles an hour.

It's all as simple as that.

Of course it's not as simple as that. Not nearly. And NASA

constructed detailed simulators to duplicate exactly the actual CSM and the experience of maneuvering one in space. A large part of my already busy day was soon given over to sitting with Benny and Choo-Choo in a mock-up of a CSM at the Cape. It was just like flying the T-37 simulator at Ellington instead of the actual Tweet itself, with the difference that, unlike the USAF's jet simulators, NASA's CSM simulators had cost millions of dollars. Every switch, button, gauge, and warning light functioned exactly like the real thing. There was a takeoff sim, an abort sim, a lunar orbit insertion sim, a reentry sim, and a docking sim. And they couldn't have felt more real. When you looked out of the window, you saw not a televised picture of the LM but an actual three-dimensional replica of the LM, complete in every detail. When, for example, you attempted to complete the docking procedure with the LM, the CSM actually moved in response to the controls; it even jarred when you made contact.

The sense of reality in the sim was increased by the fact that the three of us had to wear training suits, just like in the centrifuge at Johnsville.

By now I had three suits, all of them specially tailored for me: a training suit, a flight suit—also called a pressure suit, or space suit—and a spare flight suit. The flight suits cost an astonishing thirty thousand dollars apiece. Kit expressed most of the astonishment, as by now I was beginning to realize that everything around me cost a lot of money. But not all of it seemed money well spent. Even the ballpoint pens developed by NASA to work in zero gravity had cost hundreds of thousands of dollars.

"Why don't they just use a pencil?" asked Kit, with faultless logic. "I bet you any money you like that a pencil works just fine in space."

I wouldn't have mentioned it to them. But he did. Kit enjoyed throwing curveballs their way. To that extent he took his cue from the simulation instructors with whom he was obliged to spend part of his day. Seated at computer consoles outside the actual simulator, these guys were nerds whose job was to create simulated malfunctions for me and the two chimponauts. Engine failures, communications problems, computer problems—they tried everything. One light came on, I'd pull a lever. Another light came on, Choo-Choo or Benny would press a button. The two chimpanzees took it all really seriously and from time to time would screech out loud in frustration when they got something wrong. With other malfunctions there seemed no choice but for me to admit that I was stumped for an answer about what to do, and the sim operator would confess that if such and such a problem happened, I'd have little choice but to call Mission Control and let them decide which switch I should throw. It was soon perfectly clear to me that thanks to the computer the spacecraft could fly itself, and that if that failed, then all was truly lost. They called me the commander, but just like in *2001: A Space Odyssey* it was the computer that was really in charge.

About the only real control I had over all our destinies was during docking and takeoff. A lot of the time, with takeoff malfunctions the only thing to do was abort the mission. This meant taking hold of the abort handle and twisting it. The abort handle would fire a small rocket on top of the escape tower, which was a small red gantry on top of the CSM's nose. The escape tower would then lift the CSM clear of the rest of the rocket, enabling us to parachute to safety somewhere in the Atlantic.

Dr. von Braun often came down to watch. He seemed pleased with our progress. And once or twice he brought my dad with him, to demonstrate my proficiency and competence and reassure him that I was okay. Dad was back in uniform, of course. And back on duty. He seemed genuinely impressed with what I'd achieved.

"I'm proud of you, son," he said. "Real proud. I don't think any man was ever as proud of his son as I am of you, Scotty."

And then he saluted me. A real solemn salute, like from one officer to another, which kind of made me want to cry.

When I wasn't in a simulator, I was in a class. Of the various subjects, by far the dullest was geology. I told the geology teacher, Dr. Freichshoh, that I couldn't see the point of learning it if I wasn't going to land on the Moon myself. He said that all astronauts learned geology, and that there could be no exceptions; otherwise all the astronauts would want to drop it. The deal was that Kit had to do the classes with me. But he didn't care for the classes at all and did little to conceal his boredom.

The teachers who came to give the classes were the best in their fields, but they certainly couldn't teach. Kit and I may not have known much in the way of geology and meteorology, but after several years at Ima Hogg we certainly recognized a good teacher when we met one. Some of them tried to bring it down to our level a bit. None of them succeeded. Least of all Dr. Freichshoh.

One day, after yawning his way through a two-hour lesson on flight mechanics, Kit came back to our living quarters in Hangar S and put his head straight under the cold-water faucet.

"What are you doing?" I asked.

"Kick-starting my brain," he said. "I think it must have shut down when that guy started talking about the mathematics of satellite orbits and other trajectories."

"It was kind of hard," I said.

"Hard? On the Mohs' scale, that was a twelve."

The Mohs' scale was something we'd had in geology: the one-through-ten scale from the softest to the hardest material. One is talc, and ten is diamond.

I grinned. "So you really *were* paying attention in geology."

He let the cold water cascade over his head for another half minute before standing up. I tossed him a towel.

"You know something, Mac?" he said. "I'm beginning to understand how they manage to persuade some guy who's bright enough to know better to sit on top of a rocket and be blasted into space. *Boredom.* You do enough goddamned geology and physics, and anything, anything at all, no matter how crazy, sounds a lot better than sitting in a room and learning that the chemical formula for Topaz is $Al_2SiO_4(F,OH)_2$."

"You know, I think geology is your subject," I said. "That's the second time I realized you were paying attention."

"Yeah, but what's the point of it?" he asked. "What's the point of learning geology? It's not like you're even going to set foot on the Moon and see any rocks. Least of all topaz. Dr. Freichshoh said himself that he thought it was unlikely there would be any topaz up there. Even the chimps are going to leave the rocks alone. So why even mention topaz? If the command module gets hit by an asteroid, then maybe you'll know what it's made of. Which'll be small comfort because you'll be dead, of course. But apart from that they're wasting your time. If you ask me, this whole class is a waste of time."

He threw the towel aside and helped himself to a Coke from the icebox. "It's the same with the lessons about computers. Why do you need to know how to repair and replace components on the computer when you aren't actually taking any components on the flight? And why the hell are you learning about survival in the desert and the jungle?"

I shrugged. "In case the takeoff goes wrong and we have to abort somewhere over the desert or the jungle? Hey, I thought survival was your favorite class."

"Survival?" Kit laughed. "Mac, you're catching a ride on your own personal Hiroshima. You're gonna be sitting on top of a rocket bigger than the Statue of Liberty, carrying five million pounds of liquid hydrogen fuel and generating more power than eighty-five Hoover Dams. That's enough power to light up the city of New York for seventy-five minutes. All this survival stuff is bunk."

"Not at all," I said. "It might come in very useful if I have to pull the abort handle and fire the small rocket in the escape tower. We could come down anywhere."

Kit pulled a face. "Mac, if the *Saturn Five* blows, you're history. With or without the escape tower. You know it. I know it. And they know it. If the takeoff goes wrong, you're going to be toast, my friend. A very small crumb of blackened toast with no room for any jam. They'll bury you in a matchbox, pal."

"Well, gee, thanks for mentioning it, *pal*," I said. "Have you finished?"

He nodded sheepishly.

"You know, I wanted you along with me for support," I said. "Not so you could freak me out with a rundown on what a loony I am."

"I'm sorry," he said. "But what they ought to be telling you is something useful."

"Like what, professor?" I asked. "You being an expert on space-flight 'n' all."

"Like how to take a crap in conditions of weightlessness. Or, better still, what happens when those two chimps decide to take a crap. What happens to their crap? Is it going to be floating around beside you or what? You ask me, that's what they should be telling you. Forget the goddamned geology. That's what I'd want to know, MacLeod. How are you going to take a leak? More importantly, how are you going to take a dump?"

"The engineers call it the waste management system," said Pete. "But in my humble opinion the person who designed it should be made to take a space walk without a pressure suit. Because it sure isn't much of a system, and the word 'management' certainly doesn't give you the least clue of the full stinking horror of what's involved here."

"Jesus," said Kit.

"You boys asked me to tell it to you straight." He shrugged. "And that's what I'm doing."

The three of us were sitting in the command module simulator—a perfect facsimile of the real Caliban capsule. It was like being inside a very small but futuristic mobile home: Every inch of ceiling and surface was home to a switch, a button, a dial, or a warning light. When I wasn't in class this was where I was supposed to be, learning everything there was to know about what was going to happen and what might or might not happen. One thing I was certain was going to happen—Kit was right about that, of course—was that sometime during an eight-day flight to and from the Moon I would probably want to go to the bathroom.

"Okay," said Pete. "You want to take a leak? Here's what you do." He frowned as if the full enormity of what was involved in the explanation was only just beginning to make itself plain to him. "Er, do you boys know what a condom is?"

"You mean a rubber?" I said. "Sure."

Pete smiled thinly. "I forgot. You read *Playboy*, don't you?"

"Whenever we can," said Kit.

He unhooked a hose from the wall. The hose had what looked like a rubber attached to the end. Kit was already grinning.

"You get your own device out and then roll this on," he said.

"That looks kind of big," I observed. "For me."

Pete nodded. "I'll tell the engineers to measure you up," he said.

"Now that's what I call personal tailoring," said Kit.

"All right," sighed Pete. "You're attached. You're ready to go. You open this valve, and then start to pee. All the urine goes straight into space." He pointed to the window. "You'll be able to see it freeze into thousands of tiny droplets of ice as it leaves the spacecraft. Actually, when the sun catches them, it's almost attractive. But that's the only attractive thing about the whole deal. Because here are the drawbacks. For one thing, your own equipment kind of shrivels up in space."

"You mean forever?" asked Kit, who seemed unduly fascinated by Pete's whole explanation.

"No, it's just temporary," Pete said patiently. "For another, when you open the valve, you're attached to a vacuum. That kind of sucks at you. Quite literally. Like a vacuum cleaner. And it's very cold, of course. Neither of which is very comfortable. What's more, when you shut off the valve, it can sometimes catch, like your zipper."

"Ouch," said Kit, grimacing.

"Then there's what we call the shake problem." Pete shrugged. "Everyone shakes before they zip, right? Just to get rid of the drips. But you can't do that with this thing. So there are always one or two drops that get away when you pull your dick out of the rubber. And then they just float around the cabin. Until you

track them down with a tissue. *If* you can track them down."
He held the device up to his nose. "To say nothing of how this
thing smells at the end of your flight."

"Bad, huh?" I said.

"Like the elephant house at the zoo," he said.

"Don't you mean the monkey house?" asked Kit.

"I'm coming to that part," said Pete. "Don't rush me, kid. This
is hard enough to talk about."

"What if you want to pee and poop at the same time?" I
asked.

"You can't," said Pete. "Simple as that." He reached behind
him, flipped open a storage locker, and took out some plastic bags.
"When you want to take a dump, the best thing to do is strip off,
get down onto the floor out of sight, and then get to work with
this specially designed poop bag."

Pete showed us the poop bag. It was shaped like a bucket with
an adhesive brim, and built into the side of the main body of the
bag was a finger-shaped pocket.

"Once you're stripped off, you kind of stick this on your butt
and then poop your poop," he said. "A buck says you can't guess
the problem with something as simple as that."

"Air pressure on your body makes it hard to go," said Kit.

"Nope. That just makes you fart."

I thought for a minute. "There's no gravity to make the poop
drop out of your butt," I said.

Pete handed me the buck.

Kit pulled a face. "You mean you—"

Pete placed a finger in the little pocket and demonstrated the procedure.

"That is so gross," said Kit.

"When finally it's in the bag," said Pete, "you squeeze some disinfectant gel in beside it, squeeze it all together, and then seal your bag. The whole process can take up to an hour."

"Shit," I said.

"That's the general idea," said Pete. "You know how Gordo Cooper and I set an endurance record of eight days in space on *Gemini Five*? Well, I do mean endurance. The smell was so bad that just the memory of it can make me gag, even now, four years later. It must be hardwired into my brain."

"Yeah, but wait a minute," said Kit. "Are you telling me they've trained a chimp to do all of that?" He shook his head. "I don't think so."

"I've been kind of wondering that myself," said Pete.

We went back to the chimponaut compound to find Maurice and Ed. Ed was off duty, but Maurice was there. He seemed pleased to see us. So did Benny the Ball and Choo-Choo. Benny climbed up onto me like before. And Choo-Choo kept putting his hand on top of my head, which Maurice assured me was a good sign. We fooled around for a few minutes, giving the two chimps some banana pellets, and then Pete got to the point.

"Tarzan's got a question," he told Maurice. "Kind of a delicate question."

"Uh-oh," said Maurice.

"It's about waste management," I said. "Pete's told me what *I've* got to do. But what happens when Benny and Choo-Choo have got to go poo-poo?"

"Nicely put," said Maurice. "If you hadn't become an astronaut, then maybe you'd have become a poet, I guess. Well, it's like this, Tarzan. The good news is that when a chimp goes poo-poo, he likes to go on the palm of his hand. So that he can take a good look at it afterward."

"Sure," said Kit. "I can understand that."

"For the same reason, they're quite happy to try to use the baggies," said Maurice. "They're even happy to use the tube to go pee-pee. Only it's not always successful. So, about four or five days before the mission these two astrochimps will begin a low-residue diet. Which, as it happens, is probably what they'll do with you too, Tarzan. Then, on the day of the mission, we'll start them both on Lomotil. Lomotil is a drug that blocks nerve signals to the intestinal muscles. Slows the passage of food through the gut. At the same time it eases painful muscle contractions from not going poo-poo."

"Maybe you should take it yourself, Mac," said Kit.

"He's got a point. Maybe you should," agreed Maurice. "But four or five days of Lomotil is enough for anyone. Man or monkey. The plan is that we cut the supply the day before Benny and Choo-Choo land on the Moon; when they do land on the Moon, we plan to let them celebrate this enormous and significant scientific achievement by taking a dump down there, using special poop bags built into their space suits. To spare you any unnecessary discomfort, Tarzan. Then we start them on Lomotil again." He shrugged. "I'm not saying there won't be accidents. But we're doing our best to make sure that the three of you don't get on each other's noses."

"Thanks, Maurice," I said. "I do appreciate it, you know."

Maurice smiled. "Don't thank me," said Maurice. "Thank Benny and Choo-Choo. Which reminds me. It's time you three learned to talk to each other."

Two . . .

Chimps can't and never will be able to talk. They can make a large variety of sounds, but human speech will always be beyond them. According to Maurice, this has something to do with their vocal tracts, which are different from our human ones. But they are able to learn American Sign Language, which is used by many deaf people in the U.S. Most of the chimponauts at Hangar S had been taught to express themselves with signs by Sally Birkin, who was one of the people attached to the chimp program at the Cape, and to whom we were now introduced.

Sally was by any standard gorgeous, and both Kit and I were reminded of Gale Olson, who was one of the Playmates he and I had lusted after in *Playboy*. As Miss August 1968, Gale Olson had claimed to want to become an astronaut. Like Gale, Sally was fair-skinned and freckled with a beautiful smile and blond hair.

After our first meeting with Sally, Kit told me he was already in love with her. It was hard to believe that she was a captain in the air force.

Prior to his breakdown, or whatever you wanted to call it, T. C. had been Sally's star pupil. She had taught T. C. almost a hundred signs to express himself, and she still hoped against hope that somehow he would become his old self again and stop biting people and other chimponauts. But he steadfastly refused to talk to Sally except to ask her for a cigarette. This, she said, broke her heart. Her next best pupil was Choo-Choo, who knew almost seventy signs. Benny knew more than fifty signs. They knew the signs for colors, for fruits, for one or two objects, for emotions, and for the names of people and chimps. Quite a few of the chimponauts could also use colored magnetic chips to make simple sentences.

"Chimpanzees are relatively quick to learn words," said Sally. "Usually one lesson per word is enough. Let's hope you boys are as quick as they are."

It wasn't very long before Kit and I were having basic conversations with Choo-Choo and Benny and discovering that chimps had a talent for extending the words they knew to things for which they had no words, or for which they couldn't remember the words. For example, Choo-Choo always described an apple as "the orange which is green," and Benny described Coke as "the 7UP which is black."

Choo-Choo and Benny seemed to enjoy these conversations, and they always got very excited when they realized that they had been able to communicate with us. Sometimes it seemed like the highlight of their day. So one time I asked Sally why she thought T. C. had stopped speaking to everyone in Hangar S, especially when he had been so gifted in this area.

For a moment or two she looked evasive, and when at last she answered, I noticed that there were tears in her green eyes. "I can't tell you that," she said. "But maybe you ought to ask him yourself."

So I did.

As usual I found T. C. in the corner of the cage at the back of trailer one. Someone had taken his newspaper away, and he was just sitting there, staring at the bars sadly. I sat down as close to him as I dared—he was quite capable of reaching through the bars and twisting your ear or pulling your hair—and waited a while before I tried to initiate a conversation. I was hoping he would get used to my presence and accept it, maybe even become a little bit curious as to what I wanted from him. I'd even borrowed a packet of cigarettes left lying in the trailer office as an added incentive for him to sign. Eventually, he pinched his thumb and forefinger together and tapped them to his lips. I clapped my hands, pointed to T. C., and then imitated his smoking gesture. He moved his hand to the right, which was a sign that this was correct. Now we were getting somewhere. I lit a cigarette and handed it to him. He puffed it with enormous satisfaction and placed the cigarette in the corner of his mouth, like a guy in some dumb TV commercial. The way he looked up at the sky while he smoked, I almost thought he was going to say, "I'd walk a mile for a Camel." Instead he said nothing, not even thank you. "Thank you" is signed by touching your chin. I touched my own chin sarcastically. He puffed out some smoke and then moved his hand from his ass to his armpit. "Crap," he was saying. He looked away, and I waited until his eyes were on me again before putting my right fist in my left palm and moving it toward my body; keeping my fist there, I moved my palm back toward him. "Help me, help you," I was saying. I repeated the sign several times.

When he had finished his cigarette, T. C. flicked it expertly out of his cage and then fixed me with a hard, steady look. He pointed at himself, lifted his palms close to his mouth, and then quickly moved them down and forward; then he moved his finger downward and side to side. I felt my jaw drop slightly as I realized what he was saying: "I hate people." There was no doubt about this; he repeated the signs several times in succession. I touched my shoulder with my index finger and thumb: "Why?"

T. C. grimaced and shook his head. People usually made the mistake of thinking this meant a chimpanzee was smiling; Sally had told us that the reverse was true. Then he leaned back, lifted his feet in the air, and smacked and pinched the soles of his feet, hard, yelping in little, short, exclamatory bursts of sound, like silenced gunshots.

"You have a pain in your feet?" I said. I was beginning to feel like the ape doctor Zira speaking to Taylor, the human astronaut, in the movie *Planet of the Apes*.

T. C. snapped his thumb and fingers together and then tapped his head, several times. This was the sign for "learn." Then, with palms upward, he interlocked his fingers and pulled them apart: "How."

"Pain in feet, learn how," I repeated dumbly.

He stopped signing, clasped his legs to his chest, rocked on his butt for a moment or two, and then made the cigarette sign. I lit him another and tried to understand what he'd just said to me.

And then it hit me like a boxing glove. What T. C. was trying to tell me. *Why didn't I realize it before? How stupid can you get?* I swallowed, and with my fist I drew a circle on my chest. "Sorry," I was saying. "Sorry."

"We're leaving," I told Kit. He was sitting on the sofa in the astronaut living quarters, watching TV with a Coke in his hand. I went through to our room, collected my bag from under the bed, and started to throw some clothes inside it. After a moment or two Kit appeared in the doorway.

"Leaving? Why?" he asked. "What happened?"

"I just had an argument with Ed and Maurice," I said.

"Those guys," he said. "They tease a lot. But it doesn't mean anything. They're just guys fooling around."

"That's not it," I said. "I just found out how they train Benny, Choo-Choo, all of the chimps in Hangar S."

"They give them treats when they get something right," said Kit. "Banana pellets."

"Yes, but did you ever stop to figure out what happens to the chimpanzees when they get something wrong?" I asked.

Kit shrugged. "They don't get a banana pellet?"

"Nope," I said, zipping my bag up. "Think again."

He shook his head. "I don't know."

"You've seen them put those little metal plates on the soles of their feet," I said, "when they're in the simulator?"

"Yes," he said.

"I thought they were sensors," I said. "You know, for checking their blood pressure or something like that. I mean, you get used to having all sorts of things attached to you when you're in the sim. Attached to you. Up your butt. How's your heart? How's your breathing? If we do this, does your blood pressure go up or down? Me, I thought they were just biosensors, goddamnit." I shook my head bitterly. "Well, they're not. They're anything but. Turns out they're pyschomotor stimulus plates."

"What the hell are psychomotor stimulus plates?" asked Kit.

"I'll tell you what they are," I said. "They're zap plates. If Choo-Choo or Benny doesn't throw the right switch on cue, they get a dose of electricity in the soles of their feet."

"You're kidding."

"Nope. That's why they screech sometimes—you know how we thought they were just frustrated? Now we know the real reason. They're torturing them. No wonder they've been able to learn so much. That's why T. C. went crazy, started biting people. He couldn't take it anymore. I know, because I asked him." I made the signs that T. C. had made for me. "'Pain in feet, learn how. Pain in feet, learn how.' That's what he told me, Kit. The poor little guy."

"So what are we going to do?"

"We're leaving, that's what we're going to do."

I looked at the Omega Speedmaster watch on my wrist for a moment, then took it off.

"You really mean it, don't you?" said Kit, who knew how much I loved that watch.

"Sure I mean it."

"How much money have you got?" he asked, turning out his pockets onto my bed.

I turned out my own. "Five bucks," I said.

"I've got three," he said. "Eight bucks is not going to get us home again. That's where you want to go, isn't it?"

"Yes."

He thought for a moment. "It's not enough," he said. "We're gonna need something to hock."

We both looked at the watch. "Can you bear to do it?" he asked anxiously.

"Serve them damn well right," I said.

We left the base and headed out along the highway. Cape Kennedy is on a large island, and we had to walk across a bridge over the Indian River to reach the mainland and the city of Titusville. We walked from one end of town to the other looking for a hock-shop, and finding no such thing we decided to try our luck in a local jeweler's. The shop owner listened to the unlikely story we had concocted to explain how we came to have such an expensive watch in our possession and why we were selling it. When we had finished, he nodded patiently.

"This watch retails for almost two hundred dollars," he said. "Now, you don't strike me as the kind of boys who would have stolen this watch. But I can tell you are in some kind of trouble. So I tell you what I'm going to do. I'm going to loan you fifty dollars on the security of this watch. That means I'll keep it until you return and pay me back the fifty dollars. I'll give you a receipt, explaining all of that in writing, just in case your parents think I was trying to cheat you."

The man stepped into his office, typed out a letter to this effect on headed notepaper, and handed it over with the fifty dollars. We thanked him and then went to the bus station where we got on a bus for Orlando. From there we planned to catch a train or a Greyhound bus to Houston. By the time we got to Orlando, we had decided that the train would be better, and upon our arrival in Orlando, we went straight to the railway station to check times.

As we walked into the station, a policeman got out of a patrol car and walked into the ticket hall. Out of the corner of my eye I saw him buy some cigarettes and a newspaper and waddle slowly over to the information desk, where Kit was asking about trains to Houston. He didn't seem to be looking at us, so we didn't pay him too much attention. He carried on looking at his newspaper and seemed to be waiting his turn to speak to the woman behind the counter, who was telling us the train times and the ticket prices. When she had finished, he folded his newspaper under his arm and smiled at us.

"Would you two boys oblige me by telling me your names?" he asked.

"My name is John Smith," said Kit without hesitation. "And this is my friend David Jones."

"Smith and Jones, huh?"

"That's right, sir."

"Catching a train to Houston, right?"

We could hardly deny this, as the policeman had probably heard every one of our questions at the station information desk. "That's right," I said.

"Mind telling me why?"

I repeated the same lame explanation we had given the jeweler in Titusville; it didn't get better with telling a second time.

He nodded. "I'm sorry, boys," he said, and gently but firmly he took hold of my arm and then Kit's. "I'll have to ask you to come along with me. I think your names are Kit Calder and Scott MacLeod, and you're wanted by a U.S. Treasury official named Bragg."

(The Secret Service is part of the U.S. Treasury. Don't ask me why, but it is.)

"I've got orders to take you downtown and hold you there until someone from the U.S. Treasury Department can come and get you."

He started to move us to the exit and the patrol car that was waiting outside.

"Sir," said Kit. "Officer. Wait a minute. Surely there's been some kind of mistake. Do you honestly think it's the least bit likely that I or my friend here could be wanted by the U.S. Treasury? We're both thirteen years old, sir. Doesn't this strike you as just a bit weird?"

"That it does," said the policeman. "But orders are orders."

✪ ✪ ✪

It was close to midnight when a blue Plymouth Fury pulled into the floodlit parking lot outside the police station in Orlando. Kit and I were watching from an upper window. Out of the car stepped Agent Bragg and Dr. von Braun. They walked stiffly toward the entrance. After a while they came into the room where Kit and I were waiting wearily. Neither of them looked particularly pleased to have been brought fifty miles from the Cape to deal with our truancy. Agent Bragg leaned on the wall by the door and smoked a cigarette. He looked about as tired as I felt. Dr. von Braun did most of the talking:

"Boys, boys," he said, putting his hand on my head and then Kit's, like someone's kind uncle. "We've been terribly worried. What would I have told your parents if something had happened to you both?"

"We're all right, as you can see," I said coolly.

"If you want to go back home," he said, "then it will be done." He bowed his head curtly. "Immediately. You do not have to stay at the Cape a minute longer than you wish it." Dr. von Braun sounded more German than usual. Probably he was dog tired too.

"I'll drive you home myself," said Agent Bragg. "Tonight, if you want. All you have to do is say the word."

"Precisely so," Dr. von Braun said. "But first we must talk, yes?" He smiled his metallic smile and then thought better of it. "Instead of running away like this," he said, "why didn't you come and speak to me first? Or to Special Agent Bragg?"

"After we found out how you'd been treating those chimpanzees," I said, "we hardly felt we wanted to stick around."

"The welfare of the chimpanzees is not really my department," said Dr. von Braun. He lit a cigarette and smoked it thoughtfully. "I do understand how you must feel about the apes, however. It's quite natural that you should feel a close bond with these specimens. Indeed your sense of leadership is to be commended, my boy. They are your flight crew, after all. I, too, find it very hard to reconcile myself to inflicting pain on an animal—especially an animal that is our closest relation, yes? However, sometimes, for the greater good, for the United States and the whole free world, *for science*, we must do things that we find personally distasteful. I tell you honestly, Scott, that until now we have been unable to devise a better method of persuading the chimpanzees of the dangers of not obeying instructions."

"You'll have to find a better way, or I'm out," I said. "I won't be a party to the torture of animals."

"Nor will I," said Kit.

Dr. von Braun nodded. "You're quite right, boys," he said. "Quite right. The human element seems to have failed us here. In a matter of weeks sufficient improvements for the living space and welfare of these creatures could be provided, yes. Indeed it is not only possible; it is essential. Other methods will have to be devised. Why not? The chimpanzee is, after all, an amazingly adaptable creature. And, combined with a spirit of bold curiosity for the adventure ahead, I am certain that this problem can be sorted out to your joint satisfaction. Are we agreed?"

I looked at Kit. "What do you think?"

"This is your call, Mac," he said.

I nodded. "All right," I told Dr. von Braun. "As long as we have your word on that, Doctor, then yes, we're agreed."

In the car on the way back to the Cape, Special Agent Bragg had the radio on. He liked listening to the same middle-of-the-road crap my dad liked. Ray Conniff. Herb Alpert. Then, the music program he was listening to was interrupted by a man who said that after a long illness ex-President Dwight D. Eisenhower had died at the Walter Reed Army Medical Center, aged seventy-eight.

Both Dr. von Braun and Special Agent Bragg were sad that ex-President Eisenhower was dead. So sad that for a while they stopped the car by the side of the road and got out to collect their thoughts and smoke cigarettes.

"Did you know him?" I asked the doctor. This didn't seem an unreasonable question, given the fact that he knew ex-President Johnson.

"No, I didn't know him," said Dr. von Braun. "I showed him around the Army Ballistic Missile Agency once, in Huntsville, Alabama. My hometown. But he and I were never what you might call friends. Not like me and Johnson. There was, as you Americans say, too much water under the bridge between us. I don't think he liked Germans. Even so, Eisenhower was a great friend of the space program. People talk about Kennedy and that speech: 'We choose to go to the Moon.' But it was Eisenhower and Johnson who helped establish NASA and made us operational. It was

Eisenhower who gave NASA the Saturn project. Not to mention a great deal of money." He sighed loudly. "We shall not see his like again. I fear this new president, Richard Nixon, is no friend of the space program. He smiles and appears friendly to us, but already there is talk in Washington of budgetary cuts. Which makes it even more essential that *Caliban Eleven*, and after that *Apollo Eleven*, of course, is an unqualified success. Everything depends on it. An expedition to Mars, a space station, a space shuttle. Everything. And you are an important part of those plans, Scott. A very important part."

"Thank you, Doctor," I said.

"But a secret part," added Agent Bragg. "Let's not forget that, sir. If the BOB ever finds out that we've been running another program alongside Apollo, then we are history. You, me, maybe the whole goddamned program. Nixon is just looking for an excuse to close us down next year."

"What's the BOB?" asked Kit. "Is that like the CIA?"

"The BOB is the Bureau of the Budget," said Agent Bragg. "The people who hand out money for government projects like NASA. With no pay it's no play. If those boys ever decide to come down here and audit us, we are in big, big trouble."

"What's an audit?" asked Kit.

"It's when people come snooping around the company books and stuff like that," said Dr. von Braun.

"You mean like a detective?" I asked.

"Worse," said Bragg. "Accountants."

One . . .

I never did so much work in my entire life. At six o'clock every morning I awoke thinking about the mission. And at nine thirty every night I went to bed exhausted, still thinking about the mission. Some nights I even dreamed about the mission. In between time I learned all there was to know about *Caliban 11* and the half-sized command and service modules that I would be piloting: launch procedures, reentry procedures, docking procedures, navigation by the stars, veterinary medicine (if Choo-Choo or Benny got sick, I was supposed to try to help them get better); I even learned how to fly the lunar module, although in practice I was going to remain in orbit around the Moon in the CSM while the computer landed the LM containing Choo-Choo and Benny on the Moon's surface. I swore that if I ever went back to school, I would never again complain about homework. But no matter how much I learned, I always had the feeling that there was so much more I didn't know, and that with the mission just four weeks away there wouldn't be enough time to learn it. Pete and Dr. von Braun said that I was a quick learner and not to worry. Maurice, Ed, and Sally said I had a way with apes. Kit said he had come to the reluctant conclusion that I wasn't nearly as dumb as I'd always led him to believe. I don't know about that. But in spite of the long, long hours I was putting in on the simulator, in the classroom, and with Choo-Choo and Benny, I still felt good about myself. The sun felt warmer on my face. Food and drink tasted better. Life couldn't have been more enjoyable. I even got my watch back from the jeweler's shop in Titusville.

But it wasn't all good. Nothing is ever perfect. I guess life is like that.

For example, I couldn't help thinking that so long as I was working for NASA, the prospects for a reconciliation between my mom and dad were unlikely, to say the least. From time to time Dad turned up at the Cape and asked NASA some questions regarding my welfare and safety. For this reason he had felt obliged to delay making a decision on leaving the air force, and my mom, interpreting this as some kind of rejection, had stopped speaking to him. He never complained about it. But I could see it troubled him.

Another problem was that without the occasional zap of electricity in the soles of their feet, Choo-Choo and Benny started to misbehave. After I had spent one particularly frustrating afternoon in the sim working with a less than cooperative Choo-Choo and Benny, Maurice took me aside to talk about it.

"You want to think hard about what happened in there just now," he said. "Think hard about the need to do the mission and come home again, to your ma and pa."

He sat down and laid a big hand on my arm. "Listen, kid. No one feels better than me about getting rid of those psychomotor plates. I never could stand to see an ape being made to suffer pain. But the fact remains that an ape doesn't see things the way a man does. That ain't his fault. It's just the way he was made. Concentration, paying attention, getting the job done—none of these things come naturally to a chimpanzee. Fooling around is a way of life to these guys. Hell, you know what I'm talking about, Tarzan. I don't mean to be rude or anything, but I reckon you and Kit understand what it's like to be an ape better than any of us. Difference between you and them is that you can put the fooling around aside. You can see the bigger picture, Tarzan. That's what makes you human. An ape doesn't have that facility. Never will. That's why we had ourselves a two-tier system to deal with them. Carrot and stick. Reward and correction. I didn't much care for it. But we haven't yet discovered a more reliable way of getting the job done."

"What are you saying, Maurice?" I asked.

"I'll be frank with you, Tarzan. Me and Ed admire what you did, telling it to Dr. von Braun like that about the electric shocks. Probably we should have done it ourselves. But the fact remains, I worry about you, kid. It's a long way to the Moon and back with nothing in your bag of tricks except a handful of banana pellets. Know what I'm saying? What happens when you're in orbit around the Moon and Choo-Choo and Benny take it into their heads not to cooperate? Like they did this afternoon. Have you thought about that? I'm not for one minute saying we should go back to how it was. But maybe before the mission I should just attach the plates on their feet like before, so that Choo-Choo and Benny at least *think* you could zap them with some juice if they decide to get out of line. Which, on the evidence of this afternoon's performance, they just might."

"They're tired," I said. "That's all. We're all tired. You, me, Choo-Choo, Benny the Ball."

"Maybe so," said Maurice. "But that isn't about to let up. And going to the Moon in something not much bigger than a garbage can ain't no holiday. It's not like *Top Cat*, Tarzan. You won't get much sleep in there. It's work, work, work, all the way. An ape gets fractious when it doesn't get enough sleep. Fractious and uncooperative. You dig?"

I shook my head. "We'll manage," I said.

Maurice nodded. "I hope so."

But the most awkward problem our mission encountered was the threat of an astronauts' strike. It came about like this:

Not long after Agent Bragg mentioned the possibility of Washington snooping on NASA, the BOB sent a guy down to the Cape to check the books, just like he said they might. Sometimes it seems that talking about your worst fear has a way of making it come true. The man who came to the Cape was called Mr. Hurt, and while he was around, opening the books and asking awkward questions, it was decided that Kit and I should be kept firmly out of his way, so we were sent back to the Manned Spacecraft Center in Houston. There, despite NASA's best efforts to keep *Caliban 11* a secret, the other astronauts found out about the mission and threatened to walk out of NASA and the whole space program if their demands regarding me were not met.

According to Pete, who said he was ashamed of his colleagues, it seemed his fellow astronauts had several objections regarding my presence within the program. Some of the astronauts had been training to go into space for almost ten years, and they resented the fact that I was going into space with less than five months of training under my belt, and that I didn't even hold a pilot's license. This made several of them feel like they had been wasting their time, and those who had yet to go into space felt like I had jumped the line. The astronauts who were going to the Moon in July were worried that *Caliban 11* might steal some of their glory; one of them got very uptight about it and argued that two chimps landing on the Moon made two men doing the same thing sound like something of an anticlimax. Which was a fair point.

But by far the biggest concern raised by the astronauts was money. It seemed that *Life* magazine had set aside a large pot of cash for all of the astronauts, and they were concerned that if *Life* ever found out about me, I would rate an equal share. About twenty thousand dollars. Some thought I might even rate a bigger share, since my being a kid would generate greater media interest.

Since I had no family relying on my income, they all thought this was unjust.

"These guys put the ass in astronaut," said Pete. "I told them what a gutsy kid you were and how hard you'd worked to make this mission work. Not to mention how the whole purpose of the Caliban flights is to protect their hides, but they just didn't want to know."

"What's going to happen?" asked Kit. "Do you really think they'll walk out?"

"I don't know what's going to happen, boys," admitted Pete. "But it leaves me in a very awkward position. I'm supposed to go to the Moon myself in November, on *Apollo Twelve*, but I don't want to do it with a crew who won't talk to me."

Then, just as quickly as the dispute had started, it was all settled. Pete said they'd seen sense, that was all. And as the days passed and the mission loomed nearer, I forgot about it.

With two weeks to go I went into preflight quarantine with Choo-Choo and Benny the Ball. Everyone who came near us had to wear a surgical mask so as not to pass on any germs. It would be the same after we all got back from the Moon, except that the quarantine period would be longer and more rigorous. In case we brought back any germs from the Moon, we would have to spend three weeks isolated like biological samples in the Lunar Receiving Laboratory.

When Kit was wearing a surgical mask, it was hard to tell that he was upset about something. But I sensed he was, since not even a surgical mask should have stopped him from making a joke or two. Finally, when we were alone, I asked him what was bugging him. At first he was reluctant to answer.

"Nothing," he said.

"Come on," I said, thinking that it might be something to do with the file he was carrying under his arm. "There's something, I can tell."

He sighed loudly and looked away so that I wouldn't see the tears in his eyes.

"Was it something I said?" I asked.

"It was nothing that you said," he answered quickly.

"What, then?"

"I've been doing a bit of snooping myself," he said. "Like that guy on the Cape, Mr. Hurt. I went into the astronaut office and took a look through some of the files in the drawers. While I was in there, I heard someone outside. So I hid inside a closet. And I heard everything that the astronauts agreed on with Dr. von Braun. I found out how they avoided the strike, Scott. Dr. von Braun promised to 'airbrush'—his word, not mine—all the Caliban flights from the official record. Not only that, but those assholes insisted that there's to be no place for you in NASA. Not now. Not ever. And he agreed with that, too."

"I see," I said.

"Don't you get it?" He waved a hand at the room. "All this is for nothing. You'll get nothing out of it. No money from *Life* magazine. No medal. Not even the satisfaction of being able to talk about it. You're risking your neck for people who are going to betray you, Mac."

"They can hardly stop us talking about it afterward," I said.

"That's what one of the astronauts said." Kit shook his head. "Dr. von Braun laughed and asked them who's going to believe us. They'll just say we're a couple of crazy kids."

"Good point," I said. "There's my dad, of course. He'll back up what we say."

"Your dad is a serving officer, and as such is covered by military law," said Kit. "If he talks about any of this, he could go to prison. For treason. Don't you get it? No one is going to believe a word we say."

"I still want to do it," I said after a moment or two. "Nothing's changed. Not for me. I just want to go into space. Now that I think about it, it's all I've ever wanted."

"Are you crazy?" asked Kit.

"Probably."

"We're friends, you and me," he said. "Good friends, right?"

I nodded. "Best friends," I said.

"Look, I know how much all this stuff means to you," he said. "And I'm proud to be your best friend." He snatched off his surgical mask. "But it's because I'm your best friend that I think I ought to tell you the rest of it."

I smiled. "There's more?"

"While I was hidden in the closet," said Kit. "I read through some of their files. And it turns out they've got a lot more worries concerning an actual Moon landing than they've told you about. Some of these worries are to do with the amount of radiation you'll be exposed to. And some of them are to do with mascons."

A "mascon" is a NASA word for mass concentration—a region on the Moon where the gravitational pull is higher than normal, where heavy rock in an asteroid created a large impact basin on the Moon's pockmarked surface.

"They're worried that one of these mascons is going to affect the orbit of the CSM," said Kit. "To say nothing of the effect it might have on the lunar lander."

I shrugged. "It's a risk, sure," I said. "But no spaceflight is without risk." I shrugged. "Didn't Columbus think there was a risk that his ship might fall off the edge of the world? Something like that."

Kit shook his head. For some reason he seemed exasperated that I refused to be angry with NASA or even a little put off the mission.

"But the main thing they're worried about is contained in this file." Kit pushed a pink file across the table toward me. It was stamped TOP SECRET and had a picture of a cartoon Santa Claus on the cover.

"Where did you get that?" said a voice.

We looked around and saw Pete Conrad standing in the doorway.

"I borrowed it from the astronaut office." Kit spoke without hesitation or embarrassment at having been caught in possession of something he knew he shouldn't have. "Look, I know it wasn't right for me to take it. But now that I've read it, I'm glad I did."

Pete walked into the room and collected the file off the table without uttering a word.

"Don't you think he should read it?" asked Kit. "Don't you think that anyone going into space has a right to read that file? Especially someone whose own father features in it. Not to mention you yourself, Pete."

Pete opened the file and glanced at it for a moment, as if reminding himself of what it contained. But still he said nothing.

"What's the matter?" said Kit. "Don't you stand by what you said?" Kit looked at me. "Part of what's in there Pete wrote himself. Didn't you, Pete?"

Pete nodded slowly and then closed the file.

"If you take the file away, I'll just tell him what was in it," said Kit. "Just see if I don't."

"I don't doubt it for a minute," he said. "NASA calls this file the Santa Claus file. And he's right, Scotty. You should read it. If it was up to me, everyone would get to read the Santa Claus file. But for now they can't." Gently he tapped Kit on the head with the file and then handed it to me. "For now, it's the most secret file in NASA. So read it, sure. Just don't tell anyone about it."

Zero . . .

After a final medical exam I ate my last meal on Earth: the traditional astronaut's breakfast of steak and eggs. Choo-Choo and Benny the Ball each ate a low-residue banana. White-suited technicians helped me put on a space suit and communications hat, pressure gloves, oxygen hoses, and last of all a bubble helmet that left me in my own little world, with only the sound of my breathing and the occasional crackle of the intercom for company. Like that scene in *2001: A Space Odyssey* when Bowman closes Hal down. Then we picked up our portable oxygen units and walked down a long corridor to the doorway of the Flight Crew Training Building, where a very small group of well-wishers had gathered to say good-bye: Dad, Kit, Maurice, Ed, Sally, and Dr. Stuhlinger.

Pete Conrad and Dr. von Braun were waiting back at Mission Control in Houston.

My dad handed me something: his lucky mascot, the troll I had given him, which, he said, had saved his life. "Here," he said, "you'd better take this, Scotty. It's been lucky for me. It'll be lucky for you. It's just a loan, mind you. I want it back when you get home."

Then we embraced, and I tried to pretend that I didn't see tears in his eyes. I couldn't figure out what he was crying about. This was the best day of my life. With everyone else I just shook hands. There were no TV cameras or reporters, of course. This had to be the least-reported launch in the history of the space program. But I almost preferred it that way.

We made an odd little trio as we boarded a van for the eight-mile ride to the launchpad: two apes and a thirteen-year-old boy. Kind of like the Three Stooges, I thought. Curly, Larry, and Moe. Always one of my favorite programs. Naturally, being the mission commander, I saw myself as Moe, although I wasn't inclined to slap anyone, least of all a chimp, around the face.

I took a good look at the rocket as we neared it. The Moon was still visible in the early-morning sky, and the *Saturn V* was so tall it looked like it was halfway there already. It stood snorting plumes of fuel vapor into the dawn air like clouds of gas from dry ice wafting around some giant magician's prop. It seemed more than a little hard to believe—even a bit crazy—that we were going to ride it all the way up into the sky, and beyond.

We followed the technicians into a service tower resembling a giant oil rig and boarded a small, creaking elevator that carried us all the way to the top of the gantry, some three hundred feet above the ground. Once there we crossed the access arm into a sterile white room that had been built around the open hatch of the command module. Choo-Choo and Benny entered the command module first. Benny took the left couch and Choo-Choo the right. I took the center couch and then lay still while the technicians strapped me in and hooked me up. From the center couch I was supposed to keep a close eye on the CSM's onboard computer and our trajectory into space, but I was near enough to the electrical and communications systems that were normally the operating responsibility of the occupant of the right-hand couch to keep a watchful eye on those, too.

I glanced across at Benny, then at Choo-Choo, giving them both the thumbs-up. Both of them looked oddly more intelligent in their bubble helmets, as if at any moment one of them might start speaking English. Perhaps they knew something I didn't. Benny grinned at me, lifted his right glove, spread the fingers, and made a small circling movement in front of his face.

"Worried," he was saying.

"Me too," I said, and clapped my hand on the top of his helmet to reassure him.

They closed the hatch, locked it, and then sealed us inside. We were T minus two hours, eight minutes, and counting.

An hour dragged by. We listened to technical chatter on our communications hats, as somewhere below us the rocket filled with fuel. Dr. Stuhlinger and the test conductor spoke to me from the Launch Control Complex, four miles away, and then I heard Pete and Dr. von Braun, in faraway Houston. I busied myself following their instructions, setting switches and checking gauges. Choo-Choo yawned loudly. He was bored. So far this was just like a simulation.

The count reached T minus twenty minutes.

How the heck did I get up here? I was a long way from that window ledge at Miami Junior High. Dr. von Braun was right, of course. If I tried to tell anyone about this, who would ever believe me? They'd lock me up for sure as a certifiable loony.

With five minutes of the count left, I glanced over at the instrumentation one last time. With most of it I was just looking for warning lights. "We are go for launch," I heard myself say.

Benny moved his glove sideways and forward. "Go," he was saying.

I took hold of the abort handle; one hard pull and the escape-tower rocket would fire, lifting the CSM clear of the *Saturn V.* In theory.

The access arm swung away. Now we were truly on our own. The three of us lying on our backs staring up at the ceiling. Everything was more or less automatic now. All stages of the rocket fully fueled and pressurized.

"T minus eighty seconds."

"Power transfer is complete."

"Thirty seconds and counting."

"Guidance is internal."

My heart was in my mouth. Choo-Choo's fingertips were scratching up and down his body. He didn't have an itch. He was signing, "Excited." By now they both knew this wasn't a simulation.

You could feel it in your back. The vibration. The movement on the rocket on the launchpad. That was something even NASA couldn't simulate!

"Ten, nine . . . ignition sequence start . . . six, five, four, three, two, one, zero . . . All engines running. Liftoff! We have a liftoff . . ."

We felt the launch rather than heard it. Small sideways jerks. No real sensation of speed. Just a small increase above one g gently pushing us back into our couches. And then the speed as we burst through the clouds. The g level began to increase, as did the movement within the CSM. A high-frequency quivering as everything began to vibrate furiously, including the eyeballs in my sockets, so that nothing was in focus anymore.

"Roll and pitch program," I called out as the computer turned the rocket in the upper atmosphere so that we could take up our programmed flight path. Benny let out a scream. The g level was already over five.

"Altitude is four miles."

"*Caliban Eleven*, Houston. You're looking good at ninety seconds. Velocity four thousand feet per second."

"Roger that, Houston."

"*Caliban*, you are good for staging."

The g load stopped suddenly, and we were all thrown forward against our seat belts as the first stage shut down on schedule. We heard a bang, which was my prompt to let go of the abort handle. If I had pulled the handle, nothing would have happened, as the escape tower had just been jettisoned.

The second stage cut in, and the speed started to increase again. More g-forces built up. It was Choo-Choo's turn to scream. I felt a little like screaming myself.

"*Caliban Eleven*, your trajectory and guidance are go." That was the voice of Pete Conrad, in Houston.

"Thank you, Pete."

Eight minutes into the flight the second stage dropped away, and a few seconds after that the third stage kicked in, until, almost twelve minutes after takeoff, it too fell away, and we were one hundred and fifteen miles above the earth, orbiting the planet at more than seventeen thousand miles per hour.

Inside the cockpit tiny weightless objects were already floating around: coins, paper clips, screws, bits of dirt, my space ballpoint pen, Dad's lucky mascot troll. Even my arms floated up in front of me, as if I were about to type something. I grabbed the troll and glanced out of the window. We'd already crossed the Atlantic and were approaching the cloud-free southwest coast of Africa. More than that I couldn't say. I'd never been much good at geography. For all I knew, I was gazing down at Timbuktu. Looking up from there I got my first view of the curvature of the Earth. The edge of the curve was blurred with a thin, almost fragile shell of atmosphere. Beyond was the empty blackness of space.

The next minute we were in darkness as we flew east and into nighttime. Up there a whole day could last less than an hour.

"Time flies when you're enjoying yourself," I said.

"It sure does," said Pete.

According to my schedule this was my cue to take out my sextant. I found a star, measured the angle between it and the horizon—several times in case I made a mistake—and then keyed the number into the computer. Then I picked another star and repeated the procedure again.

Forty-five minutes later we were over Mexico. I reckoned we'd be over Texas in a matter of minutes. I looked out of the window again and saw the familiar Gulf Coast. Somewhere below a flock of snow geese was probably taking off from the Anahuac National Wildlife Refuge. Talons and Tweets were being flown in and out of Ellington. Kids I knew were sitting down in a class with Mr. Porteous at Ima Hogg. It all seemed a lot farther away than a mere hundred and fifteen miles.

"Hey, down there," I said. "Can you see me waving, Pete?"

"Sure can," said Pete. "You're looking good, *Caliban*."

Benny moved his open glove slightly to the right.

"Benny says to say hello to Maurice," I said.

Somewhere over the Pacific Ocean less than an hour later, and with *Caliban 11* checking out perfectly, Pete came on the radio again and said that we were go for TLI.

TLI stands for translunar injection. It meant that the third-stage rocket would come to life again for five minutes—long enough to push us out of Earth orbit. With ten seconds to go, the computer asked me to confirm this, and I pushed a button marked PROCEED. The third stage ignited, although it was barely noticeable. Almost holding my breath, I waited to see if MCC was going to tell me to make a course correction. But after five minutes the computer shut the engine down automatically, like it was supposed to do, and I let out my breath again.

"You are looking good here, *Caliban*," said Pete. "Right on course."

I kept my eyes on the computer readout. It was hard to believe that we could be traveling so fast and in such total silence. *Caliban 11* was traveling away from Earth now at a speed of more than twenty-four thousand miles an hour.

At such an enormous speed it hardly seemed possible that the CSM could break free of the third stage, rotate one hundred and eight degrees to face the top of the *Saturn V*, dock with the lunar module, and then withdraw it from its metallic shell.

"*Caliban Eleven*, this is Houston," said Dr. von Braun. "You are good to go for docking *Trash Can* with *Officer Dibble*."

"Roger that, Houston."

Back on Earth it had been the crew's privilege to name the CSM and the LM. Inspired by the cartoon names of the two chimponauts, I had named the CSM *Trash Can*—for obvious reasons—and the bowlegged LM *Officer Dibble*.

Docking was the most difficult part of the mission and had only been done twice before, by *Apollo 9* at the beginning of March and by *Apollo 10* in May. Mostly it was down to the computer, but if something went wrong, it was my job to take over the maneuver and perform it manually. I'd done it in the simulator many times, but now I couldn't help remembering all the times I'd screwed it up. If docking were unsuccessful, Choo-Choo and Benny would not be landing on the Moon. Instead we would very likely orbit the Moon just once and then fly straight home again. The whole mission depended on it.

There was no problem undocking from the *Saturn* third stage, but as *Trash Can* turned and then drifted back toward *Officer Dibble*, I began to pray. There was a loud clunk as the two spacecraft came together. For a moment nothing happened, and I bit my lip as I waited to hear the buzzer indicate that the docking latches on the two spacecraft had shut.

I felt my heart sink. I was just about to radio Houston that the docking maneuver had failed, when I heard the telltale "rivet gun" sound of twelve docking latches snapping shut. I almost cheered. Instead I closed my eyes and floated up to the window to watch the remains of the third stage fall away. Sometimes, the waste and litter of spaceflight appalled me. So much just got thrown away.

"Houston," I said. "We have a hard dock."

"Roger that, *Caliban*."

Trash Can and *Officer Dibble* would now stay linked until we reached orbit around the Moon.

"We're really on our way now, guys," I told Choo-Choo and Benny. "We are going straight to the Moon."

Caliban 11:
First Day

I climbed out of my space suit and floated free for a moment before unstrapping Choo-Choo and Benny and getting them out of their space suits. Benny hugged me briefly for a moment. Choo-Choo touched his chin: "Thanks."

"Don't mention it," I said. I was wearing light flame-resistant coveralls over a pair of long johns. The two chimps were wearing the same lace-up flight suits they'd worn in the simulators. Now we could relax a little.

Choo-Choo and Benny were quite used to weightlessness. They'd put in more hours in the vomit comet than I had. Benny propelled himself slowly to the window and took a long look back at Earth. The view was certainly worth it.

"Beautiful, isn't it?" I said, joining him at the window. He started to sign.

"Orange," he was saying. "Eat."

"Yes, it is a bit like an orange," I said. "A blue orange. A very blue orange. But I don't think you'd want to eat it, Benny."

Everything about Earth seemed so blue that if I had been an alien life form, "the blue planet" is what I would have called it. Even the land masses looked a bit blue. We could just make out the shape of Africa. "Look," I said. "That's Africa. Where you come from, Benny. I'm not exactly sure where the Cameroons are in Africa—north, south, east, or west—but take my word for it, they're down there somewhere."

Benny sighed a little sigh, as if somehow he knew he was looking at his home. Working with chimpanzees you find lots of times when you feel less than good about your own species and the pain it sometimes inflicts on others.

"Gee, I wish I could take a photograph of this," I told the folks in Houston. "You're really missing out on a great view."

Not only was there no official still camera, something they'd had on the Gemini missions and *Apollo 8*, but there was no TV camera either. Dr. von Braun had told me that he thought I would have enough to do without worrying about taking pictures as well, but of course I figured it would be a lot easier to "airbrush" the Caliban mission from the official NASA record if there were no photographs or film footage to contradict anyone who asserted that the mission had never happened. A picture of Earth would not have revealed anything, of course. But a picture of a spaceflight crew composed of two chimps and a boy might have been viewed a little differently. Especially a weightless chimpanzee. There was no way you could have easily faked that.

Choo-Choo tucked his legs underneath his body and propelled himself down into the lower equipment bay like a hairy basketball, farting loudly as he went. Pressure could have that effect on an ape or human body.

"Hey," I said. "Cut that out, Choo-Choo. It's not like I can open a window or anything."

I set about stowing away the space suits. There is always something to do in a spaceship. Then I used the sextant and keyed the results into the computer once again. My next job was to check the batteries and stir the fuel tanks, which involved pressing another button. After that I fed Choo-Choo and Benny with some banana pellets and ate my own rather tasteless meal. Next I persuaded myself to try to use the urine collector, which, although ultimately successful, was more uncomfortable than the one in the sim.

Benny came and put his mouth on the end of the tube as if he hoped there might be a drink in it.

"Now, you know that is not a drink dispenser," I said, scolding him. "If you want a drink, just ask."

I found Benny a water dispenser and then floated down to window number five, where something had caught my eye.

When I got there, I saw it again. A flickering, flashing sort of light outside the spacecraft. For a long, cold, sickening moment I thought we might have a fire, and so I checked the computer and the fuel gauges, but finding nothing at all wrong I went back to the window. The flashing seemed to have moved away to the opposite side of the window, although it was impossible to say where it was coming from. And what the flashing was. Just that it continued for several minutes.

"What do you make of that?" I asked Choo-Choo, who seemed to have seen it too. I was sure of that, because as I looked closely at him I saw the flashing reflected on the corneas of his amber-colored eyes.

"Say again, *Caliban*," said the voice in my headset.

For a moment I thought about mentioning the light, and then I thought better of it. The last thing I wanted was Houston ordering extensive systems checks in pursuit of a malfunction I was sure we didn't have.

And then, just as suddenly as the flashing light had appeared, it stopped.

I decided I was tired. That maybe my eyes were playing up. Something to do with air pressure on my eyeballs. Or breathing a rich oxygen mixture. Or the low-residue diet. Or the Lomotil I was taking. Or one of a million other possible reasons that had to do with being the first boy in space.

Benny was already sleeping. I decided to try and do the same.

Caliban 11:
Second Day

When I awoke, my first thought was that I must be
still asleep. There was a shower of tiny lights outside the *Trash Can*, as
if the spacecraft itself was surrounded by a galaxy of stars. Thousands
of them. These were quite different from the flashing light I had seen
earlier on. And when I looked out of the window, I saw that they
extended for miles in every direction. But for their luminescence
I might have thought I had encountered a shower of microscopic
meteoroids. Only I had never heard of luminescent meteoroids. And
meteoroids would have struck the skin of the spacecraft, maybe even
penetrated it, fatally. But none of these little lights seemed to impact
on the *Trash Can*. Moreover, I had the firm idea that meteoroids
tended to travel in just one direction. These lights, or whatever they
were, seemed to swirl around the *Trash Can* in several directions at
once. It was very odd.

I closed my eyes and opened them again. The lights were still there. I looked around for my fellow astronauts. Benny the Ball was floating in his sleeping bag, eyes closed, as if he didn't have a care in the world, just like his cartoon namesake. But Choo-Choo was awake. He was floating by window five! I could see his head moving as his eyes followed the lights around the space surrounding the *Trash Can*. Surely he was seeing them too! He glanced up at me, gave a little grimace, shook his head, and then covered his eyes. For a chimpanzee it was a very eloquent gesture, as if to say that he, too, had no idea what these lights might be and almost preferred not to think about them. I didn't blame him.

I decided to consult the flight file, a large loose-leaf plastic folder that contained details of every possible malfunction and phenomenon that *Caliban 11* might encounter. It turned out that John Glenn had seen fireflies from the *Mercury 6* spacecraft, *Friendship 7*, way back in 1962. It was suggested later on that they had actually been tiny ice flakes falling off the skin of the space capsule. But that had happened in Earth orbit, not a hundred thousand miles away, in space. Any ice flakes attaching to the skin of the *Trash Can* would surely have disappeared hours ago. I still couldn't identify what the fireflies were. I knew they weren't real fireflies, of course. And I was damn sure they weren't ice flakes. And anyway, why would ice flakes endure for so long? It didn't make sense. By comparison the brilliant shower of frozen urine crystals vented into space from the collection tube lasted only a minute or two. But I was certain the fireflies had been there for ten or fifteen minutes now.

And then, just like before, as suddenly as they had appeared, the fireflies were gone. It was as if someone had switched them off. I was left staring into the black void, which, weirdly, seemed to be staring back at me. It gave me a shiver down my spine to think about that. For the first time I felt incredibly alone in the *Trash Can*. And for a while I didn't look out of the window at all.

But once again I decided to ignore what I'd seen, at least as far as reporting it to Houston. The last thing they needed to hear was anything out of the ordinary that would put them in a flap and make them scrub the Moon-landing part of the mission. The fact was, I didn't want anything to happen that would interfere with my own very personal, not to say secret, plans for the mission. Plans that only Kit knew about.

Besides, it was time to take another sextant reading. A lot of the computing on the mission was being done by Mission Control; the results were then sent to my computer in the *Trash Can*. The point of taking regular sextant readings was in case *Caliban 11* lost communications with Houston and I had to use the shipboard navigation system to get us home. My star sightings were proving to be my best skill. Houston had checked them and found them accurate to within a few thousandths of a degree. A sextant is like a telescope in some ways, and of course I was at home with a telescope. Back on Earth I had often looked at the stars and the Moon through my own telescope.

The Moon itself was not yet in sight, however. I was told this was to do with the angle of our approach and the glare of the sun. That part was a little disappointing. I'd been looking forward to seeing it get bigger in the window.

"This is Houston," said a voice I didn't recognize. "We'd like you to begin a battery charge and then do a water dump before you start PTC."

"Roger, Houston," I said. "Stand by."

I started the battery charge, did the water dump, and then turned my mind to PTC. PTC is passive thermal control, or "barbecue mode" as Pete Conrad called it. Strong, unfiltered sunlight heats one side of the spacecraft, while deep space chills the other. In order for the hull to maintain an even temperature—crucial if the *Trash Can* was going to withstand reentry—it would be necessary to change the spacecraft's attitude every thirteen hours, rotating it slowly so that the cool side would face the sunlight. The integrity of the hull and the heat shield was not the only reason for this. The RCS quads and SPS propellant tanks as well as the structure, propellant, and battery systems of *Officer Dibble* also needed to be evenly heated or cooled.

PTC is a slow process. Only two tenths of a degree per second. Rates have to be kept slow to save fuel. But as soon as it was done, it was time to take another sextant reading and then to receive the recent telemetry from Houston. This meant I had to switch the computer into accept mode. Then, while this was in progress, I had to take off the biomed sensors attached to Choo-Choo and Benny and reattach them because Houston reported that they had been getting poor respiration readings from the two chimpanzees. Of course, this procedure was a lot more complicated than it might sound. It's not easy getting a chimpanzee to sit still at the best of times, but in weightless conditions it's even more difficult. Especially when the chimpanzee wants to have fun.

Both Choo-Choo and Benny loved being weightless and had already proved themselves to be much more adept at handling it than I was. Each chimp loved nothing better than to tuck himself into a tight ball and allow the other to bat him down to the opposite end of the *Trash Can* like a beach volleyball. This was not without its hazards, as there were several switches and levers to collide with that could have spelled disaster for the mission. But so far I had been unable to persuade them to stop fooling around like this. I was beginning to think that Maurice might have been right. Not that I would have admitted it, of course.

As a result, this biomed-sensor procedure took the best part of a whole hour. Halfway through I tried to persuade Houston to let me abandon this task, but they were adamant that it was crucial to know how the bodies of the chimps would stand up to conditions on the lunar surface.

"Houston, is that the main purpose of these biomed sensors?" I asked.

"Affirmative, Scott."

"Well, since I'm not going down to the Moon, there's no point in me wearing the sensors," I said. "After a while they feel sore and uncomfortable. So for now, I'm taking them off."

"*Caliban*, we don't think that's a good idea."

But it was too late. I'd already removed them.

We argued about it for a minute or two, and then they seemed to give up.

Pete was on communications in Houston again.

"Hey there, buddy," he said. "I have a couple of people here who say you owe them money."

It was my dad and Kit, who was back in Houston from the Cape.

"Hi, son," said Dad. "How are you doing?"

"I'm good, Dad."

"The guys down here are really pleased with how everything's going so far. What's it like up there?"

"Busy," I said. "There's always something to do. The doc and Pete are keeping me pretty well occupied. Which is just as well, as otherwise it might get a bit lonely up here."

"I just wanted to say I love you, son. And I'm very proud of you."

"Thanks, Dad."

"There's just one bit of news I have to give you, Scott. Your mother is insisting on speaking to you the day after tomorrow."

"But that's when Choo-Choo and Benny are landing on the Moon, Dad. Couldn't we delay it a little?"

"We already tried to put her off, you know. Me and Agent Bragg. But you know what she's like. We can't really put her off without arousing her suspicions."

"Can they do that?" I asked. "Can they really patch a phone call up here?"

"They say they can do it," said Dad. He laughed. "Listen, if they can send two chimpanzees to the Moon, they can fix it for your mother to phone you from Florida."

"Yeah, but what about the time delay?" I asked. "I mean, it takes at least a couple of seconds for the signal to get here."

"Bragg says there's not much they can do about that," said Dad. "But they can explain it with some story about the condition of the undersea telephone cable. Some nonsense like that. He says the actual quality of the call will sound better than a real telephone call to Scotland."

"Okay," I said. "I guess there's no way around it."

"There's no way around it," insisted Dad. "No way at all. She's an immovable object. Scott, there's someone here who wants to say hello."

"Hey, Scotty," said Kit. "This is Captain Kirk. Where's that warp engine power you promised me?"

"Captain," I said, affecting a Scottish accent, "ye canna change the laws of physics. I don't know how much more emergency power we can take before we start to break up."

"What are you doing right now?"

"Oh, you know, hanging around."

"The next mission, they should do a hook-up from space with *Rowan and Martin's Laugh-In*," said Kit. "I told them that, but they didn't go for it."

"They take themselves too seriously," I said.

"Seen any aliens yet?" he asked.

"Not yet," I said. "But if I do, I'll tell them it's you they have to speak to. Not the president."

"Right. What does he know? Are those two lunkheads behaving themselves?"

"Sometimes," I said. "But their conversation drags a bit, you know?"

"Have they been yet?"

I laughed. "You mean to the john? Not yet, thank goodness. But Choo-Choo is farting a lot, which is bad enough, I can tell you."

"Tell him to take it outside," said Kit. "That's what my dad always does when he farts. Keep your chin up, kid. I've got to go now. I've run out of dimes."

"Be seeing ya, buddy."

"I hope so. I sure hope so."

Caliban 11:
Third Day

Seated on our couches once again, we were nearing
the Moon at five thousand miles per hour. The Earth was more
than two hundred thousand miles away. The journey was almost
complete. In a matter of ten minutes we would be go for lunar
orbit insertion burn, which was NASA-speak for slowing the
spacecraft down to orbit the Moon. I was already hard at work
on the checklist to start the service propulsion system engine. But
before I started the engine, we would go out of radio contact with
Earth as the *Trash Can* passed around the dark side of the Moon.
This was what the guys in Houston called LOS: loss of signal.
It was a nerve-wracking moment. Especially as the moment was
going to last forty-five minutes.

"*Forty-five minutes*," I told Choo-Choo and Benny. "But that's
only if we get an engine burn. If the SPS fails, there won't be

any goddamned orbit, and we'll just keep on going until we get ourselves picked up in deep space by the USS *Enterprise*. About two hundred years from now. A comforting thought, don't you think?"

Benny, always the more sensitive ape of the two, leaned across and placed a friendly hand on top of my head and for a moment left it lying there like a hat. Then he spread his fingers and made a small circling movement in front of his face.

"Worried," he was saying.

"You think you're the only one?" I asked. "Hell, I'm worried, too, Benny. And I don't need your negative waves, Ben. I need you to start thinking positive thoughts about this procedure. We've got just four minutes to slow down to about thirty-five hundred miles per hour. Otherwise we're going to miss our orbit slot."

"One minute to LOS," said the voice from Mission Control. Houston. Home. Everything I knew and loved. Well, almost everything, given that my mom was in Florida. The voice started another countdown, which did little to make me feel any more relaxed about what was going to happen, or not, depending on how you looked at it.

"Thirty seconds to LOS, *Caliban*. You are go all the way."

"Roger that, Houston," I said. "See you around the corner, guys."

The next second they were gone. There was just the crackle in my headset of empty static, like a badly tuned radio in an empty room. And I felt a chill as the totality of my loneliness hit me like the flat of Benny's hand.

"Well, here I am," I said. "Two hundred forty thousand miles from home, traveling at seven and a half thousand feet per second, just to make sure you two apes pull off this crazy mission without a hitch."

Choo-Choo tapped his head with his fist. "Stupid," he said.

I smiled and took his hand in mine and squeezed it with affection. Maybe my crew couldn't talk. But they could still make me laugh. And that's not easy when you're about to do something that could send you on a one-way ticket into the void.

"Rotational hand controller number two, armed," I told myself, and glanced up in search of the computer's flashing 99 message—the one I always got when everything was ready to go. I hardly hesitated, hitting the proceed button as if our lives depended on it. No, stabbing it hard with a forefinger, too hard, because our lives *did* depend on it.

There was no noise, because the SPS wasn't that kind of engine, with an ignition and fuel pumps and fire and stuff. There were just valves that opened, and chemicals that got mixed together in the combustion chamber by some pressurized helium, and then a lot of hot gas that came out of the *Trash Can* with more than twenty thousand pounds of thrust. There was a short, agonizing pause, and then we felt a smooth, steady motion that pushed us back against our couches. After several days of weightlessness, it felt like someone sitting on me.

I didn't say a word. If the engine burned for too long, we were in trouble. And if the engine didn't burn long enough, we were in trouble. It was all down to the computer, and I hoped the computer's watch was better than mine. Since the curious incident of the fireflies in the night, the Omega Speedmaster hadn't worked at all. There was a digital countdown clock just above my head. The whole time I was watching it, I was thinking about all the important things that could last four minutes. A record-breaking mile, an extended-play Beatles single, an egg boiled—the way I liked them, anyway. At zero the engine shut down, and I realized another important thing that could last four minutes: I could hold my breath for that long. I swear it was the longest four minutes of my entire life.

"Shutdown," I said, and then checked the computer for a few reassuring facts and figures. We were orbiting in an ellipse at a height of just seventy miles. And then, out of the window, for the first time on our three-day journey, I saw it and heard myself gasp.

"My God," I said, unfastening my harness. "Guys, we're really here."

I was looking down at the surface of the Moon.

Despite the computer readout it was hard to tell how far away the surface of the Moon really was. With no blue oceans, greenish-brown land masses, continents, gray weather systems, or white cloud formations, there was no feature against which I could have measured our altitude. Orbiting the Earth you knew how high you were when you could make out the whole west coast of Africa; that gave you a real sense of perspective. But the Moon wasn't like that. There were just big craters and smaller craters and hills that were just the continuations of hollows, and then the hard edge of the Moon, which looked like you could just step straight off it and be swallowed up in the depths of space. And there were no colors, either, unless you counted the color of ash: Everything was the same dead, lifeless shade of gray. It looked perhaps like the Earth might have looked after some devastating fire had incinerated everything. As if the Moon and all that had once existed on it had been destroyed in some huge atomic war. A dead planet. An evil fossil that had been set in orbit around the Earth to remind us all of what might happen if some idiot in Russia pressed one button and an idiot in America pressed another. Looking down at the Moon, I had the strong idea that if I stood on the surface, everything would look much the same as it did from orbit. And that whatever landed there would be the most colorful thing to have been on the Moon in hundreds of millions of years. Which sort of made me wonder why Kennedy and the others had wanted us to come to the Moon so much. Already it was very clear that there was nothing much here.

Or was there?

As I came away from the window, I saw something that looked a bit unusual. And, pushing myself back to take a second look, I saw something that appeared brighter than a star and was moving relative to the stars that were behind it. I watched it for a minute or two, then fetched the sextant to take a closer look. Adjusting the sextant's focus one way and then the other, I saw that the object appeared vaguely cylindrical, but exactly what it was I had no idea. I estimated it was perhaps a hundred miles away. For a moment I considered the possibility that I was looking at one of the four *Saturn V* third-stage panels that had enclosed *Officer Dibble* until the docking maneuver that had attached it to the nose of the *Trash Can*.

I put down the sextant and fetched the monocular—a sort of telescope—in the hope that it would give me a clearer view of the object.

"I wonder. Could that be one of *Dibble*'s panels in orbit around the Moon?" There were no transponders on the panels to emit any kind of signal NASA could have tracked. Besides, we were LOS, on the dark side. "Could a panel have followed us all this way? And then, instead of just sailing past the Moon, been acquired by the Moon's gravity?"

Choo-Choo and Benny were still sitting patiently in their seats. I hadn't yet unstrapped them after the lunar orbit insertion burn. They both seemed unnaturally silent, as if perhaps they sensed my own disquiet.

"Don't all answer at once," I said.

With unsteady hands I focused the monocular on the object. The view wasn't much better than through the sextant. The object wasn't exactly like a cylinder. It was more L-shaped than cylindrical. And the light upon it appeared to move, as if this was the reflected light on something metallic. A panel orbiting the Moon would have been rotating ever since the docking procedure, and that would of course account for the sense of movement and reflected light. But this just didn't look like a panel. And there was a sort of bump in the middle, with some sort of protuberance off to the side.

"This would have to happen now," I said. "When we're out of radio contact." I glanced at the clock. "Still thirty minutes LOS to go. Not that I will report it, of course. I don't want to give Houston any kind of excuse to scrub the Moon landing, guys. If they get it into their heads that that's a stray LM adapter panel, they might decide that there's a risk of us colliding with it. Or some other crap like that."

Choo-Choo farted loudly.

"Exactly," I said. "As usual, Chooch, you put your finger right on it."

I was trying to talk myself into a relaxed frame of mind about all of this. But the truth was, I knew exactly what I was looking at. I was looking at a UFO, or what the NASA astronauts and USAF pilots sometimes called a bogey. The same kind of bogey Lovell and Borman had seen on *Gemini 7*. The same kind of bogey Pete Conrad had photographed on *Gemini 11*.

The same kind of bogey that had been described in NASA's top-secret Santa Claus file.

It seemed that a large number of pilots had mentioned "seeing Santa Claus." Santa Claus was the code they used among themselves when they were talking about sightings of bogeys or unidentified flying objects. In the words of one X-15 test pilot, it was hard not to believe in Santa Claus if you saw him coming down the chimney. All of the pilots named in the Santa Claus file, however, even those employed by NASA, were subject to military security regulations and were under strict orders not to discuss their sightings with any civilian, for fear of causing panic in the general population. This was how the Santa Claus file had come into being.

In the beginning most of the bogey sightings had been by test pilots flying the X-15. Then, as the flight ceiling for military aircraft got higher, USAF and U.S. Navy Marine pilots flying routine missions started seeing them too. Pilots like my dad, who had reported seeing a bogey while flying an F-86 Sabre over North Korea in January 1953. "It was dark, about twenty-two hundred hours," he'd said. "I saw a light that came in from about twenty-five thousand feet moving very quickly down to about one thousand feet. I thought it was some kind of missile until it stopped and went straight back up again in less than five seconds. It lit everything up. I've never seen anything like it, but I don't feel like speculating on what it could have been."

Lately, however, nearly all of the sightings had been by NASA astronauts.

Wally Schirra, aboard *Mercury 8* in October 1962, was the first of the astronauts to use the code name Santa Claus to describe unidentified flying objects. But it was John Glenn who had seen the "fireflies" on his Mercury mission in February 1962. And just what was the curious cylindrical-shaped object he had photographed from the window of his spacecraft?

In May 1963 Major Gordon Cooper told the tracking station at Muchea (near Perth, Australia) that he could see a glowing, greenish object quickly approaching his *Mercury 9* capsule on its twenty-two-orbit journey around the Earth. During the final orbit the UFO was real and solid enough to be picked up by Muchea's tracking radar. Major Cooper was a firm believer in UFOs. More than ten years earlier, in 1951, he had sighted a UFO while piloting an F-86 Sabre over western Germany.

In June 1965, *Gemini 4* astronauts Ed White and James McDivitt were passing over Hawaii when they saw a weird-looking metallic object.

Gemini astronauts Jim Lovell and Frank Borman also saw a UFO during their December 1965 mission. It was the second orbit of their record-breaking fourteen-day flight, and Borman reported an unidentified spacecraft some distance from their capsule. Cape Kennedy told him that he was seeing the final stage of the *Gemini 7* Titan booster rocket. Borman said that he could see the booster rocket too, but that the spacecraft he was talking about was something different.

In September 1966 Pete Conrad photographed a cluster of bright objects outside the window of *Gemini 11.*

The last and most recent incident in the file was from December 1968, when the *Apollo 8* command module came around the dark side of the Moon. Commander Jim Lovell's apparently innocent words, "Please be informed that there is a Santa Claus," were included in the file without any explanation; however, the very presence of this incident in NASA's Santa Claus file seemed to imply that the crew of *Apollo 8* had seen more than just the dark side of the Moon.

All of these "encounters" were common knowledge in NASA,

but none of the astronauts ever mentioned them, other than to record them in the Santa Claus file.

And now here I was, seeing the same "fireflies" as John Glenn, the same bright objects as Pete Conrad, and the same cylindrical object as White, McDivitt, and Borman.

By now I was certain that I was not watching a detached part of the *Saturn* rocket but something else. From my basic knowledge of Newtonian physics it seemed less than likely that one of the SLA panels could have kept up with the *Trash Can* for three days and then ended up a hundred miles ahead of us in orbit around the Moon. But just thinking that thought made me shiver. Because if I was right and what I was viewing through the monocular was indeed a bogey like the others in the Santa Claus file, then I couldn't help but feel a little scared. Especially now that I was out of radio contact with Houston for at least another thirty minutes. If I had thought the four minutes of lunar orbit insertion burn had felt like ten, then the remaining thirty minutes of LOS felt like a lifetime.

Five minutes passed. Choo-Choo began to grow restless. He grimaced, shook his head, barked quietly at me, and tapped his chin several times.

"Bored," he was saying.

"Hey, Chooch," I said. "Can't you see I'm busy here, scaring myself? Believe me, if I hadn't taken so much Lomotil, I'd be sticking one of those poop baggies on my rear end."

I looked back into the window just in time to see the tiny

distant orbiting object quicken for a moment and then disappear around the horizon of the Moon. It was gone. I felt my face and my arms and my legs go numb for a second. "No doubt about it," I whispered, "that was a bogey, all right." Then I got a hold of myself again.

"Well, what did you expect to see in space, MacLeod?" I asked myself. "Stay away from the window if you don't like what you see out there."

I put the monocular away and started to unstrap my two colleagues. I needed to put what I had seen out of my head very firmly. When we got around the far side, it would be time to start preparing things for the lunar landing in the morning. I didn't need any distractions while I was doing that.

"I don't much like the idea of leaving you here in orbit by yourself with a bogey," I told Choo-Choo. "But that's the way it's got to be. Like I said before, we don't want anything scrubbing the mission, do we?"

Choo-Choo looked at me and grimaced.

"Didn't I tell you?" I said. "That's right. I'm taking your place in *Officer Dibble*. I've decided that I'm going to land on the Moon with Benny the Ball. And you're going to stay up here in the *Trash Can*."

Choo-Choo clapped his hands.

"Yeah, I thought that would please you," I said.

He tapped his index finger on his shoulder.

"Why?"

I paused for a moment to consider my answer to his question.

"It's simple enough. I figured that if Dr. von Braun and NASA are really going to airbrush me from the official record and never employ me in NASA, like they said, then I might as well get as much out of this whole experience as I can," I said. "Boy, will those astronauts be ticked off when they find out that none of them is going to be the first man on the Moon. That I was down there first. Kit's idea, of course. Good old Kit. He always thinks like we're still in school."

I smiled.

"Besides, it's time for a little bit of payback. NASA cheated my dad out of a place in the space program, did you know that? I found out that the only reason he didn't get chosen to be an astronaut himself was because he'd reported that bogey in Korea. Can you believe it? No, neither can I, guys. Especially given what the Santa Claus file says has been happening since then."

Choo-Choo slapped a hand on his face and covered his eyes, Three Stooges–style.

"I know, I know, you think I'm crazy. But I can fly that thing if I have to. Really, flying *Officer Dibble* is just like flying a helicopter. Honest. I know—I've used the simulator back on Earth. Not that it'll come to that, I don't think. The computer should handle everything." I shook my head as I tried to imagine Dr. von Braun's face when they realized what was happening. And Pete's face. He would tell the other astronauts for sure. And boy, would they be mad.

"They won't like it," I said. "They won't like it a bit. But hell, they won't be able to stop me."

Choo-Choo looked at the computer, and then, palms upward, he interlocked his fingers and pulled them apart again.

"How?" I shrugged. "Because I'm not going to tell them a damn thing. Not until I've received all the telemetry for a landing from the Houston computer. That way it'll be too late. They won't be able to do anything about it."

Benny put his hand on my hand.

"Good," I said. "I'm glad you approve, Benny. What's that? What'll we do when *Dibble* gets down there? I've been thinking about that. And you know what? I thought I'd go outside and stretch my legs for a while. Get some fresh air. See the sights." I shook my head. "No, I think you'd best stay in *Dibble*. Just in case you get a taste for Moon-walking."

Caliban 11:
Fourth Day

We were all back in our pressure suits in case something went wrong with the undocking. Benny and I floated and crawled our way into *Dibble*. But before I closed the hatch and sealed it, Choo-Choo handed me Dad's lucky mascot troll. I'd forgotten it, and I realized I wouldn't have liked to go down to the Moon without it. For a chimpanzee it was a very thoughtful gesture.

Then Choo-Choo sealed the hatch inside the *Trash Can*. Apart from pressing a button to separate—and later on join—the two spacecraft, this was pretty much all he would have to do. All the same I knew that if Choo-Choo failed to obey instructions, Benny and I were dead. It was asking a lot of a young chimpanzee, but there was no way I was going to threaten the little guy with electric shocks and stuff like that. We would do it with kindness or not at all.

Inside *Dibble* there were no seats. Without gravity there was no need for them. So we stood in special foot restraints next to the controls and attached ourselves to the floor with Velcro straps. I powered up all the electrical systems before deploying *Dibble's* spiderlike landing gear. Next I set about keying in the telemetry from Houston on *Dibble's* primary computer in readiness for separation. This was something I would have had to do anyway before the two apes separated from the CSM. But Houston didn't know that I was doing it with both hatches closed. They still had no idea that I had switched places in the LM with Choo-Choo. I was doing it that way in case Choo-Choo jumped the gun and threw the switch to release *Dibble* before we were quite ready.

"We've got just a few seconds to go, Choo-Choo," I said. "You all set?"

Choo-Choo pushed the button to release *Dibble*. With a sound like a truck door being slammed shut, the twelve docking latches sprang open, pushing the two spacecraft gently apart. I took hold of the thrusters and then maneuvered us away until the *Trash Can* was about a hundred feet away.

"*Caliban*, this is Houston," said Pete. "Please confirm that *Dibble's* landing gear is properly deployed."

"Looks like a good sep," I said. "You take care now, Choo-Choo. We'll see you sometime tomorrow. Got that?"

"*Caliban*, this is Houston. Say again, please."

I ignored them for several minutes, letting *Dibble* drift away some more before I let the PGNS computer take over the landing procedure. PGNS stands for primary guidance, navigation, and control system, or "pings" for short. I'd like to have seen that the LM's landing gear was properly deployed, but I could hardly do that from inside it. Apart from the weightlessness and the fact that we were flying feet first and facedown, it was just like being in the simulator back at the Cape.

"*Caliban*, this is Houston. Come in, please."

I hit the proceed button that put the pings in charge of our descent. From now on everything would happen automatically: descent orbit insertion (DOI), powered descent, landing, everything. I would only take over if one of these procedures went seriously wrong. As for Houston, they were now quite powerless over us.

"*Caliban*, this is Houston," said Pete. "Come in, please."

"Go ahead, Houston."

"Scott, we didn't get an answer about *Dibble*'s landing gear."

"I didn't look at it, Houston. On account of the fact that I couldn't. You see, I'm in *Dibble*. I left Choo-Choo in charge of the *Trash Can*."

There was a longish pause. I tried to imagine Pete and Dr. von Braun and his team of flight controllers seated at their consoles staring at televisions full of data. Behind them, in the glassed-in gallery that looked out over the control room, where relatives and VIPs normally sat and observed space missions, there would be very few people: just Dad, Kit, and some of the guys from the Aeromedical Research Lab—Maurice and maybe Ed, or Sally. I started to imagine their faces as they began to understand the full meaning of what was happening.

"*Caliban*, this is Houston. Say again, please."

"You heard me right, Pete," I said. "I decided that if I was going to be airbrushed from the official record, then I'd better make this trip count."

"Scott, is this a joke?" he demanded.

"It's no joke, Pete," I said. "According to the pings we are just a few minutes from the dark side again, and a DOI burn that'll take us down to the surface of the Moon. Look, I'll press an acknowledge button on the pings so you know I'm telling you the truth. There, I've done it."

"Stand by, *Caliban*," said Pete.

"Standing by, Houston."

There was another long silence. When it ended, it was not Pete Conrad on the radio, but Dr. von Braun. There was a distinct edge of irritation and anger in his voice.

"Scott," said Dr. von Braun. "Listen to me very carefully. What you are doing is utterly foolhardy. I insist that you operate the lunar module's abort guidance system immediately and return to the CSM. Operate the AGS, please, Scott. Do you hear me? That's an order."

"Roger, Houston," I said calmly. "You are five by five." This meant I could hear him loud and clear. "We copy your order, Doctor. But that's a negative. *Dibble* is go for DOI and landing."

"You are not go for DOI and landing," Dr. von Braun said curtly. "Repeat, you are negative for DOI and landing."

I glanced over the flashing yellow-green numbers indicating the LM's position on the pings digital display and nodded. "Houston, you are two minutes to LOS," I said. "Listen, Doc, everything is going swell up here. *Dibble* is on his way down the alley, just like we planned. Benny and I will be fine."

"This is outrageous," said Dr. von Braun. "I could have you shot for disobeying a direct order. Do you know that?"

Dr. von Braun started speaking German for a moment, and it occurred to me that he must be swearing.

"Houston, say again, please?"

Dr. von Braun was still swearing—in German—when *Dibble's* orbit took us behind the dark side, blocking the radio signal from Houston once again.

"That went well, don't you think?" I said to Benny.

Benny shook his head.

The burn for DOI lasted about thirty seconds and took us down to about fifty thousand feet. When we rounded the near side of the Moon, we would be ready to start our final powered descent. After that, if everything proceeded smoothly, the lunar module would touch down in less than an hour.

We were on the near side of the Moon, and according to the radar altimeter we were orbiting at fifty-one thousand feet. I hoped that none of the NASA mapmakers had made a mistake and that there were no high Moon mountains getting ready to surprise me.

"Houston," I said. "This is *Dibble*. We have a good altitude to begin a powered descent."

A minute or two passed with just static in my headset, and I considered the possibility that the people in Houston were sulking and had decided not to speak to me anymore. Given that Mission Control had just lost control of the mission, I could hardly have blamed them if they had gone silent on me for a while.

"Roger that, *Dibble*, and welcome back." Pete was back on the mike. Dr. von Braun had probably left the microphone to go and have a heart attack. That or shoot someone. "And you are go for powered descent," said Pete.

"Copy that, Houston."

"Any other surprises you'd like to share with us, Scotty?"

"What if I said that I saw Mommy kissing Santa Claus?" I said.

"I'd say I hope you got a present from him, kid, because I think Wernher's crossed you off his Christmas list."

"Yeah, I know," I said. "He's going to have me shot."

"Do you want to report a bogey, *Caliban*?"

"Why not? Everyone else in NASA seems to have reported one."

I told Pete about what I'd seen. Not just about the cylindrical object orbiting the Moon, but also about the fireflies and the flashing lights.

"Roger that," said Pete. "Trust you to make the flush."

"That's it for surprises," I said. "For now."

"Not so fast, Batman," said Pete. I could hear the laughter behind his voice. "I've got a surprise for *you*. Special Agent Bragg says that as soon as you've landed on the Moon, your first job is to field a telephone call. From your mom."

"Hell. That's all I need."

"That should be an interesting conversation," said Pete. "As well as a historic one."

The descent engine fired quietly and slowed us down right on schedule. A few minutes later the pings computer turned us over so that we were traveling on our backs, staring into the immensity of space. It was an odd sensation, not even seeing where we were soon to land. The landing radar started transmitting information to the computer, which began throttling us back, and correcting our course with bursts from *Dibble's* maneuvering jets. With nothing to see out of the window I kept an eye on the pings display, hoping that none of the alarm codes would come up and oblige me to take over control. We were less than ten thousand feet above the Moon's surface, headed for the southern edge of the Sea of Tranquility. This was a flat plain with not many big rocks around. Another good reason for landing there was that the location, right in the center of the part of the Moon that you see from Earth, was an excellent place for communicating with Houston.

We throttled back again, and *Dibble* pitched forward. Now we could see where we were going. Morning sunlight filled *Dibble's* interior. Now it felt more like a helicopter than a spacecraft.

"Fuel is good," I said. "Eight hundred feet. Altitude is good. Rate of descent is twenty-five feet per second."

"Roger that, *Dibble*."

"Visibility is excellent," I said. "Five hundred feet. Surface looks good and level."

I tried to keep the excitement out of my voice as the full

meaning of what was about to happen tried to crowd into my thoughts. I shook my head. There was too much to monitor for me to think about that now. I took a precautionary hold of the hand controls, just in case. But the computer was handling everything perfectly, just like Dr. von Braun had said it would. All of my training in the lunar-landing vehicle simulator looked like it would turn out to be unnecessary. I sneaked a quick look out of the window and caught sight of *Dibble*'s crablike shadow on the surface.

"I've got the shadow out there," I told Houston. "Three hundred feet. Looks like a swell spot for a picnic."

We were headed toward the center of a crater about the size of a small town. A hundred feet separated us from the lunar surface.

"This is it, Benny," I said. "Two hundred feet. Get ready to be the first ape on the Moon. Starting to lose visibility."

Dibble's descent engine was kicking up dust in all directions. But it didn't come up in a cloud, as it would have on Earth. There was no air to catch it.

"Fifty feet," I said. "Fuel is low, attitude is good. Stand by for thirty seconds."

I swallowed hard, wondering if we really would sink like a stone in all that Moon dust, as some scientists had predicted we would. Or did the dust conceal some large, jagged rock that was about to push a giant hole through the bottom of our flimsy lunar module? It was flimsy because it had to be light enough to take off again. And what if we were parking right next to a mascon, one of those regions where the gravitational pull was higher than normal?

The fuel did seem to be abnormally low. For all I knew, we might never be able to take off again. I took hold of Dad's lucky mascot and squeezed it as tightly as my glove permitted.

"Contact light."

The blue contact light came on the second that one of the sensory probes hanging below *Dibble's* four footpads touched the lunar surface. The next moment the computer cut the engine, and we were landing on the ground, a little harder than expected, but not nearly as hard as the first time I had landed the Cessna back at Ellington Field.

"We copy you down, *Dibble*," said Pete.

"Mr. President, if you're listening, this is the Moon," I said. I sort of felt obliged to also mention the man who had made all of this possible: John F. Kennedy. There were, of course, two presidents who had made it possible, at least for me, but I didn't want to upset the one who was still alive—President Lyndon Johnson—by only mentioning his predecessor. So I just said "Mr. President" and hoped that that would do. I thought for a moment longer and then added, "*Dibble* is on the case."

I stared out the window at a landscape no human being had ever seen before. Well, not this close, anyway. The curious thing was that if I screwed up my eyes, I could very easily have persuaded myself that I was still in orbit. The Moon looked exactly the same on the surface as it did from a hundred miles up above. Just gray and more gray and then the curved black edge of untrespassed space. There were no boulders, no rocks, and no real features to speak of. Just the flat, hard, sunlit lunar surface, and in the distance, a mile or two away, the lip of the crater.

"What do you think, Benny?"

He made a zigzag in front of his face with a finger: "Ugly." He looked down at his feet and let out a heavy sigh.

"Damn right," I said. It seemed a long way to come to see very little, and after a few minutes I was easily able to tear myself away from the view to start work on the checklist of *Dibble's* systems and data, just in case we had to leave in a hurry.

The first thing I discovered was that I wasn't exactly sure where we had landed.

"Houston, do you have an idea precisely where we are?" I asked. "Because I sure don't."

There was a short pause, and then Pete said, "We're not exactly sure about that one ourselves, Scott. We think you're probably a little to the west of where you ought to be. We're working on a more accurate position for your flight vehicle, but for now we just don't know precisely where you are. We think it might have had something to do with mascons. What we'd like you to do is stand by for further instructions regarding that matter."

"Roger that, Houston."

"We have one more bit of housekeeping for you, Scott," said Pete. "Are you ready to speak to your mom?"

I groaned and let out a sigh.

"It's up to you," said Pete. "You don't have to if you don't want to."

"I guess I'd better speak to her," I said. "For my dad's sake."

There was a long pause.

"Go ahead, caller," said a voice I recognized. Agent Bragg, affecting a Scottish accent and doing an even worse job than the actor who played Mr. Scott in *Star Trek*, was pretending to be the international telephone operator.

"Mom?" I shouted. "Can you hear me?"

"*Scott*." She sounded both relieved and exasperated. "What is going on? I've been hanging on this phone for almost fifteen minutes."

"I'm sorry about that, Mom. But where I am isn't exactly easily accessible. I mean, everything up here takes a lot of time to get done."

"How's everything? Are you keeping well? Are you getting enough to eat?"

"Everything's just fine, Mom."

"I got the *Scotsman* newspaper delivered at work," she said. "I've been keeping an eye on all the weather you've been having in Scotland."

"Really? That's great, Mom."

"Such weather," she said.

"I have my suit," I said without thinking.

"I thought you said you didn't have to wear a suit."

"I bought one," I said. "It's made of tweed. To keep me warm."

"Isn't that just a bit too warm *for a heat wave*?"

"It gets pretty cold by the sea, Mom."

I hoped she wouldn't ask me any specific questions. For one

thing, I had left my Gordonstoun file back on Earth, and for another, I had forgotten to ask Agent Bragg for a briefing on what had been happening in Scotland, if anything. Weather was something we should have anticipated talking about.

"Have you met Prince Charles yet?"

Here I was on firmer ground. I'd read quite a bit about Prince Charles back at the Cape. I knew he played the cello, for example. And that he was keen on polo, and had a fondness for cherry brandy: Apparently, on the school sailing trip to the island of Stornoway, at the age of just fourteen, the prince had ordered a cherry brandy in a local bar. Good for him, I thought. But the British newspapers had gone nuts about it.

"Yes," I said. "I've met him. He's all right, you know. I was listening to him play the cello yesterday. He's pretty good. If you like the cello, that is. I think he'd be better if he didn't drink."

"Prince Charles drinks alcohol?"

"He drinks sometimes, yeah," I said. "It was in all the papers. Maybe you didn't see that. He likes a glass of cherry brandy now and then."

"Uh-huh," said mom. "Isn't he underage?"

"Oh, sure," I said. "But the law doesn't really apply to him. He can do what he wants, on account of the fact that he's a prince."

"I see."

"Nobody can punish him either, for the same reason. Here they send you on a very long walk as a punishment, right? And the guardian—that's what they call the school principal here—

he sent Charles on a twenty-mile walk. But Charles refused to go. He threatened the guy with the Tower."

"Did he, now? Scott, what would you say if I said that Prince Charles left Gordonstoun last year?"

I grimaced. Stupid mistake. She was a fact-checker; she had checked the facts. "I'd say that that's absolutely true, Mom," I said, as coolly as I could. "He only came back to collect a school prize, and to stay for the weekend." I winced. "Mom, I'm going to have to go. I'm using the guardian's phone, in his office, and he wants to make a call."

"Can I speak to the guardian? There's something I'd like to ask him."

"He's not here right now," I said. "He just stepped out for a moment."

"What's his name, Scott?"

"Hun," I said. "Curt Hun."

"Do you mean Kurt Hahn, Scott?" she asked, almost politely. "The school founder? He's currently visiting the United States. Did you know that? Interesting man."

"No, I don't mean him." I was drowning now. She knew it and I knew it. But something drove me farther from the shore. "I mean Curt Hun."

"Where are you, Scott?" she asked. "You're not at Gordonstoun. I checked."

"Mom, I've got to go," I said. "Look, don't worry about me, okay? Everything's fine. I'll be back in a week. I promise."

"Scott—"

Hurriedly, I hit the mike button to end the conversation, certain that I had just managed to drop my dad in the crap from an enormous height. But now was not the time to worry about what he was going to tell her. Pete Conrad was back on the microphone with some rather interesting information.

"*Dibble*, this is Houston," he said. "We have managed to pinpoint your accurate position, and if you're at all interested in geometry, we have some fascinating data for you. It would seem that you are on the lunar equator, at the exact center of an unknown crater that describes a perfect circle. What's really interesting, from a mathematical point of view, is the proportions of that crater. The diameter of the crater is exactly 3.236067978 miles in every direction. That means that the radius of the circle you're in is exactly 1.618033989 miles. And I repeat the word *exactly*, because in case that number is unfamiliar to you, 1.618033989 is an irrational number better known as the golden number or the divine number. It's supposed to be a number that expresses an underlying truth about existence. The math guys here are really excited about it."

"I'm glad for them, Houston," I said. "Tell them from me that I'm looking out the window and the number appears a little less than exciting up here, okay? There's just the old gray Moon in every direction you look. I mean, it's great being here, don't get me wrong. But I've seen more interesting views inside a fireplace. This looks like a lot of ash."

"Roger that," said Pete. "They want me to tell you—just so you know, you being of such an inquiring disposition 'n' all—that the ratio of the lengths in the Great Pyramid of Giza is 1.618. Also that Da Vinci's painting of the Mona Lisa uses the golden ratio. It's just a very unusual number to find in a crater on the Moon, that's all."

"Copy that, Houston." I tried to suppress a yawn. "Any idea why it should have happened, though? I mean, why we drifted off course?"

"We think a mascon must have caused you to go off course. As a result we're going to recommend that you take off within the next two hours at T-2, when the *Trash Can*'s orbit will bring you both into an excellent position for a docking maneuver. Until then we think that you should get a little rest, Scott."

"It's odd, but I do feel kind of tired," I said. I looked at Benny and saw that he was already asleep on the floor. "Must be all that fresh air. Maybe I will close my eyes for a while. Roger that, Houston. Stay until T-2."

With Benny lying on the floor, there was no room for me down there, so I used one of the Velcro tethers to construct a makeshift hammock. It was oddly comfortable. Of course I had no intention of taking off at T-2, but I didn't dare tell Pete that. Not yet. When I awoke, I had every intention of going out for a walk. . . .

The Dark Side
of the Moon

I awoke after the strangest dream, nothing of which I could remember. I felt very refreshed, albeit in a Rip Van Winkle kind of way, as if I'd slept longer than I'd imagined.

At the same time I had the even stronger feeling that something strange had happened while I was asleep.

I looked around *Dibble*, and it wasn't difficult to see what this might be. Benny was gone. What was more, I realized that I was wearing my helmet and backpack—the portable life support system, or PLSS, pronounced "pliss"—and that everything in the suit was configured for going outside the LM. The suit was fully inflated, and my oxygen and heating systems were on. This was just as well, as the cabin pressure was zero, which was hardly surprising given that the lunar module's hatch was wide open. Moreover, my boots and the legs of my pressure suit were covered in black dust, like powdered charcoal, which seemed to imply that even more had happened that I wasn't aware of. It was as if I had already walked on the Moon. But I had no memory of doing it. I blinked several times, yawned, took a deep breath, and switched on my mike.

"Houston, this is the Moon, over."

"Scott?" I heard a gasp in my headset. "It's Scott. We've got them again."

Then I heard the sound of a collective cheer, as if several mission controllers had just thrown pencils and paper into the air with enormous relief. It wasn't too difficult to guess that this had something to do with me.

"Where the hell have you been, kid?" demanded Pete. "We've been worried sick about you. What the hell happened to you?"

"I think I fell asleep," I said.

"Asleep? We've been hailing you for hours."

I glanced at my watch, remembered that it had stopped working, and then looked at the clock on the pings, trying to remember what time it had been when I went to sleep, and wondering how the hell it was possible a) that I could have overslept on a mission to the Moon, and b) that Benny could have left the lunar module without me noticing.

"How long have you been hailing me?" I asked.

"We started hailing about ten hours ago," said Pete. "At that time we thought you'd been asleep for two hours. We've been calling you on the radio ever since then. So we thought something terrible must have happened. Damnit all, Scott, we thought you were dead. That you had been hit by a meteoroid, was our best guess. We've been worried sick about you, kid. What the hell has been going on?"

"I don't know," I said. "I've been asleep, I think. I guess I was exhausted, maybe."

Even as I said it, I knew this could hardly be true. There was no getting away from the fact that my boots were covered in Moon dust. And when I swung open the hatch, one look down at the lunar surface told me where it had come from: In the gray dust were two sets of footprints. Yet I had no memory of having been outside. Nor any explanation as to why I should have forgotten something so obviously memorable as being the first person to walk on the Moon.

"What is your current status?" asked Pete.

"Status is as follows," I said. "I am alone in the lunar module."

"Say again, Scott."

"Houston, I am alone in the LM," I said calmly. "The hatch is open. *Dibble*'s cabin is depressurized. I am wearing an inflated pressure suit and am breathing thanks to my pliss backpack. But I have no memory of having carried out EVA prep procedures, or of Benny having gone outside. I can only assume he went AWOL while I was asleep."

"Stand by," said Pete.

"Copy that, Houston," I said. "Standing by."

What happened? How did I get here? Where's Benny the Ball?

"Scott." It was Dr. von Braun again. "We want you to check the oxygen levels inside your pressure suit. We think your mixture is either too thin or too rich. Either way, it might be causing you to hallucinate. Of course, if you hadn't taken off your biosensors, we might have some idea of your medical condition."

I checked the oxygen gauges. "Everything checks out okay, Houston," I said. "Oxygen levels are one hundred percent."

"Well, Scott," said the doctor, "that's just impossible."

"Copy that, Doc."

"How is it possible to wake up in a pressurized suit with one hundred percent oxygen level after an LOS of twelve hours in duration? Tell me that, please?"

"Copy that, Houston. I sure as hell don't know. Unless I was in such a deep sleep that I was hardly breathing at all. It's a mystery."

"Scott, I want you to close the hatch door, seal it, repressurize the cabin, and then blast off. The command module will be in an excellent position again for computer docking within the hour."

"What about Benny?"

"You must forget about Benny, Scott."

"Is he dead, or what?" I waited impatiently. "Come on. His biosensors are still attached. You know damn well if he's alive or dead, Doc."

"He's alive," said Dr. von Braun. "But there's no sense in going to look for a mere ape. You need to forget about him. The ape is expendable. You're not. You need to think of your own safety. You need to get back to the command module as quickly as possible."

"Negative on that one, Doc," I said. "I'm not leaving here without my crew."

"Scott, listen to me; this is not like going to look for a lost dog in the park," said Dr. von Braun. "By now Benny could be several miles away from the flight vehicle. And you really don't have the time for this kind of wild goose chase. Your pliss pack contains only enough oxygen for a three hour EVA. Do you understand me, boy? To go after that ape would be quite irresponsible. You have to think of your parents. Your mother."

"Negative, Houston. I won't stay out there for very long. If I don't see him in a few minutes, I'll come back. I promise."

"I forbid it, Scott," said Dr. von Braun. "I forbid you."

"Don't worry, Doc," I said. "I'll take my door key. Just in case you think someone's going to steal your car."

I switched off the mike. I'd had enough of Dr. von Braun for a while. I double-checked my suit and picked up my kit bag and then set about leaving the spacecraft. To do that you had to face the rear of the cabin, then kneel down, and—taking care not to damage the all-important pliss pack—slide backward, allowing your feet to go through the hatch first.

Standing at the top of *Dibble*'s ladder and holding on with just one hand, I looked down. I felt so light that I was not concerned about falling. I climbed down and paused at the bottom of the ladder, noting that *Dibble*'s footpads were depressed into the surface about one or two inches. The dust wasn't nearly as deep as some scientists had predicted.

Then I stepped onto the surface of the Moon. By now I didn't doubt that I had stood there before. My boots were bigger than Benny's and clearly matched one of the two sets of footprints that were already there. These led away in a straight line from the LM to the very edge of the crater, immediately below the sun. What was more curious was how straight these two lines of footprints were. It was almost as if someone had drawn them with a ruler.

I glanced up at the lunar module. Against the gray-white lunar surface the gold foil–clad ascent stage looked like some fabulous ancient Egyptian funerary artifact discovered in the dust and sand of a forgotten pharaoh's long-lost tomb. This and the little Stars and Stripes attached to its crumpled surface were the most colorful things for miles around. In the bright sunlight the inflated arm of my brilliant white suit looked like it belonged to an angel. But my own breathing sounded like I was in a hospital, which was a little unnerving, since it sort of reminded me that if it ever stopped, I would die. Back on Earth, you just don't notice yourself breathing, which is, I think, important to your sense of well-being and happiness.

I lowered my sun visor and started walking. I moved without difficulty. Once you get used to your own Pillsbury Doughboy shape and bulk, walking on the Moon is easy, since you almost float as you walk.

When my back was to the LM, the Moon exhausted my powers of description in just a few seconds. There was just gray and more gray and then black. It was like an enormous black and white photograph of an empty gray ocean at night. There was just desolation, boundless and bare, and the two lines of footprints stretching across the lone and level dust, far away, to the very rim of the crater. I kept thinking that if Kennedy could have seen this, he might have suggested Mars instead. Mars just had to be more interesting than the Moon.

As I walked, my boots kicked up a dust so fine it was more like chalk.

If you keep on following this trail of footprints, you'll find a lot more than just Benny. You know that, don't you?

"What will I find?"

Something important about yourself. Something important about all human beings. Something important about that still, small voice you hear inside your head. Who that voice belongs to. What it amounts to. Where it will take you. Now and in the future.

"But that's just me thinking, surely. My own conscious mind talking back to me."

It wasn't always like that. As a matter of fact, most people have forgotten how to listen to the voice you're listening to now. But up here, on the Moon, things are very different.

"You're telling me they are."

Things are quiet. There's less distraction. Less to pay attention to. In a way this is how it used to be on Earth. I don't mean the desolation. I mean that up here there's space to hear yourself think. Do you ever say that to yourself? "I can't hear myself think."

"Only all the time," I said.

The plain fact of the matter is that thousands of years ago nobody thought in the same way that people think now. Nobody had a conversation with their own thought processes, the way you do back on Earth, Scott. It wasn't like that at all. When someone had a conversation with the voice in their head, they thought that voice came from

*somewhere outside their head. That it belonged to something else. I
know that must sound incredible, but that's just how it was.*

"You mean they thought that the thought voice belonged to
some kind of god?"

*That's exactly what I mean. They had no mental language. None
at all. A thought sounded like someone else speaking to them.*

"So this conversation I'm having now," I said, "in my own
head. If I'd been around thousands of years ago, I would have
been convinced that you were a god talking to me. Zeus, Apollo,
Jehovah, Jesus, an angel. Depending on where and when I lived."

*That's quite correct. Take Moses, for example. The voice he heard
from inside that burning bush on Mount Horeb. The god who spoke
to him was almost certainly inside his own head. Only it didn't seem
that way to Moses. It seemed very real indeed. Real enough to take
him all the way back to Egypt to free the Children of Israel.*

"Does that mean the voice he heard didn't really exist?"

*On the contrary. The voice did exist. Very much so. It was easier
to listen to back then, of course. There was less competing for human
attention. Minds were simpler too. Not so much in them, I suppose.*

"So does that mean you are a god too?"

*Yes and no. I suppose it depends how you look at it. The god is
part of the man. The bottom line is this: You can regard the voice
as independent of you, or part of you. It's your choice. In a way it
really doesn't matter. You could say that it's how you choose to listen
to the voice inside you that makes a difference. That's what makes
people special.*

"I see."

No, not quite. But you will. That's why I'm talking to you again.

"Again? Have we talked before? Like earlier on today?"

Of course. You know we have. But the first time was too much for you to take. It often happens that way. I could give you such a long list of famous people who ran away when they heard my voice. Some people prefer to blank it from their minds altogether. It's just too much for them.

"So everyone can hear the voice?"

If they want to hear it. It says different things to different people, because everyone is different. The voice always sounds much the same, only people don't always pay attention to it. Just as often, when they do pay attention, they don't always listen. Something interrupts them. Like a telephone. The doorbell ringing. Then there's television, radio. You need peace and quiet to hear the voice. Or voices. Sometimes there's more than one.

"You mean like Joan of Arc? She heard voices, didn't she?"

Good example. Joan paid attention to her voices. That changed her life. Not everyone does that. Not anymore. Not everyone can. Not anymore. These days a lot of people don't even want to listen. They'd rather go to a movie. Or watch TV. The faculty of listening—of really listening—is dying out. In the same way that a sense of smell is no longer so important for humans. It's something that has to be learned again.

"So if I listen, my life will be changed, is that it?"

It's not just about listening. Strictly speaking, listening is just half of what's involved. Listening affects what you see. If you hear thunder, you expect to see lightning, right? If you hear a dog barking, you don't expect to see a cat. Similarly, if you pay attention to the voice you hear, eventually you should expect to see what you're listening to. Because of that, thousands of years ago human minds looked differently upon almost everything. It even affected the way they saw things. It meant that they could also see things you can't see today.

"You mean like angels and visions and stuff like that?"

It all depends what you expect to see when you listen to the voice. That's what's so wonderful about all of this. It's entirely up to you how you look at this experience. What you take away from it . . .

For a moment I stopped and checked my oxygen gauge. Then I turned, lifted my sun visor, and glanced back at the LM. In the distance, with the sun glinting on the gold Mylar covering, it looked more insectlike and alien than anything built by people. It reminded me of how very far I was away from home. And from everything that made me what I was. Yet I wasn't afraid. There was something about the voice in my head that was oddly comforting. As if someone really was watching over me. Someone powerful and important.

I lowered my visor and started walking again. And for a while I walked in silence.

Not much farther.

"Hey, what happened there?" I said. "You went away for a moment."

No, you did. You stopped listening. It takes a lot of practice to learn this. To put yourself aside and do what you're doing now.

"What exactly am I doing?"

Learning to listen again. Having a revelation. Hearing voices. The names for what's happening are really not that important.

"This is all just a little bit scary, do you know that? Especially up here, on my own. Miles from anywhere."

Of course. I understand. You certainly wouldn't be the first person to feel a little intimidated by all this. Grown men have buried their heads in the sand out of fear when they heard a voice for the first time.

"So what shall I call you?"

I have no name. I am what I am.

"Then, if I wanted to, I could call you God."

You could, if you wanted, yes. If a name makes you feel better. Call me what you like. Is God something you believe in?

"I always said I might believe in God if I met an angel," I said.

Then maybe you will meet one.

"Or I could just as easily tell myself that you are an alien intelligence."

Yes. If you prefer that idea to God and that helps you listen, then why not? But I'm not sure you can really see a difference. Do you believe in aliens?

"I didn't used to. But I think I do now. Since coming on this mission, anyway. I saw something in orbit around the Moon. An object. Something unidentifiable."

Try to remember what I said: that this is not just about listening. It's about seeing, too. It could be that what you saw is part of what you're hearing now. It's just a question of fitting what you see into your environment. Perhaps that's why you saw what you saw when you saw it.

"If I do see something, how will I know that it's not just a hallucination?"

What's a hallucination? Just a voice with an image attached to it, that's all. And usually it's an image that people expect to see. Have you ever wondered why people don't see angels anymore like those ancient prophets did? Or why modern people don't see visions? It's because they don't expect to see them. But can you imagine how scared you might be if I turned up in a flying saucer and landed in front of you? You'd run away. This is better, don't you think?

"Yes, I think so too."

Speaking to you from inside your own head is a much more subtle way of making contact than from the deck of a flying saucer. Can you think of a better way to convince you of something? Of gaining your confidence?

"No, I guess not."

Really, you know, it's just a question of deciding where you end and where God begins.

"So you are God."

You may call me that for the sake of shorthand, if you like. It's a good enough way of describing what I am, I suppose. Just as long as we recognize that God is just a kind of shorthand for what lies beyond man's understanding. But I might just as easily be described as an alien intelligence. Both of these names come loaded with lots of preconceptions, however. A much better way of describing what I am is information. Every atom of existence contains a level of information. Human beings are merely information come alive.

"Okay. I'll buy that."

Each person is part of a universe of information seeking contact with itself. With the bigger picture of information, so to speak. That's what drives people to fly to the Moon. And do the other things, as President Kennedy once said. Not because they are easy, but because they are hard. I like that.

"I have to buy that," I said. "I'm here."

Mostly it's one-way traffic, of course. Human beings have a terrible habit of listening only to other human beings, instead of to themselves and the information, the conscious wisdom that lies within everyone. But if you do listen, and listen hard enough, you'll see something. I can almost guarantee you will.

"I'm looking forward to it."

That's the spirit.

"So what exactly do you want from me?"

I want you to take a message back with you.

"What kind of a message?"

It's an equation. You know, like algebra.

"I hate algebra."

It's just a quick way of sending important information. Like $E = mc^2$. You've heard of that equation, haven't you?

"Of course."

Well, this one's rather similar.

"Suppose they don't understand your equation?"

That's a fair question. There are lots of people in NASA who could understand it. The same people who commented on the golden ratio present in this Moon crater. The kind of people who love the information contained inside big numbers. But in a way that's the whole point of the message. If they don't get it, they don't get it. You see, you should think of going to the Moon like the beginning of a treasure hunt. And since you're the first one here, it's you who's first to get the clue about what happens next. That's the way that the information has been designed. After all, there's nothing else here. Especially now that the message has been delivered. Really, there would be no point in coming back here except to say that you'd been to the Moon.

"You got that right."

My own opinion, for what it's worth, is that you're not ready. Not you personally, but human beings in general. You rushed it. As usual you set yourself an impossible goal and then, against all the odds, achieved it.

"You mean going to the Moon before the decade is out, don't you?"

If people had taken more time getting to the Moon, then perhaps the message would have meant more. But as it is, I rather fear that the message will fall on stony ground. At least for now. Oh, in time someone will get it. Maybe. Eventually. I suspect that by then human beings will have fallen out of love with space exploration. But this is the stepping stone. Quite literally. This is the next stage.

"The other astronauts who come after me, will they hear something wonderful too? Will they be given the message?"

Not like you, Scott. Because you're the first. There's only one message like the one I'm going to give you. After that, it all depends on them. Right now they only want to see what they expect to see. That's why they keep that file called Santa Claus. Because they don't quite believe what they've already seen and heard. Oh, yes, they've heard voices too. But hearing voices and seeing bogeys are two different things in their minds. Hearing voices equals insanity, to their way of thinking. Even more so than seeing things like bogeys. You're lucky, Scott. You came on your own. You've had a wonderful opportunity that very few people are ever given. To be alone with yourself. To understand yourself.

"To touch the face of God."

What's that?

"Oh, nothing. Just a poem my dad likes. This equation you want me to take back with me. Suppose I forget it?"

You won't. How could you? It's written on a rock.

"Rock? What rock?"

The one lying on the ground by your foot.

I looked down, and sure enough, there was the rock: a conical stone about the size and shape of an ice cream cone or a large tent peg. I bent down and picked it up. Holding it up in front of my visor I could just make out a series of small grooves and markings on the surface of the rock. I have to admit that it didn't look like a message to me.

Would you care to guess how long that rock has been lying there, waiting for you to come along and pick it up?

"I dunno. A thousand years?"

Think again. That little rock and the message it contains have been sitting there for three million years.

"You're kidding." I put it carefully in my kit bag. "Wow."

That's around the time that you and Benny shared a common ancestor.

"Which reminds me. Where is Benny? I've been walking for almost thirty minutes and I still can't see him."

He's right behind you. I think he's been looking for you.

"He's been looking for *me*?" I started to shuffle around to look for Benny. Turning in a space suit takes longer than you might think.

It's not just you who's learned to listen on this trip. It's Benny, too. I think you'll find that Benny knows a lot more than you could imagine he knows.

About ten yards away I saw a figure in an inflated white space suit exactly like my own. In the sunlight the white was almost celestial, as if the figure had just arrived aboard some kind of fiery chariot. Outside of a hospital, I had never seen anything that looked so pure and white. I wouldn't have been surprised if Benny's backpack had split open to reveal a pair of matching white wings.

From the direction of the footprints in the dust it seemed as if Benny had been walking behind me for a while. Which was a bit weird.

"There you are," I said. "Where have you been?"

He made no sound or gesture. Of course, it was a dumb question. Because a) Benny, being a chimpanzee, couldn't answer the question, b) it was blindingly obvious where he'd been—he'd been on the Moon, and c) my own radio wasn't actually switched on.

The gold visor on Benny's helmet hid his face, and it was a bit like staring into a small TV set with a very clear picture of another superwhite astronaut—me—on a plaster-of-Paris landscape, with an oblong, black shadow extending toward Benny like, well, a monolith. To be more specific, my shadow was like the monolith in *2001: A Space Odyssey.* Except that it was flat on the ground, of course. I walked, bounced, and floated toward Benny, all at the same time. Cue some startling church organ music as shadow nears ape.

I lifted my visor and stared closely into his helmet, almost wondering if behind the visor it really was Benny. Of course what I saw was the reflection of my own face staring clearly back at me. Which was a curious feeling. As if it were me inside Benny's space suit.

"C'mon," I said. "Let's go back to the ship."

Benny stayed put. Perhaps his keener eyes had spotted something on the horizon. Because it was then that I saw something else reflected in Benny's visor: a large, bright, cylindrical light moving rapidly up into the sanctuary of space from the crater's rim, about one hundred yards behind me. It looked like a small rocket taking off. Except that it moved not in a straight line but in a kind of parabola.

"What the hell was that?" I said.

I shuffled around to take a look, but so cumbersome was my suit and backpack that by the time I was pointed in the right direction, the light had gone and the sky was the same anonymous, starless, velvet black it had been before.

"What the hell was that?" I said again, staring up at the heavens. Of course, I was pretty sure what I thought I'd seen.

It was something pretty close to Santa Claus.

We went back to *Dibble*, where I collected a few small rock samples and a scoopful of dust that I placed inside a plastic box. I put these next to the conical rock with the strange markings.

I wanted to leave some small memorial of my presence on the lunar surface. No one had thought to provide me with a flag, since no one had expected me to walk on the Moon. And since the mission was supposed to be remain a secret. The only flag I had, apart from the ones on our suits and on the LM, was the one held by Dad's lucky mascot, the troll. So I left that behind. Under the circumstances I didn't think Dad would mind. I stood it up about twenty or thirty yards from the LM so that it would not be blasted away when we took off again. In a curious way the troll looked like it belonged there. I also left Lee Stervinou's flying scarf. Next to these I signed my name in the dust. Then I fetched my Polaroid Land camera from my kit bag—Kit had helped me sneak it aboard—and took a couple of pictures of the troll, my signature, and in the distance, *Dibble*. I also took a couple shots of Benny. And he took a couple of me.

In my bag I also had a roll of Kennedy half-dollars that I figured I might give to some people as souvenirs (after all, there are not many coins that go all the way to the Moon and back). People like Dad, Kit, Pete, Maurice, Ed, and Sally. Maybe Mom, too, if she ever spoke to me again.

I brushed Benny and myself off a bit so we wouldn't bring too much dust inside *Dibble*. Some of the scientists were worried that Moon dust carried inside the oxygen-rich atmosphere of the LM might catch fire. But my own feeling was that Moon dust looked volcanic, the remains of a fire that had long gone out, and would probably never catch fire again. It seemed that my geology classes from Dr. Freichshoh were paying off after all.

The last thing I did was take a walk around the footpads of the LM, checking stuff.

Benny had adapted better to Moon-walking than I had. He put his arms around the sides of the ladder, bent his legs as far as they could bend inside the suit, and then jumped all the way up, which was easily seven or eight feet. But for the weight of the backpack he could probably have jumped a lot higher. When he was inside, I tried the technique myself and only managed about four or five feet. Once at the top of the ladder, I took a last look around, scrambled through the hatch, and then closed it behind us.

Safely inside, I repressurized the cabin and took our helmets off so we could eat. Our pristine white suits were covered with grime. We looked like a couple of coal miners. Benny shook his head, wiped his face with the palm of his hand, and let out a breath. Then, with his thumbs against his body he turned his hands over his chest before turning one hand into a fist to draw a circle over his stomach.

"Tired," he was saying. "Hungry."

"Me too," I said.

I had some dehydrated chicken, and Benny ate some banana pellets. He was as fed up with banana pellets as I was with chicken. He shaped his hand like he was holding a bag and then moved his hand up to his mouth. "Potato chips."

"I'm afraid not," I said, shaking my head. "Tell you what, though. Why don't we swap?"

So we ate each other's dinner.

By now both of us were smelling pretty bad, and I guessed that we needed to get rid of the pee and poop bags built into our suits. Removing these was not a pleasant job, but it was certainly a necessary one. When this was done, we put our helmets back on, depressurized the cabin once again, jettisoned the bags, closed the hatch again, repressurized, and removed our helmets a second time.

Benny struck one thumb downward against the other, like someone striking a match: "Better," he said.

"I'll say."

He touched his chin and moved his hand forward: "Thanks."

"You're getting kind of gabby," I said. "Do you know that?"

There was dust everywhere, despite our earlier efforts at some housekeeping. It was impossible not to breathe some of it in. Benny coughed a couple of times. The dust smelled like matches, which made me worry a little that it might catch fire after all.

"You know what they need in here, when they come back to the Moon?" I said.

Benny made a sucking face.

"That's right. A vacuum cleaner." I reached for the radio switch. "Time to face the music, I guess."

I flicked the switch back on. "Houston, this is *Dibble*. Over."

I endured a minute or so of Dr. von Braun's anger in silence. While he was ranting, I looked across at Benny and pulled a face.

Benny made a V shape with two fingers in front of his face and moved them toward me. "Snake," he was saying.

I nodded. "Damn right," I muttered.

"Of course I'm right," said Dr. von Braun. "Takeoff is in one hour. I suggest you carry out an immediate systems check."

"Roger that, Houston."

"By the way," he added with a sadistic chuckle, "your mother is on the warpath, fit to be tied."

I let out a groan. "Does she know everything?"

"Everything," he said.

"Poor old Dad."

I took a couple of star sightings with the sextant and fed the results into the computer. Then we put our helmets back on, which made breathing a lot easier. There was just too much dust for us to breathe comfortably otherwise. After almost an hour it was finally time to leave.

The ascent engine beneath us was a chemical engine. You just opened some valves and let the hypergolics mix up a bit, and then, bingo, you'd blast off, with just thirty-five hundred pounds of thrust needed to get off the Moon. The ascent itself was simple enough too. The pings computer was supposed to handle everything, from our trajectory to our speed. It all seemed just a bit too simple to me. If the engine didn't fire at all, we were stuck on the lunar surface. Forever. And if *Dibble*'s engine didn't burn for long enough—at least seven minutes—we wouldn't achieve enough altitude and speed to rendezvous with the *Trash Can*; chances were we would simply crash back onto the lunar surface and be killed. Sixty-nine miles in orbit above the Moon, the *Trash Can* and Choo-Choo were beginning to seem like a long way away.

Pete took over at Houston again. Much to my relief.

"No other traffic in the vicinity," he joked. "*Dibble*, you are clear for takeoff."

"Roger that, Houston. Beginning countdown. Nine, eight, seven, six, five, abort stage, engine armed, ascent, proceed."

I pushed the button. For a brief moment nothing happened, except that we heard liquid moving underneath us. Then there was a loud bang, like a decent-size firecracker going off, and we were going up, at about the same speed as a well-struck baseball. A shower of brilliant gold foil from the descent stage flew away in all directions.

For about thirty seconds we went straight up, and then we pitched over at an angle, staring straight down at the lunar surface. But there was no time for sightseeing. I was too busy watching the computer.

"Ten thousand feet," I said. We were now traveling westward at about a foot per second.

Things went well for about two or three minutes; then Benny barked at me and began tapping his left palm with his index finger. One of the alarm lights had lit up. A second or two later the ascent engine began losing power. And then, to my horror, it stopped altogether.

"Houston," I said, trying to eliminate panic from my voice, "we have a problem."

"Say again, please, Scott."

"Houston, we have a problem," I said, with a little more urgency this time. "The pings computer reports we have zero engine activity. We are still ascending, but slowly. We are at one hundred and ten thousand feet, about fifty miles short of altitude and orbit."

"Roger that, *Dibble*. Stand by. We're looking at it."

I heard myself swallow loudly, and I cursed myself for having left the lucky mascot troll down on the surface. That was the thing about lucky mascots. You were supposed to take them with you, not use them for some stupid and misplaced ceremony. A feeling of nausea swept over me, and for the first time since taking off from the Cape I felt real fear. I didn't know how long we had left, but before very long *Dibble* would stop ascending altogether. And, very gradually, the Moon's one-sixth gravity would acquire us again, and we would start falling back down to the surface.

Unless something happened, and happened soon, we were going to crash.

Benny the Ball and I stood in the lunar module staring down at the surface of the Moon, where, unless we were very lucky, we would probably crash-land in a matter of a few hours. We were orbiting the Moon at an altitude of just over twenty miles, with no apparent way of gaining any more altitude. If the *Trash Can* had been crewed by a human, such as myself, it might have stood a chance of coming down to get us. But with Choo-Choo at the controls, it was hard to see how this was going to happen.

"*Dibble*, this is Houston." It was Pete. "We've got lots of people down here working on this."

"Roger that, Houston," I said. That meant they hadn't been able to think of anything. I glanced anxiously out of the window. The Moon seemed to be getting bigger. Then I realized. It wasn't getting bigger; it was getting nearer.

Benny let out a grunt, then smacked his fist into his palm and moved it toward me. "Help you," he was saying.

"I wish you could, pal."

Then he moved his right index finger against his left index finger: "Try." Then, with his left hand palm down, he waved above his other index finger: "Helicopter." Helicopter was what Benny called the LM. Finally, he pointed up, meaning, not surprisingly, "up."

"Try helicopter up?" I repeated dumbly. "Yeah, thanks a lot, Benny, old pal. That really helps."

He signed at me again, only this time with greater urgency.

"Wait a minute," I said. "Maybe you've got something there."

"Say again, Scott," said Pete. "We missed that down here."

"Houston, I think we have an idea of our own," I said. "About what to do. Something we'd like to try, anyway."

"We?"

"Sure," I said. "Me and Benny think the combustion chamber may not have filled completely. We're going to use the attitude control rockets to adjust the lunar module to an upright position. We think that this will move the chemicals back into the combustion chamber and the engine will fire again. You know, like shaking a car around when you run out of gas."

"Roger that," said Pete. There was a pause, and he added, "We advise you to make sure that you only use half the rockets. Use only the rockets currently pointing downward. Otherwise it will accelerate your descent toward the Moon."

"Copy that, Houston."

I took hold of the controls, squeezed them, and gently set us upright so that we were staring out of the window into space instead of looking down at the Moon. Then I held my breath, because the valves for the SPS engine were still open. To my surprise the proceed light came on again, and without hesitating I pressed it. Much to my relief the chemical engine exploded into life just as before, firing us farther away from the Moon. Benny had been right. Tilting the LM had stirred the contents of the combustion chamber. We were on our way again.

"Houston, be advised, we have a burn. Houston," I said excitedly, "we have a burn."

"Roger, that's great to hear."

I reached out and clapped Benny on the head, and he let out a grunt of pleasure and then farted, probably just for the hell of it. At least it was inside his own suit.

"You're a hero," I said. "But don't think you can take advantage of that, okay? We only just got this place smelling nice again."

Once more we soared upward with me reading off the altitude indicator as we went. It wasn't long before I caught sight of what might have been the *Trash Can* orbiting the Moon more slowly about fifteen miles above us—a bright blinking spot of light in the top corner of the window.

"This is *Dibble* coming up your alley, calling Choo-Choo," I said, pressing a button on my pings. "Over."

Hearing this, and seeing a red light appear on his computer console, Choo-Choo was supposed to press a green respond button. But nothing happened.

"Are you there, Choo-Choo?"

Benny shook his head and then signed impatiently at me, his index fingers closing to his thumbs in front of his eyes.

For a moment or two I struggled to remember what this sign meant. So Benny kept on doing it until my tired mind caught up with his. Was it my imagination, or had his sign vocabulary suddenly increased since our being on the Moon?

"You think he's asleep?"

Benny punched his forehead as if lamenting that it had taken me so long, and then nodded twice.

I signed back at him, making my index fingers spring open in front of my eyes. "Let's wake him up," I said.

Benny didn't need to be asked twice and started screaming at the top of his lungs. This went on until we got a green light back from the *Trash Can*. At long last Choo-Choo was acknowledging our signal.

"Nice to hear from you, Choo-Choo," I said. "We were wondering where you'd gotten to. Thought maybe you'd slipped out of the *Trash Can* for a quiet cigarette."

I grabbed the controls and fired the reaction control system engines to put us on a course that would cross the course of the *Trash Can* on our next orbit. After another couple of minutes it was time to pitch the LM forward again, only this time I had to do it manually.

Less than two hours later the computers of both the *Trash Can* and *Dibble* docked us perfectly. Immediately I set about disabling the LM's systems and getting *Dibble* ready to jettison. Then we opened the hatches on each side and made our way into the *Trash Can*'s cockpit. Choo-Choo was very pleased to see us, chattering excitedly like, well, an ape. He hugged me and then he hugged Benny the Ball.

Benny gave Choo-Choo a cool sort of look and then caught my eye. He raised his hand just above the shoulder and then bent his hand forward at the wrist. "Fairy," he was saying.

I laughed. "Benny," I said. "That's a very unkind thing to say about poor Choo-Choo. He's just pleased to see us, that's all. I don't think he's a fairy at all."

I laughed again. But then I held my hands together and moved them up and down. "Friend," I said. I made a fist with the thumb raised. "A good friend."

An hour or so later we closed the hatch on *Dibble* and undocked. The LM's job was over. We were leaving it behind. Then, when jettisoning was complete, the computer blasted us out of the Moon's orbit and set a course for home.

Choo-Choo was not well. First he said he had a headache, and I gave him a couple of aspirin. Then he just floated on his couch and stared listlessly at the instrument panel. For a while he retched like a dog, and I began to get worried. Maurice came on the radio from Houston and told me that Choo-Choo's temperature—unlike me he was still wearing his biomed sensors—was high and that it seemed he had a fever.

"How's Benny?"

I wondered how to answer this question. Benny was certainly not ill. But he was hardly behaving normally. For one thing, his ability to sign had increased remarkably. Whereas before the flight he had had a vocabulary of less than fifty signs, I estimated that now he knew at least two or three hundred. Perhaps more. For another thing, he was making up signs of his own. He could even answer many of my direct questions with a nod or a shake of the head. Only I hardly wanted to tell Maurice this. I liked Maurice. But I didn't want the people from the Holloman Aerospace Medical Center deciding they wanted to study Benny and find out what might have increased his IQ—because there was no doubt in my own mind that this was what had happened. Clearly, Benny had had some kind of experience on the Moon that was comparable to mine. And it had affected him more than, perhaps, it had affected me.

"He's fine," I said. "Same old Benny the Ball. Quiet. Affectionate."

"How do *you* feel, Tarzan?" asked Maurice.

"I've had a sore throat," I said. "And my nose is kind of stuffed. I presume it's some kind of reaction to all the Moon dust we had to breathe in the LM."

"I'd like you to reattach your own biomed sensors," said Maurice. "That way I can check your temperature. But on the face of it I'd say you have a cold. And so does Choo-Choo. Chimpanzees are very vulnerable to human respiratory illnesses. Give him plenty of water. Stop giving him Lomotil. And give him some more aspirin."

But then Choo-Choo vomited. One minute I was trying to fix myself a meal, and the next Benny was signing at me furiously. He drew a circle on his stomach and then pointed. "Sick," he said.

There was a brownish globule of puke drifting toward me like a balloon. The weightless conditions inside the *Trash Can* almost made the puke seem alive. I ducked it just in time. Benny handed me a plastic bag, and, trying not to gag, I sailed after the puke, trying to bag it before it hit something important. But no sooner had I bagged it—the puke looked like a horrible species of goldfish—then we heard a loud fart and saw a chain of diarrhea leaving poor Choo-Choo's body.

Benny touched his left palm with his right middle finger, and then his right palm with his left middle finger. And, in spite of what was happening, I laughed. "Jesus," was what he'd said.

"Amen to that, brother," I said, and, still chuckling, I grabbed another bag and went after the crap. I spent the next hour hunting for bits of poop and puke. The smell was terrible, of course. After a while I was obliged to use the oxygen mask just to have a respite from the stench.

Choo-Choo stopped vomiting, and the diarrhea stopped, but he got worse, and soon I had given up the oxygen mask and attached it to his pale face. Benny held his head and looked concerned.

We remained like that for a couple of hours.

And then Choo-Choo died.

Benny the Ball let out a long sigh and then moved his hand slightly forward from the side of his face. "Sad," he was saying. And then he moved his flat hand downward in front of his body. "Very sad."

I couldn't speak with grief. A dead chimpanzee is one of the most pitiful sights in or out of the world. It's just that they're so very full of beans when they're alive. Like small children, I guess.

Benny pushed himself down into the equipment bay and stayed there. Do chimpanzees cry? Yes, they do. It's a sound I'll never forget. I stayed there holding Choo-Choo's body for a while and then called Houston to tell them what they already knew.

I could hear the tears in Maurice's voice when he spoke to me.

"*Trash Can*, this is Houston," he said. "Everyone here is very sorry about your loss. All the gang back at the trailer in Hangar S will be really sad to hear about what happened to poor Chooch. He was a great little guy. One of the nicest apes I ever worked with." He sighed and then cleared his throat several times. "I know this is difficult for you right now, Tarzan. Real difficult. But I'm afraid Choo-Choo can't stay with you in the *Trash Can*. I hate to say this, but you're going to have to put on your suits, depressurize the cabin, and then jettison his body into space. If you don't, it's possible Benny might get what Choo-Choo had. Not only that, but things could start to smell pretty bad in there."

It was a little hard to imagine how they could smell any worse than they did already, but I got the point. A dead body is a health hazard in a spacecraft. So we put Choo-Choo in his space suit and helmet, and we suited up ourselves. After we had depressurized the cabin, I tethered Benny and myself to the *Trash Can* and opened the hatch.

For a while Benny and I just stood there in the hatch, holding Choo-Choo's body, while I tried to think of something to say. Finally, a few words came to me:

"Captain's log, star date June 1969. We remember the life of our dear friend and fellow astronaut Choo-Choo," I said. "While Benny and I traveled down to the lunar surface, his mission was a lonely but vital one: to watch over the command service modules, which were and are our only way of getting home. He performed it well. And we shall miss him, always. Just as we shall miss his sense of humor and his strong sense of friendship. We like to believe that he is not gone, but that he is now part of the One from which we all came, and to which we shall all one day return."

So saying, I let Choo-Choo's body go. It rose a foot or two before I pushed it away, back toward the Moon. We watched until Choo-Choo was just a small silvery speck, one human-shaped star in an infinite space of light and darkness.

I was just about to go back inside, when I noticed a sort of dent on the *Trash Can*, as if something—a small meteoroid, perhaps— had struck the CSM during our orbit of the Moon. Still tethered to the inside of the *Trash Can*, I maneuvered myself outside the spacecraft to take a closer look.

The dent itself was about the size of my hand and a couple of inches deep. The position of the dent, between the command module and the service module, was where the heat shield was located. When we dumped the service module, it would be the heat shield, positioned at the blunt end of the command module, that would bear the five-thousand-degree heat of reentering the Earth's atmosphere. A fiberglass honeycomb structure filled with a silicone material, the shield didn't so much deflect heat as absorb it. The idea was simply that it would melt away instead of the astronauts inside the command module. But if as well as denting the CSM the meteoroid or whatever it was had also cracked the heat shield, we were in serious trouble. The plain fact of the matter was that a crack in the shield could mean that it would melt away sooner than was perhaps convenient.

It was impossible to inspect the heat shield until the service module was jettisoned. And I decided not to worry anyone by telling them, Benny included. If the heat shield held up, then we would survive. If it didn't, we were toast. It was as simple as that.

Two days later we were go for reentry. We approached the outer limits of the Earth's atmosphere at twenty-five thousand miles per hour. A sheath of ionized gas surrounded the command module, giving us a five-minute radio-signal blackout. This didn't bother me so much, as I'd had little to say to anyone in Houston since Choo-Choo's death. Benny and I wore suits and sat with our backs to the heat shield. I didn't know why they thought the suits would make any difference, but Mission Control had insisted on them. Perhaps they thought they would make our bodies easier to identify.

By now I was beginning to realize why on all the TV news reports I'd ever seen of the Gemini landings, the capsule containing the astronauts was always as black as something you might have found in a campfire. It wasn't a coat of paint that made the capsule black; it was heat. Enormous heat. Outside the window of the command module I had a startling view of just how much heat there was. We had a tail, a bright red and yellow tail of fire, and we were like any meteor entering the top of the Earth's atmosphere. I don't mind telling you that it's an unnerving sensation to sit at the center of a man-made fireball. Even through the protection of my water-cooled space suit I had the strong sensation that my back was getting warmer. Much warmer. Combined with the g-forces of deceleration this made the whole experience terrifying.

Suddenly it grew a lot more terrifying, as a large chunk of heat shield flew off like a small lump of molten lava. Then another. We were burning up! Benny started to screech. And so did I. How could I have been stupid enough to sign up for this? I was going to die like a toasted marshmallow!

I thought of Mom and Dad, and our house in Houston, and Kit, and Ima Hogg, and Pamela Townshend, and flying the Tweet, and Lee Stervinou, who'd been killed. It wasn't much to show for thirteen years of life. Everything important in my life seemed to have happened in the last few months: meeting the president, and Pete Conrad, and Ed and Maurice and Sally, and Choo-Choo and Benny, and the voice on the Moon. I still didn't know how I was going to explain the rock with the message I'd been told to give to the people at NASA.

I started to pray. I prayed like I'd never prayed before. Certainly it was louder than I'd ever prayed before. I repeated the Lord's Prayer as if the Lord and his apostles were all deaf. By the time we had come through the worst of the reentry, "give us this day our daily bread" sounded more like an angry autoworker's demand shouted through a bullhorn outside a factory gate. . . .

Then we were through the enormous heat of reentry, and still alive. Now all we had to worry about was our enormous height and our enormous speed. If instead of the heat shield it was the parachute that had been damaged by a meteoroid, we would hit the sea and break up like a cheap water glass. The recovery ship would need a giant sieve to find all the pieces of our command module. Not to mention the remains of our dead bodies.

But at thirty-eight thousand feet the first chute deployed. It was designed to stabilize us long enough for our main chute to deploy at just ten thousand feet. But descending at thirty feet per second, if the main chute failed to deploy, we were still going to be killed. The whole thing was just too crazy for words! The idea of ever doing this again, like Pete Conrad planned to do, seemed utterly lunatic. Small wonder that John Glenn, the first American to orbit the Earth, had already retired from the space program.

And then, with my ears popping like champagne corks, the window filled with the red and white of our main parachute, and we knew that we were going to make it. Just as long as the command module didn't fill up with water and sink before the navy divers had a chance to get the rubber collar around us. If it wasn't one thing, it was another! God damn those NASA designers.

They really knew how to put you through it! My heart was beating like a wild animal.

Two minutes later we hit the water with a sizeable impact that sent every loose thing in the command module—including a few of my fillings, I think—flying through the air. After a longish wait we heard a helicopter circling overhead, and outside the window I registered a couple of splashes as two navy divers hit the water. As soon as the flotation collar was in place around the command module, we heard a knock on the hatch. I opened it, and an almost disembodied hand thrust a couple of BIGs, biological isolation garments, in at us. In case we were carrying any unknown bugs back from the Moon. We put them on. To my surprise Benny didn't need my help. He was getting to be very independent. No one said anything. Not that we would have heard anything in our airtight BIGs and with the helicopters beating their rotors overhead.

Then a Billy Pugh net lofted us, one at a time, into the chopper. We saw no one from NASA when we got aboard the USS *Hornet*. No one spoke to us or congratulated us on our safe return. There were no speeches, and no medals. With the smoked-glass visors on our isolation garments there was no way that any of the sailors could have distinguished me from a chimpanzee. Of course, after Choo-Choo's death there was a good reason for these precautions. No one had any idea if we were carrying infectious diseases or not, and a virus from the Moon could be disastrous for people on Earth. At the same time I think our anonymity suited NASA and Dr. von Braun very well. The BIGs meant that it was easy to keep my presence aboard a NASA spacecraft a secret. But by that stage I was too tired and too relieved to be back on Earth to care very much. I just wanted to go home and sleep for a hundred years without the stink of puke and poop in my nostrils.

As soon as we were on board the ship, we were ushered straight into the windowless mobile quarantine facility—a forty-foot-long house trailer with a couple of bedrooms, a bathroom, a kitchen, and a living room with a TV. The rocks I had collected from the lunar surface, including the one with the message, came with us. In the MQF we were allowed to remove the BIGs. They wouldn't let me wash my hair. And when I took a long, hot shower, they insisted that I bag the towel for later analysis. They didn't let Benny wash at all. Then I had a meal and watched *Star Trek* on TV. To my surprise Benny the Ball did the same.

The next morning when we awoke, it was hard to believe we'd ever been to the Moon at all.

For two nights we stayed on the ship before it docked at Pearl Harbor, in Hawaii. I'd always wanted to go to Hawaii, but of course there was no chance of me leaving the MQF. Besides, we were only in Pearl long enough for the trailer to be lifted onto a flatbed truck and driven to Hickam Airfield. At Hickam Field the MQF was loaded into the belly of a C-141 Starlifter transport aircraft and, with us still inside, was flown straight to Ellington Field in Houston. Here we were hoisted onto another flatbed truck and then transported to the Manned Spacecraft Center, where, finally, we were transferred to our home for the next twenty-one days, the Lunar Receiving Laboratory, an eight-million-dollar purpose-built luxury facility with a laboratory, a projection room, several bedrooms, a doctor, a cook, and a lab specialist. There was even a janitor to keep the place tidy. Special Agent Bragg was also there, but in the beginning it was a little hard to understand why. We were informed that a veterinarian from the Cape would be joining us the following day. All of these people seemed quite happy to take the risk of being exposed to a potential Moon virus.

It was obvious to me that we were in for three weeks of intensive medical tests and checks. And I was anxious that Benny should be made aware of how this might affect him more than me. I wanted to warn him that it might be in his best interest if he seemed exactly like the old Benny the Ball, instead of the massively more intelligent Benny who had returned from the Moon.

"Listen to me, Benny," I said. "Did something happen to you on the Moon?"

Benny touched his head and then his chest with his clenched fist. "My head," he was saying.

"Someone spoke to you?"

He touched his chin and then moved his hand forward with the fingers opening; then he held his hands together and moved them up and down. By now I was more or less certain that he understood everything I said, and although he was not able to speak himself, his use of sign language was so fluent and quick that there were times when I had to ask him to slow down. "Beautiful friend," he was saying.

"You made a beautiful friend on the Moon?"

He nodded twice.

"The same thing happened to me." I shook my head. "Only I don't think we should tell anyone about this. At least not about you. You've got to play dumber than you are. Otherwise the men in white coats . . ." I touched my body with my middle finger and flicked it forward; then, clenching my hands, I made a movement like someone putting on a coat. "The men in white coats . . ." I touched my wrist with my index and middle fingers. "Doctors. They'll study you. Look inside your head. Maybe never let you go. But I don't want that. I don't think you want that either."

Benny shook his head and grimaced.

"I want you to come home with me," I said. "Would you like that? If I could fix it, would you come home and live with me?"

Benny held his hands against his face and then opened the fingers: "Wonderful." Then he laid the flat of his right hand across his left hand and moved it up to his chest: "Pleased."

"Me too, Benny," I said. "Me too. Just remember." I moved my fisted hand toward my head. "Act stupid."

Benny punched his head with his fist and then fell on the floor—a spectacular bit of clowning that had me laughing out loud.

The rock samples were with us in the LRL, of course, along with a geologist from the MSC who had volunteered to share our quarantine. (Kit had volunteered to share our quarantine too, but NASA had refused to let him take the risk.) The geologist was the same guy who had given Kit and me our lectures, Dr. Freichshoh. To us he was a beard with glasses and a white coat. Dr. Freichshoh spent nearly the whole time in the laboratory, staring at the lunar rocks and dust through a powerful microscope. Which was where I found him when I tried my best to explain the true origin of the cone-shaped rock.

"There's a message on one of those rocks," I said.

For a moment or two he tried his level best to ignore me.

"Mmm-hmm," he murmured.

"If you look hard enough," I said, "there's an important message. On that cone-shaped rock."

"Well, of course there is," he said without lifting his eyes from the microscope. "Didn't I tell you before, Scott? Geology is full of history. Every stratum of limestone, every shale, every chunk of basalt contains an important message. A message that's billions of years old."

Naturally, I didn't want to sound like a nutcase, so I felt obliged to leave out the fact that the only reason the cone-shaped rock was on his workbench at all was because an alien, possibly divine voice had told me to collect it and bring it back to Earth so an important equation that was marked on the surface could be read and then deciphered. However I said that, it was going to sound crazy.

"You don't think those marks on the surface of this particular rock are just a bit unusual?" I said.

Dr. Freichshoh sighed and looked up from the microscope. "In what way unusual?" he said, humoring me. After all, he probably thought there were more important questions he had to ask me about the lunar surface; from the minute he'd arrived in the LRL, he'd bored me to death with a lot of questions about the surface, and the crater, and the rim of the crater, and the color of the dust in comparison to the rocks.

I shrugged. "You don't think those marks on that rock look a little like writing?"

"Writing?"

He picked the rock off the bench with his rubber-gloved hands and turned it in his fingers like a piece of porcelain china.

"Yes," I said. "An ancient writing. Millions of years old."

"And who do you suggest could have done this writing?" he asked, trying to contain a smile inside his beard. "The man in the Moon?"

I shrugged. I sure wasn't about to tell him.

"Whatever gave you such an idea?" he said. "No, this rock is obviously volcanic, and the marks you see on the surface were almost certainly made while the rock was still hot and therefore soft. Most likely as it got pushed along in a lava flow. Perhaps the shape is a little unusual. But I can assure you that there is nothing remarkable about these markings. As a matter of fact, I've seen their like before. Right here on Earth, I can assure you. They're not writing. If you really want to know, they're what we geologists call striations."

"Yes, but look here—not all of these markings go in the same direction," I said. "I mean, if the rock had been forced along in a lava flow, you can hardly imagine that the lava flow would have suddenly changed direction, can you?"

"Why not? The lava might have met an obstacle of some kind and been turned to the side." He sighed. "I think that's a much more likely explanation for these markings than the possibility that they could be some ancient form of writing. Now, if you don't mind, I really have a lot of work to do, Scott. Perhaps we can talk about this again, only some other time. NASA wants my preliminary report by tomorrow morning."

Perhaps if he had been a mathematician or a linguist, he might have seen something in the markings. But as it was, all Dr. Freichshoh saw was the rock itself. If he was married—which I doubted—I guessed his wife must have been some kind of marble statue. Because all he seemed capable of seeing was rock and more rock.

The veterinarian sent from the Cape turned out to be Maurice, whom Benny greeted coolly, scorning an invitation to jump into his arms.

"Ain't you gonna come and say hello to me?" said Maurice.

He picked Benny up and fed him some banana pellets in an attempt to ingratiate himself. Benny took the pellets and ate them quietly.

"You seen any changes in him?" Maurice asked me.

"He's maybe a little quieter since Choo-Choo died," I said.

"That was a hell of a shame," said Maurice. "A hell of a shame."

"Apart from that," I said, "nothing at all."

Maurice placed Benny in a chair, and kneeling down in front of him signed a couple of times—touching his chest with his hands and then moving them forward to make fists with raised thumbs. "How are you?" he asked. "How are you, Benny?"

Benny looked dumbly at me and then at Maurice before farting noisily in his face. Chimpanzees may be mute, but they always know how to make a point.

Catching the full stink of it, Maurice stood up abruptly, looking more than a little aggrieved. I almost felt sorry for him. I knew he cared a lot for Benny. But I also knew that he was a serving officer in the air force and that it was his duty to report any significant changes in Benny's behavior. Such as suddenly becoming the chimpanzee equivalent of a genius. And putting anything like that on a report that was destined for the Aeromedical Research Lab at Holloman Air Force Base in New Mexico would have spelled disaster for Benny.

"What's eating him?" Maurice was looking at me now.

"I dunno," I said. "Ask him."

"Hell's the matter with you, Benny?" asked Maurice. "You didn't used to be so damned rude." He touched his hand with his fingers and then, making a fist, made a small circle on his palm. "Apologize."

Benny shook his head and then closed his open fingers near the side of his mouth. "Orange," he was saying.

"Damned if I'll give you an orange," said Maurice. "Not until you say hello nicely." Maurice wrapped a Velcro sleeve around Benny's arm to take his blood pressure. Benny endured it in silence. That and the rectal thermometer.

"He's tired," I said. "We're both tired. Tired of being in here. He misses Choo-Choo and the rest of the gang. And I miss my mom and dad."

"Didn't I say? You can speak to them on the telephone."

The LRL had a special call area. All you had to do was go in there and pick up the phone, and the NASA operator would put you through to whomever you wanted to speak to. So I did. Much to my surprise I found Mom was back home with my dad. She picked up the phone.

"Mom? What are you doing there?"

"Scott, honey, praise the Lord," she said.

I heard her turn away from the phone and say, "Ken, it's him." And then she was back, speaking with me.

"Are you okay?" she asked anxiously. "Are they treating you well? You haven't come down with any Moon bugs, I hope."

"I'm fine, Mom. I had a cold on the way back. But really, everything's okay. All this talk about Moon viruses. It's a lot of crap, I think. Just an excuse to keep us under observation like a couple of lab rats. Every time I blow my nose, a lab technician takes the Kleenex away for analysis. I'm not even allowed to wash my hair. They keep combing it for Moon dust. Benny's, too."

"Ugh. That's disgusting."

"I know. They're kind of irritating like that. But both of us are just fine, Mom."

"Us?"

"Me and Benny the Ball," I said. "One of the two chimpanzees

I went to the Moon with. The other chimp died."

"I heard. I'm sorry. I guess you were pretty attached to him."

"Kind of, yeah."

"What was it like up there?"

"You'd have hated it, Mom. We had these really clean white space suits and we got Moon dust all over them."

"Trust you to think I'm only interested in your laundry." She laughed. "You're just like your father."

"Well, you wouldn't believe how hard that stuff is to brush off. We're still coughing it up, from when we breathed some of it when we were in the lunar module. My snot still looks kind of black."

"But you're all right," she said. "That's the main thing."

"Mom. I'm sorry I lied to you. But I couldn't imagine you giving permission for me to go. And you can't blame Dad. It wasn't his fault. He said no in the beginning. But then the president turned up and asked me to command the mission. President Johnson, when he was still president. And after all, the president is the commander in chief. So it was real difficult for Dad to refuse him. And besides, I really wanted to go. It's not every kid who gets the chance to go into space. And even though now we have to keep it all a secret and I won't be able to talk about it or anything, I wouldn't have missed it for the world. It was the most fantastic experience of my life."

"That's all right," she said. "I understand. Any boy would have said the same as you did."

"You're not angry?"

"Not now," she said. "I was very angry when I found out that you weren't at Gordonstoun. In fact I was furious. And I was even angrier when your father told me where you really were, because of course I didn't believe him. In fact I didn't believe him until I got a call from ex-President Johnson himself. And then I couldn't help but believe what he and your father had told me."

"I thought you didn't like President Johnson."

"I don't," she said. "But then he is, was, the president, like you say. And if the president tells you something, then you sort of have to believe it, right?"

"Right."

"Scott, there's something I want to tell you," she said. "Your father and I did a lot of talking while you were up in space. I guess the danger of what you were doing made us think about how much you mean to us and the stupidity of our own differences. We realized that what's important is the life we both have with you. So. We've decided to give being married another shot."

"You have? That's great, Mom." This was the best thing I'd heard since the chute opened above the command module. "So has Dad agreed to leave the air force?"

"No," she said. "No, I've had second thoughts about that too, Scott. I'm not going to ask him to leave the air force. I guess I realized how much it means to your dad. And how much it would hurt him for me to make him leave it."

"But what about your opposition to the war?" I asked, anticipating there could still be more arguments on that subject.

"President Nixon's going to end the war," she said. "That's why we voted for him, anyway. I think he'll keep his promise. Look, let's not talk about that now. Your father's anxious to speak to you."

I heard her hand him the telephone.

"I'm so proud of you, Scotty," he said, sounding pretty choked up. "So, so proud."

"Thanks, Dad."

"I told you," he said. "You're a natural stick-and-rudder man."

"There wasn't much flying, Dad," I said. "The computers did most of it. I guess that's the future."

"All the same, from what I hear, you made some pretty tough decisions," he said. "And Kit tells me they were pretty pissed off at you, kid. Those guys at NASA, von Braun and some of the others. When you decided to take an ape's place on the Moon landing. But I just want you to know, everything you did is all right by me. Then, now, and forever in the future."

I was pleased he'd said this. It made it easier to bring up the subject of Benny the Ball.

"Dad, I'll be seeing you pretty soon," I said. "But I want to ask you something. Do you remember you told me that a good commander always brings his men back home?"

"Sure. I remember."

"Dad. I want Benny to come home and live with us."

"The chimp?"

"Yes. He was my crew. Half of it, anyway."

"Well, I was kind of talking about people, Scotty," he said awkwardly. "Guys in the air force. Not chimpanzees. And I didn't mean 'home' literally. I was talking about bringing them back to the United States. Instead of leaving them behind, in the jungle, at the mercy of the enemy."

"Dad," I said. "Benny's real home is in the Cameroons. That's in Africa. But he won't ever be able to go back there. Not now. He's been living with people for too long. The only other home he's ever had is the Aeromedical Research Lab at Holloman Air Force Base. In New Mexico. But if he goes back to Holloman, they'll probably use him for experiments or something."

"Do you know that for sure, Scott?" asked Dad. "I thought they sent them to the zoo. Ham, the first chimp in space, he went to the zoo in Washington. It was in the newspapers."

"They've got a chimponaut file, Dad. Kit managed to get a look at it when we were at the Cape. Ham did go to a zoo. But most of them get reassigned to what the air force calls 'hazardous mission environments.'"

"I dunno, Scott," he said. "It's hard enough raising a kid, let alone a chimpanzee."

"Benny deserves better, Dad. He saved my life. Look, you'll understand everything when you meet him."

I was about to tell Dad just what a remarkable chimpanzee Benny was, when I heard breathing on the line. Not my Dad's breathing, but someone else's breathing. Someone was eavesdropping on our conversation. Maybe it was Special Agent Bragg. Or someone on the outside, from NASA. There was no way of telling.

"Look, Dad, just trust me, okay?"

"All right, son. If it's what you want, then it's fine by me. But have you considered the possibility that the air force might not let you have him? Those Holloman scientists might already have other plans for Benny."

"I've considered it," I said. "And I've figured out a way that means they'll have to say yes."

After that, they watched me even more closely. The janitor, Mr. Tydings, and even the cook, Mr. Belcher. One time I caught Agent Bragg in my bedroom, and I was pretty sure he'd been about to search it. I figured it was just as well that I'd hidden my Polaroid Land camera somewhere they would never think to look for it: in Dr. Freichshoh's bedroom, at the top of the closet.

I decided that I couldn't speak freely on the LRL's public phone. But there was one other phone: the one in the lab. I had to get to that phone. The only trouble was that Dr. Freichshoh was in the laboratory nearly all the time. So I enlisted Benny's help to create a small diversion. I asked Benny to go into the lab and steal a piece of Moon rock—and to make sure that Dr. Freichshoh saw him do it. Benny was happy to help. He didn't like Dr. Freichshoh any more than I did.

Of course when Benny took off with a piece of the precious Moon rock, Freichshoh went nuts and chased him all around the LRL.

And while he was occupied doing this, I went into the lab and called Kit, who was back home with his parents.

First, I spoke to Mr. Calder, Kit's dad. He sounded a little strange. Like he wasn't exactly pleased to hear from me. Then Kit came on the phone and explained:

"After you landed on the Moon, NASA and the Secret Service got real serious with us, Mac," he said. "Special Agent Bragg and

Dr. von Braun brought a lawyer with them and made my parents sign a legal document that meant we could get into trouble if we ever talk about you and me having worked in the space program. He said they'd made your mother and father sign the same kind of paper."

"I just spoke to them," I said. "They didn't mention anything like that."

"Maybe they didn't want to worry you," he said. "They must figure you've got enough on your plate right now."

This sounded reasonable enough.

"But why didn't they get *you* to sign something?" I asked Kit.

"What would be the point?" said Kit. "Who the hell is ever going to believe me if I tell them about what happened? Or, for that matter, you? No one's ever going to buy the fact that you were the first guy on the Moon, Mac. Not if you live to be a hundred."

This also sounded reasonable enough.

"Mac, this thing with the Secret Service," said Kit. "It scared my mom and dad. Don't get me wrong—it was fun, what we did. I don't regret a bit of it. But this is all a bit too heavy, you know? My dad says that after what happened to Jack and Bobby Kennedy, the Secret Service is capable of anything. And I kind of agree with him. We might end up in a car accident, or a house fire, you know?"

"I need your help, Kit," I said. "I need you to come here, to the MSC. I want to give you something important."

"But how can you do that?" he asked. "I thought you were in strict quarantine."

"I am," I said. "They watch me pretty closely, too. But there's always a way around these things. I'm certain I can get out of here for about five minutes."

"What if you've got some terrible Moon bug?" asked Kit. "For all you know, you could be just a few days away from turning into giant stick of broccoli."

"All that Moon virus stuff?" I said. "I don't believe it. I think it's just a way of keeping me under the microscope. Like when I went to the Lovelace Clinic. C'mon, Kit. I really need your help here."

"I dunno, Scott," said Kit, lowering his voice. "Now that you've called, my parents are going to be keeping a close eye on me. Even now they're watching me like a hawk. And it's not just my parents. There's a big black car parked out in front of our house. It's been there ever since you came back from the Moon. Like there are Secret Service men watching the house or something. I think it's going to be difficult to get away. "

"All right, all right. Let me think."

I hung up and racked my brains about what to do.

And then I remembered Pamela Townshend. The girl next door. The girl who was still waiting for me to impress her.

She sounded surprised to hear from me.

"What was Scotland like?" she asked.

"Look, Pamela," I said. "Do you remember the promise you made? That I should call you when I was ready to impress you?"

"Of course I do," she said.

"Well, I think you're going to be impressed," I said. "Really impressed. But I'm going to need your help along the way."

Apart from that one occasion when Benny stole the rock, and Maurice had to help find it, things were pretty boring in the Lunar Receiving Laboratory. People just hung around waiting for us to get sick. They read books. They played cards in the living room. Or they sat in the movie theater and watched screenings of sports games and the latest movies. Movies like *Where Eagles Dare*, *The Wild Bunch*, and *Winning*. That part of it was pretty good. The only person who didn't ever visit the movie theater was Dr. Freichshoh, who spent nearly every waking hour in the laboratory looking at rock samples and not seeing what was staring him in the face. The dumbass. He kept the door locked after Benny returned the rock.

There were windows, but the windows were double-glazed, locked, and covered with venetian blinds. There was a special air-conditioning system that was meant to prevent air from escaping the LRL without first passing through a number of filters and pumps. There were double air-locked doors, like in a spacecraft, and those were also kept locked, but there were no guards or anything outside the LRL. After all very few people knew anyone was there. Mr. Tydings had a set of keys. So did the cook, Mr. Belcher. He was the one who took delivery of all foodstuff into the LRL. This happened only in the morning. After he cooked dinner at night, he always took a shower.

The rest of them were watching *Midnight Cowboy* on the evening the plan was to go down. I didn't get that movie at all. And they weren't at all surprised when I left the screening room. In fact I think they felt more comfortable that I wasn't going to see it.

While they were in there, I sneaked into the shower and pocketed Mr. Belcher's keys. I was just on my way to the main door when I found Agent Bragg blocking my way. He had my camera in his hand.

"Is this yours?" he asked.

"No," I lied. "I think it's Freichshoh's."

"It was in his closet, that's true," said Bragg. "But he says he's never seen it before and he doesn't know how it got there."

"Then it's someone else's," I said.

"There's dust on it."

I shrugged. "You said it had been in a closet, didn't you?"

"Freichshoh says it's Moon dust," said Bragg.

"That guy has got Moon dust on the brain," I said. "Besides, there's Moon dust all over this facility. That's the point of the quarantine. So people like Freichshoh can collect the last few grains of Moon dust I've been hiding in my hair follicles."

He shook his head. "No, I think this camera went to the Moon and took some pictures. Without NASA's authority."

"It's not my camera," I said. "Maybe you should ask Benny."

"I could always make a phone call, check the serial number," he said. "Find out where it was bought and when and by whom. I think it's yours. Trouble is, there's no film in it."

"Are you calling me a liar, Agent Bragg?" I said.

"If it does turn out to be your camera, we're gonna have to turn over your room," he said.

"You can turn over this whole facility for all I care," I said. "It's not mine."

Agent Bragg went off to the telephone area. I knew I didn't have long before he checked those serial numbers and discovered the camera had been bought by my mother. If I didn't manage to get my Polaroid photographs out of the LRL before Bragg came back to me, all my plans for getting Benny away from the air force would likely come to nothing. The photographs were my edge— the only means I had to negotiate his freedom.

I ran to the back door and tried several keys in the lock. Finally, I found the right one. I opened the door, closed it carefully behind me, and found myself faced with a heavy-duty polyethylene tunnel. I unzipped the entrance, stepped inside, and walked through until I came to a second zip-fastened opening. When I got through this, I fumbled with the keys, unlocked the outer door, and stepped out into the warm Houston night air, praying that Pamela would not have lost her nerve and that she would be outside when I opened the door.

She wasn't. There was no sign of her. Just an empty parking lot and beyond it a tall fence.

"Pamela," I said. "Are you there?"

"Scott?"

I ran to the fence and found her on the other side. In the moonlight she looked even lovelier than I remembered.

"What's going on?" she asked. "Are you in some kind of trouble?"

"Not trouble, no," I said. "But I'm in an awkward situation. I need you to look after something for me. Until I get back home. Only you can't mention it to anyone. Not to your parents.

Not to your best friend. No one. It'll be safer that way. Do you promise?"

"I promise."

"These pictures will tell you everything." I pushed them through the wire and watched her face as she glanced at the top one.

"My God," she said. "Are these for real?"

"Do you think I'd be here if they weren't?" I said.

"No, I guess not."

"Look, I've got to get back before they miss me. Just remember what I told you. Top secret. Your eyes only. Okay?"

I turned to leave.

"Wait," she said. "I'm impressed. I'm totally impressed. More impressed than I can say." And then she pushed her lips through the wire.

I kissed her and ran back to the door of the LRL.

I went back through the air lock, returned the cook's keys, and went straight to my bedroom. I just had time to put on my pajamas, get into bed, and pick up a book before the door opened. It was Agent Bragg again.

"Agent Bragg," I said. "What a pleasant surprise."

"All right," he said. "Where are they?"

"Where are what?"

He swore. "Don't be a wiseass with me, kid," he said. "The Polaroid photographs you took with that Land camera your mother bought, in Miami, the day before your birthday."

"Oh, *that* camera," I said.

He picked up my clothes and turned out the pockets.

Ten minutes earlier he'd have found all ten pictures in there. Some taken by Benny. Some taken by me. The LM. My name in the Moon dust. Everything. Including a nice one of the Earth, shot from the lunar surface. I was especially proud of that one. The Earth looked really blue in that Polaroid.

Finding nothing, Agent Bragg threw back the covers of my bed and jerked his thumb at the door. "Out," he said. "I'm gonna shake down your room."

And when he found nothing in my room, he searched the whole of the LRL, from top to bottom. He was at it all night.

The next day he was tired and crotchety. "I don't know where you've hidden them, kid," he said, "but I'll find them. They must be in here somewhere."

"Why do you say that?"

"Because since you came back from the Moon, you've been in complete isolation," he said. "First in the mobile quarantine facility. And then in here."

"Maybe I hid them in the MQF," I said.

Agent Bragg smiled a sarcastic smile back at me. "Nope, we already checked there. Where are they?"

"Safe," I said.

He shook his head and grinned. "Naw, they're here somewhere," he said. "I'm sure of it. Nothing gets thrown away from this facility. Even your goddamned Kleenex gets bagged and stored for analysis. Those pictures have got to be here. The double doors are kept locked. Windows double-glazed and locked. There's nowhere else they could be."

I shrugged. "Have it your own way," I said. "Hey, did you search Benny's cage? Maybe he's got them."

From the look on his face I could tell immediately that he hadn't searched Benny's cage. At the same time he had to deal with the disappointment of knowing that if I had hidden the pictures in there, I'd hardly have reminded him to search in there. Bragg didn't like Benny much either. Not since Benny had stolen the rock. Bragg had been obliged to help Maurice recapture the rock, and in the process he had earned himself a bite on the leg.

"Maybe I'll get Maurice to do it," he said.

At the end of the twenty-one-day quarantine period they told me I was free to leave. I hugged Benny and told him I'd be seeing him soon.

Benny, who was still playing dumb because Maurice was watching, said nothing.

A NASA staff car was waiting to drive me home. But first I had to go to a meeting with Dr. von Braun up in the astronaut office.

Pete was there, just like the first time I'd been in the astronaut office. He greeted me warmly, as well as with some embarrassment.

"Congratulations on an excellent mission," he said, clapping me on the shoulder.

"Thanks, Pete."

"What a pity it was spoiled by your inability to follow orders," added Dr. von Braun.

"I guess I didn't much like the idea of being airbrushed out of the space program," I said.

"Nevertheless," he said stiffly, "you agreed to abide by certain conditions. And confidentiality was one of them."

"It was you who offered me more, Doctor," I said. "And then took it away again."

He shook his head. "I spoke without proper authorization," he said. "I regret I did not foresee that the other astronauts would object so vehemently to your continued presence in the space program." He lit a cigarette. "I must ask you for those photographs. The ones you took on the Moon."

"You can have them," I said. "For a price."

"Which is?"

"I want Benny the Ball to come home with me," I said. "I don't want him going back to Holloman."

"The chimpanzee? Why should you want this ape?"

"He's my friend."

"You Americans are so sentimental," said Dr. von Braun.

"I want an official transfer of ownership of that chimpanzee," I said. "An official document drawn up by a lawyer. Like the one you made my parents and Kit's parents sign. When I receive that, you'll get half the photographs."

"How many photographs are there?"

"Nine," I said. "The first one didn't come out."

"How can I be sure that there aren't ten?"

"You'll have to take my word for it."

"Very well," he said. "I'll fix it."

"Thank you."

"That's it?" Dr. von Braun seemed surprised. "No money?"

"No money," I said. "But there is one other thing."

I told him exactly what I wanted.

"That might be a little harder to organize," he said.

"With your connections, Doctor?" I said. "I doubt it."

"Lyndon Johnson is no longer the president," he said.

"I have every confidence in your ability to do this," I said. "After all, you're the man who managed to put a boy and an ape on the Moon. Something as small as this shouldn't be too difficult. You'll get the other pictures when I'm satisfied you've kept your end of the deal."

"You know, we could always have the Secret Service put out a story and have these pictures of your Moon landing discredited," he said. "Argue that they were faked in a film studio, perhaps. These days pictures are being faked all the time. It's not so difficult to do. Hollywood can do anything. Make anything look real. Everyone in America knows this. They can do anything."

"You could do that," I said. "But why take the risk that someone might accept my pictures as genuine? Besides, if you discredit my pictures, you risk discrediting your own when *Apollo Eleven* goes to the Moon next month."

"He's got a point there, Doc," said Pete. "It might be easier just to go along with what he wants. Under the circumstances I don't think he's asking for very much."

Dr. von Braun stared at the ash on the end of his cigarette for a moment. Then he stubbed it out.

"Very well, I agree." Dr. von Braun stood up, clicked his heels, bowed curtly in my direction, and then left the room.

Pete smiled at me. "You know, Wernher's not such a bad guy," he said. "He came here to the U.S. with everything he owned in a cardboard box. Somewhere between an enemy and a friend. He's worked hard for this program, and for this country. I kind of admire him." He paused and extended his hand. As I took it, he said, "So, what's it like? On the Moon?"

"You want to know something?" I asked him. "I'm glad that no one is ever going to know I went to the Moon. No one apart from my mom and dad, and Kit and his family. I've got a feeling that for all of you guys the most difficult part of going to the Moon will be what happens when you come back to Earth. Of living with all the media attention. And forever having to answer that unanswerable question of what it's like." I smiled. "It's like nothing. Nothing at all."

Epilogue

"So what's it like?" asked Pamela. "On the Moon?"

"There's a poem we had to read in school," I said. "By W. B. Yeats. It's called 'Easter 1916.' It's about the Irish rebellion against the English. One line gets repeated again and again: 'A terrible beauty is born.' I'm not sure what it means in the poem, but that's exactly how I'd describe the Moon. It has a terrible beauty."

We were sitting in my yard. On a swing. Looking up at the Moon. It was July 1969, and most of America was doing the same thing.

"I love it that you know poetry," she said. "As well as the fact that you can fly and stuff. Weren't you scared on the Moon?"

"Yes," I said. "But I wasn't scared for myself. You see, there's this thing you can do with the Earth. From the surface of the Moon our planet looks so small that you can blot it out with your thumb. And that gives you a very strange feeling. Like nothing down here is really that important. Like the Earth could just disappear and it wouldn't matter."

"That's exactly how it looks in that Polaroid you gave me," she said. "Amazing to think you've really walked up there."

I'd given Pamela the tenth and last of the pictures I'd taken—the only one I hadn't given to NASA. It was the one of the Earth floating in space like a fabulous blue sapphire in a jewel case. The most precious thing I had, and I wanted her to have it. What can I say? When you're young and in love you do the craziest things, right? She loved it.

"I can't imagine anyone ever giving me anything more impressive than this photograph," she said. "If I live to be a hundred."

That was the whole idea, of course.

For a while we both played at blotting out the Moon with our thumbs.

Then she said, "Where's your friend?"

"Benny? He's watching TV."

"Does he have a favorite show?"

"He'll watch pretty much anything that's on."

"He sounds a lot like my little brother."

"But he likes slapstick sort of stuff best. *The Banana Splits* and *The Monkees*."

"It figures."

"But best of all he likes *Top Cat*."

Pamela lifted her beautiful, freckled forearm, which is as strong and slim as the shaft of a tennis racket, and looked at her watch.

"I'd better be going," she said, and kissed me on the cheek. "You're so brave, Scott."

I walked her home, of course.

When I got back to my own house, I went to look for Benny. Dad turned the garage into Benny's living area. There's a TV, a rope with a tire on it, an old chair, and a mattress. He likes his living area a lot. Sometimes he and I sit around and talk to each other with signs for an hour at a stretch. There's not much Benny can't say when he really puts his mind to it. Even Mom talks to him now. She was a little nervous of him when he first came to stay, but now she calls Benny my little brother, although he's not so little. Benny's very fond of her. His own mother was taken away from him when he was a baby. Whenever he talks about her, he taps the side of his head with three fingers, and follows this sign, which means "mother," by holding crossed hands close to his chest, which means "love." He's completely housebroken now. You can't get him out of the shower, although he doesn't much like soap. He helps around the house, taking out the garbage, dusting up on top of the bookshelves and curtain rods, and weeding the flower beds. A lot of the weeds he eats. One day Dad says he'll probably want to go back to Africa, to be with his own kind. But for now he's quite happy where he is. That's what he tells us, anyway.

Pete Conrad told me that NASA learned a lot from *Caliban 11*. Especially about the lunar module's ascent stage. They still think it was me who worked out how to make that SPS engine burn again. Only I know it was really Benny, and that Benny saved my life. It's best they don't know the whole story, I think.

We all watched the *Apollo 11* Moon landings on TV. Me, I didn't think much of the TV coverage. The pictures hardly did it justice. When it was on, Benny kept on looking up at the ceiling and behind him and underneath the chair he was sitting on. For a while I thought he'd developed a ghost, like T. C. back in the bad old days of Hangar S. But then I realized that seeing the pictures of the Moon had reminded him of the voice he'd heard when we were there. He was looking around because he expected to hear something or someone speaking to him. Sometimes I try to be somewhere quiet and listen out for it myself, but there's always a sound that comes along to interrupt me, and I haven't heard the voice again. Perhaps one day I will. When the time is right. When things are a little quieter.

Benny is quite certain about what he heard up there, even if sometimes I'm not nearly so sure. He holds his index finger up in the air near his head and moves it backward, like Fidel Castro when he's making an interminable speech.

That sign means "God."

It might have been one small step for a man and a giant leap for mankind, but it was Kitty Hawk, North Carolina, for a chimpanzee.

Sometimes I feel bad about the cone-shaped rock I found on the lunar surface. That I didn't make a bigger deal of it when I was speaking to Dr. von Braun. The trouble was, he didn't trust me any more than I trusted him. And under those circumstances, if I had told him about the message that's written on the rock, I think he would have thought that I was trying to make a fool of him. Either that or he'd have sent me to see a shrink. What was the equation written on the rock? My guess is that it was something really important—the next stage on from $E = mc^2$, maybe—something that would have helped take us to other planets. Perhaps leapfrog them altogether on our way to somewhere more interesting. Because I suspect we'll get to those other planets in our solar system and find them as disappointing as the Moon. It has to be something really important written on that rock, or why else would it have been ready and waiting for us on the Moon? A fuel formula, perhaps. Or maybe some important new law of physics. Our destiny, perhaps. Either way it's still there somewhere in one of NASA's rock drawers. And one day someone—someone like me, perhaps—will look at that rock again and figure it out. I sure hope so.

I might even get Kit to help me. Since the NASA classes we took, he's become a serious collector of rocks, and he says that when he grows up he intends to be a geologist.

Sure, going to the Moon changed me. But not in a bad way. The good thing about it was that it made me seem impressive to myself, which is just a way of saying I have a lot more confidence in me and who I am than I did before this all happened. I enjoy schoolwork a lot more now. But I'm not so sure about going to the Air Force Academy. I think maybe I'd like to go to Harvard or Yale and become a mathematician or a physicist. Math and physics are now my strongest subjects. My math teacher, Mr. Porteous, says that the Scottish boarding school Kit and I went to certainly worked some kind of miracle in me. He no longer tells the class that he expects me to be hanged. Now he says he expects nothing less of me than a Nobel Prize.

The gods have given me health, victory, and power, and all other good things. I have everything I ever wanted. Pamela's affection. My parents back together. And for the first time in ages my father seems happy. Of course he was delighted to get my mom back. And very relieved I returned safely from the Moon. But what really gave him a buzz, because it was so unexpected, was that the air force promoted him to colonel. Without a word of explanation. One morning he went into his office in Ellington and there was the letter detailing the promotion, lying on his desk.

"The air force is like that," he told us later that day. "They never give reasons. They don't have to. That's the deal you make when you sign up. You take what you're given. That's just the air force way."

Of course I knew different. And so did someone in the air force, I guess. But then, they weren't saying. He was right about that much. And neither was I.

I continue to love flying, although I will have to wait until I'm sixteen before I can apply for a license. There's no way around that. Dad takes me up in the Cessna sometimes. It's real flying. I've decided I prefer propeller airplanes to jets. There's nowhere I want to go so fast that I need to be in a Tweet or a Talon. If ever I hear that voice again, I know it's going to be while I'm flying a prop. Flying is magical.

We did calligraphy in school, and we had to choose a poem to transcribe in our best handwriting. I chose to write out "High

Flight," the poem that Dad has in his den. I had it framed, and now it hangs on the wall in my room. I read it almost every day. Sometimes I think of John Magee, the guy who wrote it, and his tragically short life. Sometimes I think about the tumbling mirth of sun-split clouds. Sometimes I picture the long, delirious, burning blue. But mostly, with silent lifting mind I think back to the time when I trespassed the sanctity of space, put out my hand, and touched the face of God.

"High Flight"
by Pilot Officer John Gillespie Magee Jr. (1922–1941)

Oh! I have slipped the surly bonds of Earth
And danced the skies on laughter-silvered wings;
Sunward I've climbed, and joined the tumbling mirth
Of sun-split clouds—and done a hundred things
You have not dreamed of—wheeled and soared and swung
High in the sunlit silence. Hov'ring there
I've chased the shouting wind along, and flung
My eager craft through footless halls of air.
Up, up the long, delirious, burning blue,
I've topped the windswept heights with easy grace
Where never lark, nor ever eagle flew—
And, while with silent lifting mind I've trod
The high untrespassed sanctity of space,
Put out my hand and touched the face of God.

Reproduced by kind permission of This England Books.

Author's Note

Much of the information in this story is factual, but much of it is also fiction. Everything about the technical workings of jets and rockets is true. The Tweet was—possibly still is—the jet of choice for people learning how to fly in the United States Air Force. I consulted a classified technical manual to help me understand the plane, and I also used a computer simulator that enabled me to fly the plane in simulation so that I could deliver a vivid idea of what it's like to fly.

The air-force base in Texas that I describe is indeed where the Apollo astronauts flew in and out of military jets, and yes, they really did use them to go shopping. It was something of a local scandal.

It's hard for us to remember now, but the urgency about getting to the Moon was twofold. To some extent, it was seen as

John F. Kennedy's legacy. But Lyndon B. Johnson was really the moving force behind the space program, much more so than Kennedy and Eisenhower. Johnson, of course, made sure that nearly everything to do with NASA was based in his home state of Texas. He also wanted to make sure that the United States got there before the Russians. People were worried that if the Russians got there first, they would claim the Moon as Soviet territory, and they were even more worried that the Russians would start building a missile base there.

People really were very worried about the future of Apollo after the terrible fire in *Apollo 7* in January 1967. Certainly it is true that if there had been another accident after *Apollo 7*, there's no doubt that the space program would have been cancelled. NASA was incredibly worried that *Apollo 11* might not manage to take off again after it had landed, and they had numerous other concerns too. There were many unanswered questions on the day that *Apollo 11* took off for the Moon—so many that they made me think I ought to write this book.

Much of what happened back in the space program is still shrouded in secrecy. But all of the UFO "bogeys" described in the book are true. Armstrong and Aldrin really did see something on the moon that even today they prefer not to talk about. John Glenn really did see "fireflies." To this day, nobody knows what they were. In fact, all of the Apollo flights were witness to sightings of bogeys that remain unexplained.

The chimp program did exist in the early sixties. Chimps did fly in spacecraft. All of the information of how they were trained is true. But at what stage they stopped, no one is quite sure, which is where my fiction takes over. There's no doubt that the original Gemini astronauts were pretty upset when they discovered that monkeys would fly in space before them, and that did happen. But whether the chimp program was kept going alongside the Apollo program, we are not really sure. The chronology is accurate, however.

This book is about a real boy. I was twelve in 1968. My own father did his national service in the British Royal Air Force. I was always interested in planes. And space. I had books on astronomy and a large telescope. And there's no point in denying that the boy in the story is kind of based on me. Although I grew up in Scotland, my dad worked for an American company and not only were his colleagues from Texas and Kansas City but one of my best friends was an American boy who went to school in Scotland.

I still remember the awe my friend—his name was Greg— and I both felt during Christmas 1968 when *Apollo 10* orbited the Moon. In a sense that was even more special than the actual Moon landing itself. I hope that the forthcoming fortieth anniversaries of *Apollo 10* and *Apollo 11* will help to remind Americans of what a staggering achievement this was, and remind them of what a great country the USA is.

—Philip Kerr

√

Northport-East Northport Public Library

To view your patron record from a computer, click on
the Library's homepage: **www.nenpl.org**

You may:
- request an item be placed on hold
- renew an item that is overdue
- view titles and due dates checked out on your card
- view your own outstanding fines

**185 Larkfield Road
East Northport, NY 11731
631-261-2313**